SKYLARKS OVER DAISY HILL.

Bill Habergham

PG-J Publishers

skylarksoverdaisyhill.com

My grateful thanks are due to the following people:

My family around the world but in particular my wife, Suwfieya, son, Joshua and niece, Rosie for their love, encouragement and advice over many years to help ensure the completion of this novel. My former PA Janet who helped to get this project moving and to my editor, Lisa Findlay.

To the current and past members of 619 Squadron Association, Bomber Command for their inspiration, stories and memories, some of which are incorporated into this work.

To the people of Montrueil Aux Lions, Aisne, France and in particular my dear friend Bernard and his family who hold the memory of one particular crew so dearly.

Printed in the United Kingdom

First Printing 2022

ISBN: 9781 3999 15328 and 9781 3999 14147

Cover art and design: Daniela Bertua and Alejandro Colucci.

PG-J Publishers, United Kingdom

For My Father and his beloved Brothers

Table of Contents:

Prologue.

The End! Aisne, France, July 1944

He was awoken by a machine roaring from the edge of eternity. A bellow of intense protest, one of metal shearing, bending, breaking, failing and falling, as it strained to maintain its integrity against the forces of war and the laws of physics that were tearing it apart and carrying lives away with it.

Fully awake now, he could actually feel the noise as the waves of sound crashed through the shutters and the brick walls of his small bedroom, which reverberated with their intensity. As he sat up, the room was lit up by a fearful flickering of light, as if by some huge flaming torch.

He now understood that a mechanical monster was being driven to the edge of destruction, and the sound he heard was the failing of the monster's engines. It foretold of a hellish, flaming death to come.

Rene, just 19 years old, had gone to bed

around midnight after a long day cutting hay in the meadows down by the river that ran through his father's farm. The river at this time of year ran quickly and softly through a small valley that came down from Montreuil, to join the crystal blue River Marne, just two kilometres from the farm.

With the German curfew in place, Rene had to use every hour of the long daylight to carry out all the work that was needed. His father, crippled by a stroke just three months earlier, could no longer help his son with the physical work around their small farm. His father was once a bull of a man, stocky and strong, but now he was reduced to paralysis and incontinence. Rene found it hard to comprehend that his father, who until the moment the embolism burst in his brain, had seemed such a physical embodiment of indestructible masculinity - the very epitome of the rural agricultural "Peasant" of "La France Profonde" - could no longer care for or protect his family. The loss seemed greater because the physical shell of his father was still with them, requiring the constant attention of his mother and his sister. When he looked into his father's eyes now, Rene could see the utter indignity he felt and his longing to rid himself of this life and the cold hard chains of malady that held him.

On this night Rene had fallen asleep almost immediately, as the young can do; only to be awoken by the physicality of this noise that seemed to defy nature itself.

As the crescendo grew and the flickering orange-blue light filtered through the shutters, he rushed to the window to throw them back. As he did so, he saw, coming from his left, the outline of an enormous aeroplane, totally engulfed in flames, with the exception of the forward section and the large Perspex canopy that must have held some members of the crew.

The right wing of the aircraft seemed no more than 30 or 40 metres from him and he was shocked by how close it was - only slightly higher than his eyeline, as the 400-year-old farmhouse was built up on a rocky promontory well above the river to protect it from the occasional winter floods.

As the aircraft moved very slowly in front of him, moving to his right up the valley towards Montreuil, he saw a man move forward in the canopy of the aircraft and start pointing and gesturing up to the valley. He stooped as giving instructions to someone to his left, presumably his pilot. Slowly the man turned to his right and for a moment appeared to look directly into Rene's eyes. In the light of the flaming wings and fuselage of the gigantic aircraft, Rene could see his face clearly. His intense, dark brown eyes were etched with tiredness.

Rene, at the start of his life at 19 years old, would die in the 21st century at the age of 83. For every day of his life to come, in middle age and in old, Rene would think back to those seconds that he held the man's eyes. Though the two men were separated by no more than a few metres of space, they seemed to stand together on the banks of the River Styx, the river of Greek myth that separated the living from the underworld. Their very proximity only served to highlight and magnify the hideous fate that quickly began to move them apart. Charon, the ferryman, had arrived to carry one to his death within the next sixty seconds, while the other was to live a full and fulfilled life for another sixty years. It was as if at that moment the airman was trying to transfer his life and thoughts and memories to the other. "Remember me, who I am and what I am, and take my life with you."

The airman held the gaze for one second longer, and then his face changed; the jaw tightened, the eyes became strained with fear and he spoke directly to Rene, who saw the lips move very briefly but very distinctly. The short words were clearly directed at him! As one man went to his death, fear struck at the heart of the other who witnessed it. Cold fear that he would never hear or understand the message he had just been given from the edge of hell and therefore it must forever go unheard and un-comprehended. Another second ticked by. The airman turned back to his left and Rene saw his mouth move again, as he seemingly tried to encourage his pilot to find one last burst of life in the doomed aircraft.

The young man watched as the huge ball of flame and smoke moved up the small valley to his right, illuminating the fields of cut grass. Pieces of the aircraft began to fall onto the road close to the little bridge at Caumont, whilst all the time the flaming torch was slowly sinking towards the little wood at Dacile.

The terrible screaming wrenching sound of

the dying plane began to subside as it moved up the little valley, perhaps half a kilometre away now.

Suddenly, what had been a smooth, slow descent abruptly changed as the stricken aircraft veered to the right and plummeted to the earth. Metal fragments blew high into the air as the aircraft buried itself in the slope of a meadow. Instantly, the shock wave of air rushed towards Rene, and the half-opened shutters on his window blew back and crashed into the wall of the house. Flames launched skyward, maybe 30 or 40 metres.

In that instant, six men lost their lives. Six men with mothers, fathers, brothers, sisters, wives, lovers, friends, were all obliterated. The ripples of their lives began to spread and move through time, ever onward, ever in the memory of some, to return and echo in the future in strange and incomprehensible ways.

With the final crash still ringing in his ears, Rene heard his mother's voice. 'Rene, Rene, qu'est-que c'est?' she shouted from his parents' bedroom at the back of the house.

'Mama, it is terrible. A huge aeroplane has

just crashed up near the mill at Sillon. I think it must be an English bomber, by its size. I must go and help.'

His mother's voice rose to further heights of concern, close to hysteria. 'No, Rene, never. The Germans will be there soon, the curfew is on, they will kill you.'

Rene thought for a moment. She was right, of course. It had only been seven weeks since D-Day, or "Le Debarquement", as the BBC French service referred to it. Everyone knew the Germans were being pushed back. The BBC radio transmissions told them that and anyone locally could tell by the volume of military traffic heading north and by the tense, nervous look on the faces of the German soldiers, that matters were close. Only three months earlier the Germans in town had been completely relaxed, taking the best seats in the restaurants and bars in Chateau Thierry, as confident and arrogant as they had been since 1940.

Now they were edgy; the occupiers faced retribution, loss, failure, and death. The locals knew things were changing and power was shifting and no longer, therefore ,was there any conversation or banter between the Germans and the French. The end was near. Life, which had been on hold for four years now, would have to resume in some other way.

These were difficult and nervous times for the occupiers and the occupied. Rene knew that to go out now and be caught by the German patrol that must be heading this way to attend to the crash, was to risk certain death. No questions would be asked. The Germans would assume he was a member of the Resistance and shoot him on the spot. His body would be thrown in the town square, for his neighbours to find and bury the next morning.

The airman's dark eyes haunted Rene, and he felt he must go to the site. Could the airman and his comrades have survived?

Rene's mother called for him to come to the bedroom, interrupting his thoughts. He entered his parents' bedroom. Two candles were burning. He could see the fear and concern in his mother's eyes, but his own eyes were drawn to his father lying unmoving in the bed, but clearly awake. He moved to his father and looked down at him. His father's only movement now was with his eyelids, which blinked rapidly in his fear and agitation. Rene knew that his father was imploring him not to go. 'Stay with me, keep us safe, look after your mother.' All these statements seemed to swim in his father's eyes.

Rene stayed! He could not sleep, of course. The burning aircraft glowed on the hill and occasionally there would be a crack and pop as superheated ammunition exploded and whizzed through the air. The night passed slowly.

Dawn streaked the sky at 5am. Rene prepared to move at 6am, the moment the curfew ended, but he could not wait. At 5.30am he left the house, pulled his bike from the stable and began to cycle up the little road that ran through the valley. He heard nothing, even the birds of the dawn chorus were quietened and seemingly in mourning for the deaths they had witnessed, but Rene remained on the alert for the sound of German cars and trucks.

Rene rounded the corner of the road as it approached the track leading down to the little bridge across the stream at Caumont. As he pulled onto the track the smell of burnt rubber, metal, vegetation and something else, which he couldn't yet identify, entered his nostrils.

He threw down his bike and went on foot. At the bridge he could see a small pasture on the other side of the stream. The grass was scorched black and the trees along the river were torn out and burnt black, or in some cases reduced to stumps. In the middle of the pasture he could see the shape of the aircraft. It was the rear section only, badly scorched but still intact. The gun turret at the rear of the aircraft was skewed to an angle of 45 degrees and the guns themselves were twisted and bent.

As he approached the wreckage, Rene could see that the rear section had fallen off the main body of the gigantic plane, which had then travelled on a further 300 or 400 metres, ploughing through the wood before hitting the roof of the mill at Sillon and burying itself in the bank of road that lead from the mill.

Rene picked his way through the metal and debris that lay all over the ground, which felt warm under his boots. He looked into the rear turret and immediately drew back. Rene had never seen a dead man before, but sitting in the turret – with his head bloody and his flying clothing still smouldering and slick with oil, was an English airman. One side of his face was crushed and his eye socket held only blood and arterial threads, but the other half of his face was almost unscarred. He looked young, about Rene's own age. Rene stared at the twisted corpse for maybe a minute.

He moved along the fuselage and saw another body which had been thrown from the plane. The dead man lay face up, and apart from the dried streaks of blood that had oozed from the ears, nose and mouth, he looked almost asleep. One arm was thrown half across his face, whilst the other reached upward in a protective gesture.

Rene did not know what to do for these men. What does one do for dead foreign airmen in your own occupied country? These foreigners were enemies to the occupiers, who expected the French to support them on pain of death, but they were brave liberators to most, even though they had to destroy parts of France itself in order to bring about the freedom of the French. This war was complicated for the occupied French. It created real and moral dilemmas at every turn.

Rene heard no sounds that indicated people

were moving towards the crash site, so he continued forward, past the detached rear section of the plane. He noted the letters "P" and "G" next to the English roundel of red, white and blue that could still be seen through the scorched metal of fuselage.

Rene knew now that all the crew must be dead. There could be no hope for them. He was suddenly moved by an intense desire to find the body of the airman he had seen from his window. In the midst of the death and chaos, this man would be a link, in a strange way, to life!

He followed the line of scorched and broken trees where the front section of the aircraft had continued to plough forward after the rear section had fallen away.

The blackened earth still smouldered in places and Rene noticed pieces of paper, leather, glass, broken and shattered parts of the aircraft were everywhere. Suddenly, amidst this debris, he saw parts of bodies. A boot with a bloodied sock and shard of bone protruding from it. A shattered hand and other shreds of skin and bone. Ahead of him he saw a complete body lying face down, except one leg which had been severed and lay a few metres apart from the body. The stump of the leg was still slick with blood and the smell was sickly and metallic. Rene had slaughtered oxen, pigs and geese many times with his father; he knew the sweet sickliness of blood. Wasps and insects were buzzing around the slick wet blood of the leg. Rene felt he had stumbled into a charnel house!

Inside the severed boot he noted a detailed flying map. He stood over the body and reached down to pull it over to face the light. The face of the dead aviator was grey and ashen and the eyes were open. He recognised the dark eyes he had seen just a few hours before. This was the man he had stood with on the banks of the Styx a few hours earlier. Now he was dead. Handsome, with a sharply chiselled nose and fine steady chin, and dark hair that curled slightly, this man was real.

Rene knew that all soldiers and airmen wore identity disks around their neck. He reached to the man's zipped flying suit closed at his neck, and tugged it down slightly. The airman wore a blue tunic underneath with a light blue shirt with a tie still carefully knotted. Rene wondered about this type of war. Bombing from 5000 metres with a tie on. Killing whilst nicely dressed. How strange! It was a small thing but something Rene never came to terms with for the rest of his life.

He saw the tags around the neck and read the name in the engraved disk. So, this was the name of the man he had seen, living and breathing just a few hours earlier, now dead. He had seen him go to his death and could not help him. He resolved to do all he could to look after him in death! He had known this man in the last moments of his life and he vowed to bury him with dignity and to dedicate his life to keeping his memory alive.

At that moment Rene heard the sound of voices and footsteps close behind him. He turned to see Monsieur Elgart, who lived in the house close to the farm, approaching, slightly out of breath. Running behind him was his 6-year-old son, Bernard, silently staring in blinking amazement at the chaos around him.

'Monsieur Elgart, you must not come here,' said Rene quietly.

'Why, Rene? We saw the aircraft come down last night. We came to help assist the crew if we can.'

'Monsieur Elgart, you cannot help them. Please look carefully around you. This place is a morgue. Bernard should not see this.' As he looked closely, Monsieur Elgart suddenly began to notice the pieces of human flesh scattered around; a finger, part of a skull with bloodied hair matted onto it, a sock with a mangled and gristly bone jutting from it.

The blood drained from Monsieur Elgart's face.

'Bernard, quickly, we must leave here. The men from the aircraft we saw last night cannot be helped. Your mother will be worried.' The little boy said nothing. His face gave nothing away. Rene suspected he had already seen the terrible human remains around him, but either uncaring or not understanding, said nothing.

Many years later Rene came to know that the little boy had seen and understood more than he thought possible. The boy would never forget this day and the brief trauma that he had witnessed. In later years, he and Rene would bond over this terrible day and work to keep the memory of the dead crewmen alive.

As Monsieur Elgart moved away, holding

his son's hand, Rene heard the sound of heavy vehicles arriving down the road. The Germans had finally arrived, shouting orders as the vehicles stopped and disgorged 15 or so men of a local Wehrmacht platoon.

He stood where he was and waited for the Germans to come to him. He did not want to provoke any reaction from the occupying army, all 15 of them!

The German platoon split up; half of them moved towards the forward section of the plane, still smouldering at the mill site, and the other half came towards Rene. They gestured to him to approach. The sergeant spoke good French. There were no introductions.

'Have you found bodies?'

'Yes, sir.'

'How many?'

'Three so far, I think. It is hard to tell, they are not all intact.'

'Did you witness the crash?'

'Yes.'

‘Any parachutes?’

‘No, sir.’

Rene knew what they were looking for. Any survivors lurking in the area would need to be found, identified, and brought in. They all knew that an aircraft of this size carried a crew of seven men. There had to be seven bodies!

If anyone had escaped from the burning craft, the Germans would search every building, barn and factory within a fifteen kilometre radius, making life hellish for the local population as they did so.

‘Come,’ said the sergeant. Rene followed him along the burnt and broken ground towards where the front of the aircraft lay. If anything, the debris and litter from the bomber only increased.

Two hundred metres further on, the burnt wreckage of the front section of the broken bomber lay half buried in the slope the of small bank that formed the road at the mill.

Amid the ghoulish chaos lay the torso of a human being stripped of legs and arms, with a burnt and half severed head laying to one side, barely attached to the shoulders. The physical force of the crash and the massive deceleration process involved had whipped metal, flesh, rubber and glass into a terrible mixture of broken, beaten, and tormented elements that came as close to a vision of hell as one could bear. The stench of the burnt and rotting carcass of the aircraft and its human content only added to the sense of horror and desolation that surrounded this charnel house. There was no God and no civilisation in this place.

The sergeant had moved off towards a number of large, dumpy metal cylinders lying nearby. He came within ten metres of the first of these objects and stopped suddenly, going no further. Rene had never seen such things before but knew instinctively from the shape of the objects and by the sergeant's reaction that these were the bombs that the aircraft carried. It had clearly never reached its target and carried its load with it to its own end.

The sergeant barked some orders to two of his men who then ran back towards their own vehicle on the road. He heard the engine start and the truck move away. The sergeant gestured to Rene.

'You from around here?'

'Yes, sir.'

'I need hay to put around these until the engineers arrive to blow them up.'

'Yes sir, I will go and see what I can do. I understand.'

Rene walked back to his bike through the grisly carpet of death and destruction. He rode back home and dragged his large hay wagon from under its cover. He then ran into the field next to the farm and brought his two large dray horses into the yard, hitched them to the wagon and drove into the field where his bales of hay lay. He selected six trusses and hoisted them onto the wagon. He could spare no more - one could not know what the coming winter could bring - but he knew a clash of armies must be imminent and if he would be forced to provide additional fodder by one side or the other

He put the thought from his mind and set off back up the road to the countryside. The German sergeant had been busy and Rene noted that Monsieur Balme from a neighbouring farm had also been suborned into bring hay trusses along.

The German platoon arranged the hay, two high, around each bomb. They did this in a hurry. Rene had heard that the English bombers often dropped delayed action munitions when attacking roads and railways, timed to go off over 24, even 72 hours, to prevent repair gangs going in. Rene suspected these bombs may be the same. He did not want to be close when they exploded.

By this time a small crowd of locals had gathered, maybe 20-25 people, Rene guessed. Most of them he knew as neighbours and friends, although some were strangers, probably from Orain, two kilometres away. Not much was said. Initial curiosity made way for horror and then sympathy for the dead airmen. They were liberators to most of the French people, although the local mayor - who kept his communist sympathies very, very quiet - saw it in a more complicated way: "friends now - enemies later once all the fascists of the world have been cleared out", he liked to say to those whom he could trust.

After 30 minutes of waiting, another Germany military vehicle arrived. Out jumped four men in a drab olive and brown uniform. The men looked tough but clearly embarrassed and not in the least enthusiastic to be here. They carried no weapons, just small canvas tool bags.

The German sergeant indicated to the lead man where the bombs lay scattered, hidden behind the bales. Rene realised that these men were Russian prisoners of war. The Germans had press-ganged them into being bomb disposal squads in return for slightly better treatment and better rations.

The Germans would never risk their own men in these circumstances. Instead, they stood well back, trained their weapons on the Russians and let them do the difficult and dangerous work of defusing the bombs. Clearly the Russian engineers were getting good at this. They had had a lot of practice in the past three months, as German night fighters had brought down many more bombers than usual in the Aisne and Marne districts. No one knew why the Allies were so focused on disrupting German military infrastructure at the time, but now it was clear they were leading up to the D-Day invasion.

Rene, along with the other French people and the German soldiers, stood at a distance and watched the Russians attach fuse wire to the core of each dismantled bomb, then unravel the wire back to where the German platoon stood. At a safe distance they set each detonator and with a warning shot each time, blew the wiring and fuse mechanism of each bomb to pieces.

After the Russians had defused eight bombs in just 40 minutes, the truck was backed up to each bomb and the Russians loaded each bomb core into the back and carefully drove off with their German escort. Clearly, extra vodka was on their menu tonight.

The whole exercise took no more than 2 hours. Rene never moved the whole time. He wanted to see the bombs destroyed, but more so, he wanted to remain near the bodies of the dead crewmen. He wanted to see this through to the end.

Again, the German sergeant gestured to him to approach.

'What is your name?'

'Rene Pascal, sir!'

'Well, Rene Pascal, I want you and six of your friends here to assist me in collecting and counting the bodies of the crew. This, as you can see, will not be easy or pleasant.'

'I understand, sir.'

Seven blankets were brought out from the truck.

The two crewmen in the rear of the aircraft were mostly intact. The German soldiers were not careful in extracting the rear gunner in particular from the mangled turret. At least one leg was broken deliberately by the swinging butt of a rifle in order to disengage the gunner's foot trapped in the wreckage.

The sergeant ripped away the man's identity tag, wrote the name on a sheet of paper, and threw the body and the paper together on the blanket.

The mid upper gunner received similar treatment.

They moved to Rene's man, still lying where he left him. The sergeant noted that the man's tags had been moved.

'Did you touch this man, Pascal?'

'Yes, sir.'

'Why?'

'I wanted to find his name, sir.'

'Well, you did, yes?'

'Yes, sir.'

The sergeant looked quizzically at Rene but said no more. The body of the brown-eyed airman was laid on the large blanket. The severed leg that lay several meters away was simply thrown on to the corpse. This was no way to treat a warrior, thought Rene.

'Now for the hard part,' said the sergeant. 'We now have to account for the next four bodies. Form a line with your friends and walk towards the wreckage by the mill. When you find human remains, stop. Indicate to my men and we will come and collect them.'

The next hour was the most cursed and horror stricken of Rene's life. He had seen a number of farm animals slaughtered and he would continue to see such slaughter for the remainder of his life, but nothing would haunt him like this. They raked together the broken and dismembered parts of the remainder of the crew, who had been torn literally limb from limb and sinew from sinew. Some flesh which could only be human could not, however, be recognized as belonging to any part of the body. Elsewhere lay disembodied flesh, skull segments with wet matted hair still attached, fingers, bone, cloth, and ash!

The warrior's death so ennobled in memory, literature, religion, and custom was now foul, undignified, and beyond reasoning. Instead, three mangled, burnt, and shredded corpses were found. The tags that might have identified them had melted into what remained of the torso of each man.

As it became clear that only six bodies were to be found, the German sergeant became agitated. He called on his truck radio to his headquarters, warning that there must be a seventh member of the crew who in all probability had bailed out and was now loose in the countryside.

The Frenchmen shuddered. Life would be hell for the next few days as the vicinity was torn apart looking for the escaped airman. No one was safe and no property would be left untouched.

Rene now realized that it was mid-afternoon. He had been up all through the night and had arrived at the crash site just after dawn.

The sergeant's work for him was not done, however. Pointing at Rene and his fellow Frenchmen, the sergeant shouted, 'You six – in the back of that truck.'

With a glance at the menacing figures of the German platoon, Rene asked no questions but climbed aboard with his dragooned colleagues.

The sergeant ordered them to the front of the truck. Behind them the German soldiers threw in the six brutalized and mangled bodies of the Englishmen. The truck started up and moved away.

The journey only took 15 minutes but the Frenchmen had to endure the time clinging to the roof and sides of the swaying vehicle with the rank smell of burnt, decaying human flesh pricking at their nostrils. Blood dripped from the corner of one blanket and the men nearest shuffled their feet to avoid touching it.

When the truck halted, Rene recognized where they were. They stood outside the small British military cemetery that led up the hill away from Lancy sur Marne. The British military had been here before! In September 1914 the British army had been pushed back to this place before beginning a counter attack directly between two great German armies that were sweeping down towards Paris from the north. The British did not know it, but in advancing they threatened to split the German armies. Held in check by the French army on either side of them, the Germans began to withdraw towards the sea and what became known as the 1st Battle of the Marne was over.

Over the next few months as the great trench lines of the Great War developed in eastern France, the bodies of the British dead were brought in and buried here with full military honour, or at least as much as the war would allow.

Today, Rene knew, the 163 men who had lain here for 30 years would be disturbed by another 6 bodies of their countrymen who had just died in yet another "Great War". The original men would hardly have thought that their sacrifice a generation earlier would lead to another expenditure of blood and horror so soon afterwards.

The German sergeant threw down six shovels and two picks. 'Follow me,' he said. He walked to the gate of the small cemetery, paused to locate a suitable site not far from the cross of sacrifice used in each British military cemetery, and then indicated to Rene, 'You start here.' Pointing at the next man, 'You here.' So, Rene began to dig the first grave for these young Englishmen.

Three hours it took, of hard toil and backache. The ground up here was harsh and full of flint, unlike the soft alluvial soil of Rene's father's farm near the river. Great lumps of flint and chalk had to be moved before he and his colleagues had fashioned four rough graves only just over a metre deep. Not deep enough really, but the Germans had run out of time.

Four graves for six men! Just one was enough for the mangled remains of three disassembled corpses.

The blankets containing the bodies of the Englishmen were brought from the back of the truck. Rene had one request.

‘Sergeant, sir. May I respectfully request that the body of the man I found be placed in the grave I have just finished. I found his body this morning and feel that it is my duty and desire to bury this man...’

Rene’s voice trailed away He did not know yet why he felt so much for this man. Why was he so important that it was Rene who must look after his mortal remains on this earth? He thought for a moment. The man had spoken to him from the banks of the Styx; his last words had been to him. That was enough.

The sergeant paused for a moment and nodded. He pulled one of the blankets aside and looked at his scribbled note. ‘This is him.’

Two of the sergeant’s men lifted the blanket and without ceremony or care dropped the body into Rene’s grave. The remaining bodies were then similarly tossed into the earth. ‘Now cover them,’ said the sergeant.

Rene and his sad party of conscripted labour did as they were ordered and piled the flinty soil over the bodies. The sergeant then moved to each grave and placed a small wooden cross on each mound of earth. He had scribbled on each slat of the wood the name of each man, or in three cases, the word "Unbekannt". The sergeant turned to Rene.

‘I will notify the German military authorities of this action today, and they in turn will notify the appropriate French authority. We will go now. I warn you and all of you here that you are not to move or mark these graves. These men are your enemy and will not be given any act of remembrance or condolence. Do you understand?’

Rene certainly did not understand but would not say otherwise. He gave an imperceptible nod, which the German sergeant took as assent. He called to his men, and they loaded back into their vehicles and drove away.

Rene turned to his colleagues in the conscripted burial party. He knew Henri, the butcher’s assistant, the best as he regularly came to the farm.

‘Henri, we cannot leave these men like this.’ Henri nodded in agreement. ‘Whatever the Germans say, these men are human beings. They deserve the respect we all would want in our hour of death.’

The remainder of Rene's indentured party agreed. They all knew that those men had died to free France, themselves, and their families. Only the Germans were the occupiers here. These men deserved a Christian burial.

The stained and exhausted party found Pastor Romeau in the small café next to the Hotel de Ville. He was a regular there; coffee, the odd glass of wine, and local gossip, were his physical sustenance whilst he carried out his spiritual mission on earth.

News of the crash had spread throughout the village and the surrounding countryside and Pastor Romeau, with his keen ear for local news, was aware of what had happened.

Rene led his dirty party into the café and explained everything that he knew of the crash and the burial.

'Rene,' said the Pastor, looking at him steadily, 'you know what the Germans will do if they see us carrying out a public service to honour these men.'

'Yes Sir I do, but you must know that these men are also patriots and soldiers, and like us they are all God's creation.'

The Pastor could not argue. Age may have made him cynical with regard to human nature, but his faith remained strong and his belief in the freedom of France burned like Rene's. He had fought in the First War and had ministered to hundreds of wounded and psychologically damaged young men in that conflict. He knew he could not deny these young men entry into God's house if he could ease their passage.

'Very well, Rene. Meet me in an hour at the cemetery. We will keep it brief, yes?'

Rene sank down on a chair as the Pastor left to gather his tools of office. Monsieur Leval, the owner of the café, brought the little burial team a glass of water each and a home-baked baguette to share.

Little was said for the next 40 minutes as the ragged band sat in their own thoughts. The scarring memory of what they had seen and done over the last few hours began to entrench in their minds, where it would solidify and magnify for the rest of their lives. Their attitude to life, living, and death would forever be changed by this brief experience.

Rene stood up and began to move to the door of the café to return up the hill to the cemetery. His burial detail followed.

As they walked up the hill they were joined by a small crowd of locals. The Pastor had obviously passed the word!

At the cemetery the Pastor waited with another small crowd. Rene realized that maybe 70 people were present, many carrying flowers and small wreaths quickly and crudely fashioned.

The Pastor wasted no time before beginning to read a very abbreviated version of the Requiem Mass. Rene realized that in all probability these Englishmen were not Roman Catholics but what did it matter -- God was the same wherever you were or wherever you came from.

As the Pastor came to the end of the burial mass, the small crowd stirred as they saw a German military car move up the road towards the cemetery. No one moved. They realized there was only a driver and one other man in the vehicle.

The car drew to a halt and a short young

man exited in the blue uniform of the Luftwaffe. A junior officer, thought Rene, no older than myself! Blond hair ruffling slightly in the wind, he seemed to have tired eyes and a slightly weary demeanour.

No one moved as the young officer entered the gate of cemetery and came towards the small crowd. He moved towards the Pastor. 'Monsieur, please continue,' the officer said in perfect French.

The Pastor nodded and completed the last sentences of the mass. He then asked the crowd to bow their heads in prayer and asked the Lord to bear these men into his grace and called upon all men of the world to seek peace, reconciliation, and forgiveness at this most terrible of times. As he finished, he looked to the German officer, 'Herr Lieutenant, you must be here for a reason, do you wish to say anything?'

The young officer hesitated. Rene realized he was nervous, shy, and actually somewhat overwhelmed. He clearly had not expected to see a crowd. Rene thought he was not going to speak but suddenly he found his voice.

'Mesdames et messieurs, my name is

Zimmerman. Last night I flew in the skies above here. I shot down two Lancaster bombers. I believe that these men are the crew of one of the bombers I shot down. I am here to pay my respects to my enemy and my comrades of the air.' He paused again. Suddenly struggling to find words and with his voice hesitating and cracking with emotion he went on, 'Pray for these men. Keep their memory alive in your hearts and your minds, as will I. I ask you to do this with an open and free heart. I am not your enemy. I will pray for these men also…because tonight…tomorrow…it may be my turn to die. I could not go on if I thought no one would remember me and mark my grave. These men are my comrades in life and death.'

The little crowd seemed to hold its breath. The young German moved to the side of graves and the crowd silently gave way to him. He came to attention and slowly raised his arm to his forehead in military salute. He stood in salute for a full minute or more. No one spoke or moved. Again, Rene noted the sound of the larks and birds of the fields surrounding the little cemetery seemed to dim in witness and honour of the events that were playing out. Slowly The German pilot brought his arm down, bowed his head to the graves, and returned slowly to his car, never looking back. Silence and stillness reigned.

Rene watched him leave and then some of the mourners began to lay flowers on the rough earthen graves.

He realized that he had just witnessed something profound which only added to the searing sights, sounds, smells, emotions and pure sweat that he had witnessed this day.

The war had started when he was just 15 years old. His country had been overrun and defeated. He was honest enough to know that at that age, although he had felt and seen the deep insecurity of his parents and family as the Germans took control of his country, little had really changed to alter the patterns of his life. He still went to school and his friends and peers were still close and well. He still worked on the fields with his father at the weekends and during holidays. The girls he knew at school increasingly attracted his attention. Great events had swirled around him and they swirled still, but by and large they had passed him by. He had become a man at a time of war but fate and fortune decreed that because he lived in an occupied nation he never had to fight, to suffer, or to feel real fear.

The Englishman he had seen on the banks of the Styx last night on his way to his death and whom he had buried today, had died in fear and anger alongside his comrades, all of whom were probably not much older than Rene.

The German pilot was young like him and lived last night, and presumably in the nights to come, in fear of death and his own mortality.

Perhaps if they all could have known each other in other circumstances – Englishman, German, and Frenchman – they could have been friends. Yesterday, the Englishman lived and was loved. Today, the man who killed him and the man who buried him both mourned him. The fates of all three were now drawn together. Rene was conscious that the dead man had a certainty about his future which he and the German pilot did not, and he felt afraid for the pilot and himself. He had never really thought about death before but the Englishman's quiet calm in the face of death and the German's dignified respect for the man he had killed had taught him to value life.

Rene understood now his good fortune in not having to die in the way these Englishmen had and in the way that the German pilot dreaded. But at the same time, he felt somewhere the regret that all young men have when they do not become warriors. Could he face a death such as this? Could he be courageous? Could he rise to the ultimate test of men? To risk one's life and survive, or to die perhaps in physical and mental pain, knowing the end was certain as the English airmen had suffered just hours earlier?

Yet Rene also saw the unity of war in the young men who fought it and the ultimate absurdity of it. The German pilot had come to pay respects to the men he had killed. If they could the Englishmen would have killed him. None of them wanted to die, but still they killed each other and left their mothers and fathers and friends and lovers to grieve for them and endure the hollowness and agony of loss and bereavement. Bereavement that was so violent in its suddenness that it left no time for contemplation and preparation. Life had been torn away from these men and their families probably knew nothing as yet. The aching pain of their loss was yet to dawn.

He imagined the mothers of these men, so far away, living with the wretched pain of fear and constant worry. Praying, hoping, pleading that God would not take their sons away. Today their boys had been taken from them and they did not know the certainty of their loss to come.

The thought of this almost tore Rene's heart in two. He imagined how his mother would feel, if he had gone to fight. He had never thought of this before. The torment of a mother at home thinking of her boys. Seeing the shape of their face in her mind, feeling the memory of their arms around her as they kissed her goodbye. The smell of their skin and their hair still lingering on her. How can you tell a mother the news of the death of her beloved son! The smiles and the laughter she would no longer share, the comfort she would not feel of his presence, the company in her old age. The grandchildren she would now never know and love. Rene struggled to contemplate the enormity of the ripples of a young life ended. The pain, the suffering the agony of it all to those left behind – and still their families did not know of their pain to come!

Rene realized that whilst he had been lost in his thoughts the crowd had largely dispersed and he was almost alone in the little cemetery. The raw earth of the graves was covered with fresh flowers. The scene was peaceful and somehow comforting.

Suddenly, there was a disturbance at the low gate into the cemetery. A German military truck had pulled up next to the cemetery, and the senior corporal was arguing with the German pilot who was still standing there. The pilot grew angry and their voices carried clearly to Rene.

Suddenly the corporal saluted and he and his men climbed back into the truck and drove off.

Lieutenant Zimmerman beckoned Rene to come over, so he joined him at the gate.

Lieutenant Zimmerman spoke in his perfect French. 'I am sorry you had to witness that, monsieur. 'My comrades were under instructions to remove the flowers and memorials to the British airmen. It is the policy of our High Command that no memorial should be left to RAF bomber crews, who they regard as terror flyers and who kill women and children without thought and impunity.'

Rene remained unmoving.

'Monsieur, my comrades and my superior officers are wrong. The have their orders as do I. We are all young. We fight for our country, our family and our friends. We do as we are told. Today it was their turn to die. Tonight, it may be mine. I sent the corporal away with these words.'

There was silence between them, and then Rene said, 'Thank you for your words. You have taught me to value life and for that I shall always remember you. I wish you a long life and happiness.'

The young German lieutenant looked at him and then to the graves. He turned slowly and left.

Rene began to walk back down the hill towards home. As he walked the ripples of fate and of life and the events of the day continued to travel outwards. Like casting a large stone into a pond, the ripples were more like waves sweeping and rushing outward. The deaths of these men would already have been noted at the airbase in England where these men should have returned hours ago. The engineers and support crew who worked on their aeroplane yesterday would now know they were gone.

The aircraft that had returned needed checking and repairing. The weary crews that had made it back had to be debriefed, notes taken and reports written. Life went on. War went on and death would certainly come again. There was no escape from that. The grinding machine of the air war would continue. One had to endure and go on if for no other reason that you owed it to the boys who would now never return.

Meanwhile, the administration and bureaucracy of death would now be underway. Intelligence officers and specialist crew would be collecting belongings and personal effects. Comrades and other crews would now be mourning the lives lost and nursing the clawing fear that it would be their turn next.

Ever outward the waves of these deaths would sweep. Telegrams would be sent to homes and opened with trembling hands. Words would be seen and read but the enormity of their meaning would hardly penetrate distraught minds. Grief would overwhelm the families and friends of the dead men. Fears would be confirmed, hopes would die, and lives would be forever changed.

No more would children see their fathers, mothers their sons, wives their lovers and companions in life! The sadness would ache forever.

Work colleagues, school friends, drinking pals, members of sports teams would learn the news and gasp in incredulity. Men would stand in pubs as men do and look into their pints and say nothing. Occasionally, one would speak, 'Do you remember when we...' or 'How about that time he...,' followed by a short story or joke. There would be brief smiles at the anecdotes of sunlit memory and then they would relapse into silent bereaved solidarity.

The local papers would write obituaries; schools would make announcements of lost sons. Churches and chapels would fill with the weeping, the bewildered, and the lost.

Still the waves would move forward, gradually crashing on the shore. Memorials would be built. Parades would take place. History would be written and slowly the waves would subside but tiny ripples would return to the centre; smaller, softer and running interference on each other and beginning to change direction and to mingle in strange nonlinear movements.

New generations would be born who would be affected by the now gently lapping waves of fate and circumstance. The future could not be defined but memory would always remain.

Rene Pascal returned home that day, his life changed forever by what he had seen and done. He lived all his life on the farm, marrying his beloved Isabel in 1948 and raising three daughters with her. He lived to meet ten grandchildren. Hardly a day went by when he did not think of the six British airmen he had buried and of the one that got away.

As he passed his 60th birthday and felt the hand of his own mortality on his shoulders, he decided he would at last begin to find out more of the men and the machine that he had seen come to earth on that July night so long ago. The ripples of fate and of death had returned to gently seek him out.

Chapter 1

Crewing Up

I first met David at an event which long after the war I grew to understand was a uniquely British affair. Eccentric, unusual, probably operationally inefficient, but nevertheless completely open, meritocratic, and democratic.

After seven weeks of operational training learning our individual skills, in my case as a bomb aimer, along with 28 other men in my cohort, striving to ensure that we could place bomb loads directly onto and into the bowels of Nazi Germany; our training unit CO announced to us one morning after graduation, 'Right, you lot. Tonight, 19.00 hours, all of you outside the NAAFI. Three buses will be ready to take you to Silverstone. We have deemed you to be almost ready for war and tonight you get to choose whom you will go to war with. Its "crewing up" time, gentlemen, and the very best of luck to you all.'

We had all heard of the process, of course, and it was an inevitable and vital part of our volunteer process. You volunteer, you're assessed, you train, you qualify, you pass out of your specialism and you then "crew up" and train together with six other men and learn to work together as a unit and as a team for seven weeks, in order that you can go to war as a coordinated and hopefully professional unit. The margins are very tight. If you choose the right team you might survive!

That night we all knew we would be thrown together in one hangar with a few hundred men with other specialties. Each plane would need a pilot, a navigator, a bomb aimer, two air gunners, a wireless operator, and an aircraft engineer. We would add the engineer later, but that night we needed to find the other men to live with, train with, co-operate with, fight with but never – please God – to die with!

The simple plan was that the RAF had selected you as aircrew and carefully trained you for many weeks and months, but you, as a freeborn Englishman, Scotsman, Welshman, Ulsterman, or member of His Majesty's Empire and Dominions were now to choose on an individual level, man to man, who you would fight alongside as you faced your enemy, an enemy that represented the very antithesis of this free association of individual men and women.

After the war I began to realise what a clever boost to self-esteem and morale this method of selection was. The military mindset is normally to break individualism in order to achieve the greater good and superior co-ordination of the unit as a whole. As such, you break individualism before rebuilding the cohesion of a functioning military unit. In this case the RAF went so far, but then suddenly handed back responsibility for action to you. Finding the best men to work alongside you was your choice and created even greater levels of trust and co-ordination in the most intense and dangerous of circumstances. It was a brilliant insight. Only as time ebbs away did I come to realise the terrible downside. It magnified personal loss to an almost unbearable extent!

We hardly saw or understood any of this at the time. On that day in January 1944 with the war in full swing outside we were excited, nervous, and adrenaline-fuelled. I cannot describe it – like walking out with your first girlfriend, or seeing your first child; it's not quite like the frisson of excitement and ecstatic fulfilment that comes with those events, but nevertheless a moment in your life history that you remember forever. This particular feeling was denied to those who did not serve and all those generations that came after.

We arrived at Silverstone that evening from all the local training bases within a fifty mile radius. Buses and military trucks filled the area around Hangar 2. Blue uniformed men were everywhere. Shouts, instructions, greetings, shuffling movements, the straightening of ties and brevets all took place before we entered the echoing hangar. Once inside, a somewhat different atmosphere pervaded, like an affected military boredom. Light conversation in training groups took place as the CO walked to the centre of the giant building. 'Gentlemen,' he called, his voice echoing in the high ceilings, 'you all know why you are here. Now, get on with it! You have 20 minutes, although I doubt you will need that. When you have your crew please give your names to my warrant officers sitting there.' He indicated four men sitting at desks by the hangar door with notebooks of suitable size and importance in front of them.

As the process began, initially the training

groups held together, slightly unwilling to step into the unknown, but as certain men recognized each other from earlier induction or training groups, gradually the herd began to move and mingle.

The banter was typically British – light and understated. 'You need a navigator, you say. Well, I am absolutely hopeless. No idea how I passed training. Can't even find my way out of bed in the morning.'

'No, I couldn't hit a barn door. Absolutely bloody hopeless.' This statement was generally favoured by a variety of air gunners or bomb aimers.

I stood for a minute or so, eyeing the mass of blue uniformed men around me. This was disconcerting. These men were mainly strangers. How could I possibly pick a crew of colleagues with whom to trust my life? I knew it happened but could not see how.

My eyes were drawn to one man slightly removed from his training group who seemed to be scanning the mass with an elevated level of scrutiny. A single wing with an 'O' for Observer at the base was sewn onto his tunic. A navigator!

He was standard height, maybe 5 feet, 9 inches with dark brown hair, a fine nose and chin. A good - looking chap and certainly older than the rest of us.

My training group had an average age of 22. I was 19. Most of the rest of the hangar would not be much different, all young, very eager and all volunteers. This man held himself in an entirely different way from the rather gauche, naive young men around him. He had clearly seen something of the world. He probably had a little money, I thought, and almost certainly knew something of those strange, fearful, and yet wonderful creatures called women. He had an aura of self-confidence and self-will that set him apart.

It is one of those contradictions that perhaps only war can bring about. At 19 I was fit and mature enough to be taught how to fight and kill and perhaps to die, but the reality was that in life and war I really had little idea about who I was and what I wanted to be. I knew I did not want to die but I also knew for certain that I did not want to let anyone down in this conflict – family, friends, God, country, however you wanted to put it. Although I tried hard not to show it, what I and probably 90% of the men present really wanted was someone older, more experienced, and generally more knowledgeable to lead us, guide us, and help us through the terrifying and unknown landscape to come.

We young virgins tried hard, but you could tell by the way we simply walked and talked that we were unsure of just about everything. We walked just a little too self-consciously and talked just a little too loudly in order to overcome our uncertainty. This older man moved in a way that proved he had attained self-awareness.

There is a time in a man's life, not given to all, actually not given to many, when all elements of their physical, mental, and psychological make-up fit together perfectly and all others around them can see it and feel it. They hold themselves and they talk in a way that allows all others to feel their confidence and want to follow their leadership. They are often quietly spoken, but their words speak loudly and clearly.

To some men it comes early in life and fades; we all know the schoolboy hero who makes nothing of his life. To others it comes late, after life experience and knowledge have shaped and hewed their personalities.

This man was such a person; handsome, athletic, knowledgeable, someone to respect and someone to love. Someone free of hubris and arrogance, someone touched by simple human kindness and humility but edged with physical hardness, a man in control of his environment and his destiny. A leader of men!

He caught my eye and began to walk towards me. Later and in very different circumstances, he would tell me why he had come to me. He smiled a wide, confident smile as he approached. 'Hello, lad,' he said in a slight northern accent, his brown eyes sparkling. 'I'm looking for a crew and I think I can get you where you need to be.' I was not sure what to make of that statement. I was slightly confused. I presumed as a navigator he could take me over the target, but was that it or did he have a wider context with destiny in mind? Years later, I came to believe it was the latter context.

Although we were of the same rank, flight sergeants, I immediately deferred to the older man. 'I am sure you could, sir.' I did not need to call him sir, but as an opening statement it felt right. I still could not quite believe this self-assured man had approached me.

'We'll none of that formality, lad. My name is David, and who are you?'

'Bob Astell, Sarge. Pleased to meet you.'

'Right, Bob,' he replied, 'let's go find ourselves a really good pilot to cart us around Germany. Got anyone in mind?'

'None at all,' I said. 'You?'

'Yes, Bobby lad, I've been told we should look out for Flight Sergeant Johnny Smith. Passed out in the top three of his class. If we're going to get through this, I want the best I can find at the controls. I know what I am looking for. I passed my pilot's exams myself, but my mathematics is better than my flying apparently and the brass told me they had plenty of pilots but fewer people able to wield a compass accurately, so here I am.'

The natural leadership and foresight of my navigator was already showing through. Instinctively I already thought of him as 'my' navigator.

‘How do we find him, David?’

‘Let’s ask, it should be simple enough.’

David pulled a young sergeant with the dual wings of a pilot on his chest to one side.

‘Are you John Smith?’ he asked.

‘No, I am afraid not!’ The pilot looked disappointed. ‘Are you fellows looking for a pilot by any chance?’

‘No, just John Smith,’ David said quickly, but with a broad disarming smile that let the young sergeant pilot down easily.

‘Over there with the blond hair,’ he told us with some resignation.

‘Thanks pal,’ said David. ‘What’s your name, by the way?’

‘Kevin, Kevin Beamon’ he said

‘Kevin , the best of luck to you. I know you are going to find a great crew. See the tall skinny guy over there with the black hair? He’s Bill. The best nav on my course. Grab him and tell him I sent you.’

The young pilot looked faintly elated and moved off quickly.

David motioned to me and we walked over to the unbelievably youthful looking flight sergeant with the pilot's wings. Even to me he only looked about 15 or 16 years old. Not a trace of stubble on his face and perfectly smooth, unblemished skin. Only, maybe, 5 feet 6 inches tall, which emphasized the impression of youth. Apparently undeterred by the young age of this pilot, David put on his winning smile and went straight for his target.

'Are you John Smith?'

'Yes,' came the slightly wary response.

'We've heard good things about you. Do you need a good crew?' David played the clever game that this was to be the young pilot's choice when in reality it was no such thing. The blond kid smiled nervously, which if it were possible, actually made him look even younger. A cherub on a Christmas card came faintly to mind.

'How can you have heard anything about me? I'm absolutely hopeless. Get sick in the air and only have about 50 hours flying under my belt.'

'We're not here to argue, Johnny. I and my bomb aimer, Bob here, are looking for a first-rate pilot. I'm David, by the way.'

David gripped the young pilot's hand and increased the intensity of his grin, and John surrendered.

'I'm game if you are,' he said and suddenly in the space of three minutes there I was with the foundation of a new Lancaster bomber crew. A pilot, a navigator, and myself, the bomb aimer. The three key human ingredients to get a heavy bomber to Germany and back and do the assigned job. In such a short space of time, I had met two men who were to affect my life for the rest of my days!

'Right, that's it,' said David. 'Now, Skipper,' he said, flattering the cherub even further, 'let's go find a couple of gunners to guard our backside.'

Standing in the far corner of the hangar was a gaggle of gunners. Just clear of the main group, talking intently, were two likely looking lads. As we approached, they pretended to ignore us, but the presence of our nav standing patiently in front of them could not be ignored. His aura seemed to warm the very air around us.

The two gunners turned towards us. The taller of the two with tousled curly brown hair and blue eyes spoke first. The only trouble for me was that I was not precisely sure what he actually said. I recognized the accent as that of Yorkshire, but it was so thick and heavy that a well brought up boy from Cheshire such as I, was barely able to understand it.

'Hey up thee three, what does thee want?' At least I think that was what he said and I was intrigued that he was able to turn the plural three into a singular object.

Our nav was unfazed and seemed to be able to speak the dialect fluently, which impressed me even further.

'Tha's well?' said David, which was a question apparently.

'Alrite, I suppose. What's thee after, Sarge?' said Yorkshire. Another question.

'Gunners, lad. Are thee both up for it?' said

David, answering with yet another question.

There was a pause whilst the air gunners looked the three of us over.

'Can the lad drive?' said Yorkshire. I think he might have been referring to Johnny with this question but he kept his gaze on David.

'Happen' was the response from David which I simply had no translation for, but it might have meant yes. I was actually finding the economy of this northern debate involving no narrative, tenses, or subjunctive clauses quite difficult to follow.

'What's tha think?' Another question, but this time Yorkshire was directing it towards his companion, a short and stocky thick-set man with blue grey eyes who now spoke for the first time.

'Yeh, they look good, pal. Let's go with them.'

I was relieved to hear an accent that I at least vaguely recognised with a reasonable level of diction and which took the form of a pure statement in the positive.

Unfortunately, David immediately relapsed

into northern vernacular and I was back on Ilkley Moor without a hat again!

'Reet, then. Job's a good un. Does thee know a good wi op then?'

'No! does thee?' said Yorkshire.

Would this mutual interrogation session never end I wondered, at which point David turned and winked at John and myself.

'In case you did not know, chaps, I'm a Yorkshireman too.'

'That does explain a lot,' I said.

We shook hands with our new crewmates.

'Geoff, Geoff Patterson from Northampton,' said our stocky crewmate. 'I look forward to working with you boys.'

'Cyril Knowles, from Dewsbury,' said our tall Yorkshireman, who then proceeded to give us some sage advice. 'Tret us rite and we'll tret thee rite. Tha all must stand thee rounds, no mythering, mind.' In my head I translated this as 'Treat us correctly and buy your rounds of beer and we shall all get along fine.' This new language was going to take some getting used to!

Now that we were five, we had to find a wireless operator, the man who would keep us in touch with our fellow flyers in the air as well co-ordinate our position and receive and transmit any changes to our targets.

Again, our navigator led his little party back into the centre of the hangar and began to scan the room. We all spotted a striking and unusual fellow talking to another crew carefully stroking his chin. He was a tall and very sophisticated looking chap with striking jet-black hair, which was obviously very carefully cut and groomed by a professional. Not for him the make-do look of an RAF barber! He also sported a perfect pencil moustache. Many of the men in the room that night had tried without success to carry off the sophistication of a perfect Hollywood style moustache. Either through a lack of, as yet, sufficient male hormone or through abject ignorance, most had failed, but kept up the pretence nonetheless that the creeping fur on the top lip was actually a look of maturity and style. This man, on the other hand, carried it off with perfection.

The effect was further enhanced by the perfectly tailored uniform he wore, rather than the loose fitting 'off the peg' or rather 'off the factory floor' look that most of us had to endure throughout the war.

This wireless operator stood listening to the offer that seemed to be being put to him, but his eyes occasionally flitted away from the salesman in front of him. The pitch was clearly not perfect! He seemed to say nothing.

David saw his opportunity and moved in, flashing his best smile. I never did find out why David thought this man should become our wireless man, but he certainly stood out from the milling crowd and not simply because of the perfectly fitting uniform and flashing teeth. David's target appeared to be Indian, with dark skin and fine aquiline features.

'Excuse me, Sarge,' he said to the pilot who was attempting to explain exactly why the wireless man should join his crew, 'but I hope you will not mind if I have a word with this friend of mine here. We were at school together don't you know,' he lied.

A faint smile came over the handsome

Indian's face. He did not speak but moved languidly in behind David as he turned and stepped back towards us standing just a few yards away. The alternative crew turned to watch.

Our Yorkshire Tyke, Cyril's face was a picture of intrigue and bewilderment as David returned with his exotic companion. David turned to his find. 'Now then, old chap, I would be honoured if you would join Johnny here, Bobby, Geoff, Cyril, and myself as our wireless operator. We think we are going to make the best crew in our OTU, and we aim to all get through this war in one damned piece.'

Still the handsome Indian did not speak. He rocked gently, shifting his weight from one foot to another in his tailored shoes and returned to stroking his chin whilst his deep brown eyes slowly flicked around our crew, seemingly sizing us up as comrades and friends.

The silence continued. Finally, Cyril could take it no more. Economy of word and action was in his Yorkshire blood and these polite games were not for him. He began as always with a question.

'Does tha spake English lad?' he said in his

broadest dialect. 'Say som'at, for God's sake.'

He clearly had no idea how to approach this subject and as the silence continued and our Indian friend weighed up his options with a wry smile on his face. Cyril made one last attempt to elicit a response, speaking as slowly and carefully as possible.

'Ah said...does tha spake English' – a long pause – 'lad?'

The handsome man turned to face Cyril square on, his brown eyes twinkling, but the face still impassive. He drew a small but exaggerated breath and spoke for the first time.

The timing of his response was perfect. Unhurried and unforced, he spoke in the most clear-cut diamond voice, accentless, with a perfect emphasis on each clearly pronounced syllable. His English was a thing of perfection and beauty with exquisite tone and timbre.

'Well, my dear chap. I do try at all times to speak your language with the correct pronunciation, diction, and clarity. I try to emphasis my words to ensure that I am at all times and in all places perfectly understood. I feel that in the specialisation I have now chosen to carry out in support of my King and Empire, clarity of voice over the crackling wireless will be of the utmost importance.'

The voice cut away but the twinkling smile remained.

Cyril's face, on the other hand, had changed. His jaw sagged a little and his tongue seemed to hang from his mouth and his eyes bulged with surprise. He recovered quickly enough, however, and the cockiness returned to his voice. Now it was his turn to pause for added emphasis as a confident smile returned to his face. In turn his timing was perfect as he looked at the rest of us.

'Ah telled thee he could na speak bloody English. Noe idea what that wah about.'

Laughter broke out all around, including from the alternative crew who knew now that they would still have to find a wireless operator.

'What t' bloody 'ell does tha call that? Does thee work for the BBC or som'at?' Cyril's questions resumed.

The laughter continued.

‘The name is Danuska Kissonsingh,’ said our new crewmate, ‘but you can call me Dan if it helps,’ and handshakes took place all around. ‘Pleased to meet you all, chaps.’

‘So where did you really get that accent?’ asked David, who actually had not seemed phased in the least by the perfection of the voice we had all just heard. Dan paused for a moment, but seemed to decide that he had better keep matters as transparent as possible in order to short circuit the team building process.

‘Oh, quite simple really,’ he replied in his perfect King’s English. ‘My father is the Principal Private Secretary to the Prime Minister of Mauritius, which is where I was born. I was educated at the Royal College, Curepipe, where we were served a copious diet of French and English classics, Moliere, Racine, Hobbes, Locke, Rousseau, Adam Smith, Dickens, you name it. I won a Rhodes Scholarship to Oxford in 1937, took up my place in 1938, and fell in love with it, in particular its intoxicating blend of centuries of youth and tradition with a never-ending search for intellectual truth. There I still was when the war came along. England is my spiritual and intellectual home. It is mine to protect and love. I hate the darkness that Nazism has spread on this continent. If we lose, my kind will certainly have no place in their world. I joined the OTC at Oxford and as a result find myself with you all today.'

There was silence for a moment.

'Right simple, nah tha says it like that,' said a smiling Cyril.

Dan turned to David. 'Thanks for the intervention, by the way, this feels right!'

The self-effacing English manner that pervaded the room that night came upon David also.

'I don't know what the hell I am doing myself, but I do know I need the best men around me if I am to get through this. The odds for us all are not great as you all know, but now we have the best pilot in his class,' he nodded at Johnny, who flushed red, 'and he will get us there and back in 30 missions God willing... or should I say Gods willing?'

It was now Dan's turn to look a little abashed. 'I'll tell you about that later,' said the handsome Mauritian, although he never did in the end. 'By the way, how do you know John is that good?'

'I checked! It doesn't matter how, but I was told that he was the best flyer in his class. Maybe not the best at the paperwork perhaps or the theory, but put the man behind the controls of any aircraft in the RAF and he can make it do things and at a speed that no one thinks possible. The finest natural pilot some of the trainers had seen, apparently.'

We all listened attentively to that little speech. We looked at Johnny, who blushed an even deeper shade of red.

'Well, I do enjoy flying a bit,' was all he could say.

Clearly David had put a good deal of thought into getting this team together, but getting the right 'skipper' was the key and he felt that everything else would follow from it.

We all knew the odds were stacked against us surviving 30 missions over Germany. There was a 5% casualty rate per raid, which as an average did not sound too bad unless you happened to be amongst the 5% of course, but multiply that number by the 30 missions you were required to do and the numbers simply did not compute to your advantage. We were young then, however, and no 19-year-old can ever really contemplate death, which was purely a theoretical concept to me at the time. Even if we could reconcile ourselves to death's reality in war, however, it was an equal certainty that someone always survives to tell the tale and with sublime poignancy every single man in that room that night believed it would be he, that survived. We now had the best pilot and a natural leader in David. With these men around us we felt as immortal as warriors could be. It was euphoric!

In that moment we began to weld together as a team. The RAF "method" had worked its magic. We knew we would have many hours of training to come over the next seven weeks, but we had the view in that moment that we could work together and look after each other and survive.

David turned to us all and said 'OK boys, let's go and sign up for this war,' and we walked over to the nearest warrant officer sitting at his desk.

'Gentlemen,' he said as we stood around him, 'Are you together by any chance?'

'Yes sir, we are,' said David.

'Your names then, gentlemen.'

David indicated that Johnny as the skipper should go first and then one by one, we announced our names and serial numbers to the warrant officer, who carefully wrote them down and ticked them off against a substantial ledger of all those present.

The warrant officer gave Johnny a duplicate of the chit he had just written down listing the details of the crew. 'Congratulations, Skipper, and the very best of luck to you and your crew.'

'Thank you, sir,' beamed John, who then turned to David. 'Where to now, Navigator? Give me a course.'

'The pub, I think, gentlemen, if we can flag down a bus to Buckingham. The pub should be as good a place as any to start our training!' David replied with a wide smile.

We moved out of the hangar as the last of the milling crews made their approaches and salutations to each other. As we did so David pointed out to me that the pilot, he had originally approached in order to find John Smith was in a crew with the navigator he had recommended.

Outside it was a chilly evening. Buses and trucks that had brought the men and kit into Silverstone were already being commandeered to go into Buckingham. It was a common enough occurrence and the drivers were happy to be bribed with the offer of free beer to take the new crews into town.

We dumped our kit onto the hangar floor to be collected later and crowded onto a single bus.

Forty minutes later we found ourselves in the warm fug of the Red Lion. David bought the first round as we were in effect 'his' crew and led the conversation. 'Right, boys, here we all are and here is to all of us. Good luck,' he raised his glass and we reciprocated his gesture.

'Right,' he said, 'there is a war on and we have to move fast so let's have a quick rundown on who we all are, just to break the ice. I'll go first.' He paused. 'David Lumb, I'm a bit past it at 30 I'm afraid. I was born, bred, and still live in Morley in Yorkshire just south of Leeds. I'm an accountant by trade, so pretty good with numbers you will be pleased to know. I was Deputy Borough Treasurer at the Morley Town Hall before I joined up in 1941. Play a bit of rugby in the winter and cricket in the summer.' He paused again. 'How's that?' he asked. 'Will that do? Who's next?'

Cyril piped up, but not to tell his life story.

'Thirty, tha says. Tha'll be needing thee slippers to get in t'bloody plane. What is thee doing here? Borough Treasurer is a reserved occupation in't it? Tha need not be here. Yah could ha stayed at home like.'

'Cyril, lad, you are right of course,' David said, then addressed himself to all of us. 'I come from a big family. Brother number 3 was born in 1918, on November 10th actually. The next morning at 11 the bells rang for the armistice and my mother always swore they were ringing for young Jack. The irony of all ironies is that those born in the year peace finally came in the first war, were all called up in 1939 to fight this bloody second war now and put right the wrongs of that peace. All those who were 20 in 1939 were called up no matter what; they had no choice. So, in July 1939 off young Jack went. My mother was worried sick. I could not let him serve alone while I stayed at home all nice and cosy. I could have done my bit in the Town Hall, watching the money, but what kind of war would that be and what if he does not come back? He is in the Royal Marines and has already seen the worst of it. Norway in 1940, Crete in '41 and he's in the Far East now, poor bastard. So, I volunteered for RAF like the rest of you and here we are. Besides lad,' he said, turning directly to Cyril, 'I may be old and knackered but I'll get you in and out of Germany damn quick.'

Cyril smiled softly and drank deeply from his pint.

'Alright,' said David, 'now you know my story, what about the rest of you?'

With the exception of Dan, who was 22, no one was over 21, so we believed we had nothing in the way of life experience to put alongside David's, and we were all a little reluctant to speak.

Eventually a small potted history was teased

from us as the evening and the beer took hold.

Cyril was a miner, as was his father and his grandfather before him. He had done an engineering course at night school while working above ground at the same pit as his father. His qualifications were good enough to get him accepted for aircrew training when he volunteered in 1941 aged just 17. 'I'll kill us a few of them Jerrys before I go back down pit after its all over,' he declared.

John Smith, our pilot, was from a little town in the Scottish borders, Melrose. The only son, he was a keen runner, tennis player, and reader of history. His father was a vet. In 1942, John volunteered to fly heavy bombers, which he had dreamed of flying all his life. He learnt to fly at his local gliding club and was qualified before he had even sat behind the wheel of a car. After some extensive testing by the RAF, he was accepted for PNB (Pilot, Navigator, Bomb Aimer) training and was sent to his nearest OTC in Berwick upon Tweed.

My story lasted all of 15 seconds. 'Bob Astell, aged 19, from Bollington near Macclesfield,' I gulped out. Father deceased. I work for a local architect but I really want to be a teacher of English. I love all English novels, but for the moment I just want to fly in heavies,' was all I could find to say.

Geoff Patterson we already knew was from Northampton. He was 20, had two brothers and a sister, and was a trainee draughtsman at his local engineering works. He was happy to talk about his experiences when volunteering. He wanted the RAF as we all did; it was the youngest and most exciting of all the services and had all the cachet and glamour associated with a new fashion.

Geoff was sent to Lord's Cricket Ground in 1941, which was then being used by the RAF to assess new recruits. He initially failed his eye test but pleaded with the medical orderly to be given second chance. The orderly told him to come back the next day at the same time. Geoff was desperate to get into the RAF, so for his final chance he decided to spruce himself up even more than usual, to give himself the best military bearing. He pressed his tunic, polished his boots, washed and carefully combed his hair, made sure his teeth were as white as possible, and even spent 15 minutes polishing his tunic buttons to a high sheen. It was the best 15 minutes he ever spent.

The next day the same officer who had failed him in his eye test gave him a clear pass. Puzzled, Geoff said, 'Sir, yesterday my eyesight was not good enough for the RAF but today it is fine?'

'Yes,' came the reply, 'but yesterday your tunic buttons were not as clean as they are today!' Before he could respond, Geoff was dismissed from the room. He left shaking his head and wondering how newly polished brass buttons had miraculously improved his eyesight! He never did get an answer.

Dan did not add to our knowledge of him any more than we had already learnt back in the hangar at Silverstone. Cyril continued to eye him with some caution, however.

'Any bloody miners at Oxford, then, Dan old boy?' He tried his best BBC accent with this phrase, but I am afraid to say it still sounded purest Barnsley to me.

'Cyril my dearest chap, I'm afraid not and much the poorer it is for it, I have to say,' said

Dan, rising to the class challenge admirably. 'But after this war is over, you and I are going to have dinner at my college in our brave new world that we will have shaped and created together, free of the fascist threat. What do you say to that, old chap?' His accent was exaggerated of course, but he meant what he said.

Cyril looked at his new colonial colleague with a continuing degree of scepticism but there were, perhaps, the first indications of mutual respect. If anything, Cyril was flattered to receive an invitation to dinner at an Oxford College, but he kept his distance for the moment. The Yorkshire accent came on even stronger but the timing was good. 'Time for thee to get thee next round in, ah think.'

We all laughed and Dan stepped forward to collect the next round.

'Normally I'd get the servants to do this kind of thing.' He winked at Cyril and moved off before he could respond.

Once settled down with another round of drinks, David moved the conversation off in a different direction, keen to know more about our pilot.

‘Now then, young Johnny. I have heard great things about you from some of your instructors. How good are you?’

John blushed a little again. ‘I’m not sure I’m that good, really.’ He tried to defer the interrogation, partly out of genuine bashfulness and partly out of fear of giving his crew anything to worry about.

David was serious. ‘John, I know the senior instructor at your AFU. I used to walk out with his sister. He tells me you were one of the best he has seen. The quickest to learn, the fastest to grasp new concepts, and the most confident in the air. What were risks to other pilots you made look perfectly safe. You never got sick, never missed a training flight and went solo three flights ahead of the next best in your unit. You’re good, mate!’

John had been caught red-handed. All the observations were true. He stammered a little as he began his story.

‘Well, it’s true, I just love to fly. I cannot wait to get into that seat and get up there each day. I find it so exciting, so exhilarating. You can all see that I am not the tallest bloke around, but when I get behind those controls it's like I am reborn. I control the power of those engines and the way they move in three dimensions. I cannot explain it, but I feel bigger, stronger, more in control of my destiny when I fly. If I live until I am 100 years old, I will always have to fly. It's like I exist above and beyond the world. I just need to do this.'

His words tailed away, but we could all feel the pleasure and delight he took in his skill. He was a boy transformed into a man when he spoke of flying. That night we all looked forward to seeing him in action and David's plan to give us all confidence in our new pilot had worked perfectly.

Buoyed by our skipper's confidence, Geoff urged him to give us more details. 'Tell us some more about the training in the AFU, John. What was it like?'

'Well, we flew Airspeed Oxfords. We called them "Oxboxes". It's a pretty heavy plane, closer to the feel of bombers, I believe. We flew four or five training flights a day, depending on the weather, including night flying. I loved the night flying in particular or the night simulations, although they were really tough at first.

'They gave us a special helmet with red coloured glass eye pieces. The cockpit windows were tinted green so that at night it looked absolutely pitch-black outside with nothing to pick up on in, so you have to rely totally on your instruments. It's scary at first. Are the compass bearings absolutely right, the altimeter accurate and so forth? But after a while the confidence comes. You know they can get you absolutely anywhere you want to be as long as the bearings are right and the rest of time you can feel your aircraft in your feet and through your toes on the rudder and through your hands on the stick. It's like you can talk to her and she understands everything that you want her to do, every thought, every desire.

'One exercise we had to do with everyone masked up was a beam approach blind landing. You had to listen out for a series of "beeps" like the BBC "pips" over the radio. If you are on course they sound at a certain rate, too fast and you are high, too slow and you're too low. You just have to keep the signals nice and regular and find your way down onto the runway. You cannot see a thing, remember. I tell you it makes you listen out very carefully as you know the ground is coming up to meet you and you have to adjust throttle and flaps and rudder all the time to keep in line and on the right glide path. There is an instructor to take over if you get it wrong, but you don't want to let that happen.

'First time I did this, my instructor shouted and took over and I thought I'd buggered it up, but when I took my helmet off, we were no more than 50 feet from the ground and bang on line with the runway. I couldn't believe it. My instructor was seriously chuffed I can tell you, but not more than I was.

'I tell you boys, if we ever get into trouble, I will bring you all home. I promise you, boys.'

He had been looking down and away from all of us, but at these last words he lifted his head and looked directly at us, his blue eyes flashing with his passion and self-belief.

'I promise you boys I will bring you all home safe!'

We believed him. How could we not? His sincerity and self-confidence were plain for all to see and hear. We were not to know that at that moment the gods of war and of fate turned to each other and giggled a little in their knowledge of the future.

'Thank you, John,' said Dan, the perfection of his voice only adding to the power of John's words. 'I think you may indeed be a Greek God of legend. Perseus reborn perhaps, or do I mean Lelantos, the Titan of the air? Either way your skills and quick thinking will make a mockery of us all and our Germanic Gorgan adversaries I trust. Here's to you.'

He paused for effect. 'To the Skipper,' he declared, then raised his glass. The chorus was returned by the rest of us, as we drank to John and he went back to being his bashful self as he withered under the compliments of his new crew and comrades.

David simply smiled a slightly knowing smile as if his research had just been confirmed.

We thought perhaps that might be the end for tonight as it was getting close to closing time, but there was still time for another round and David wanted to know more.

'Cyril, lad. How was your training?'

Cyril paused, not sure about the need for this. 'Lads from Dewsbury don't allus have much to say, Sarge,' he said.

'Ah but I think you do,' said David.

'Alrite Sarge, I'll tell thee all summat so we can all be sure what we are getting into.

'When I did me gunnery training I wha sent to South Wales at Stornydown gunnery school. We trained on range in fixed turrets and then in't air in a bloody ancient Whitley. Knackered she were! Six of us at a time shooting at a drogue towed by a Lysander. We all had different coloured tracer shells so instructors could tell us apart.

'Anyway, the lads I were with were a good bunch. Got on grand we all did for three weeks or so. I'd applied to be transferred to another gunnery school in Morpeth cos me eldest sister were training to be a nurse in Newcastle and it were closer like. Niver thought I'd get that transfer, but one day the adjutant comes up and tells me I could go.

'Next day I wha away, but I heard that two days after I left, them other five lads were all burnt to death when the Whitley turned over on landing.

'I often think how bloody lucky I were. Niver did get to spend much time with me sister either, we just couldn't get our leave sorted between us. Any road, let's all hope we all get as lucky, eh?'

No one replied, but we all thought silently about Cyril's gunnery mates. We had all heard similar stories of bad luck across all the services. Just guys being in the wrong place at the wrong time, but being young and blessed with eternal optimism we all insisted silently that it could never happen to us.

In the sombre moment we drank the last dregs of our beer and decided to head back to barracks.

As the bus rolled on into Silverstone, Cyril addressed Dan directly, referring to his earlier comments about Johnny.

'So who is this Lelantos bloke, then? One of thee servants?'

'Ah, not quite, Cyril old chap. Simply one

of the Titans of Greek myth. You know, like Zeus, Aphrodite, or Apollo of Olympic legend. A member of a primeval race of deities who were around even before you English came on the scene!' He smiled. 'In the case of Lelantos, he is one of the younger Titan gods of the air with a hunter's skill of stalking prey. Quite an apt description for the Skipper, don't you think?'

'If tha says so,' said Cyril. He continued his questioning. 'So how many of thee got, then?'

'What, servants?'

'Aye. How many ruddy servants?'

Dan's face remained rakishly impassive as he spoke.

'Oh, I'm not always sure. It varies of course depending on the time of year, as you probably know Cyril. I suppose there are six regular servants if you don't count the cook whom one might regard as a tradesman, don't you think?'

Cyril stared carefully at Dan as the latter moved relentlessly on.

'Of course, when I went up to Oxford I was only allowed one "scout", as college servants were called, and I had to share him with the rest of the chaps on the same landing. Still, needs must.'

The rest of the crew were enjoying this in rapt humour as Cyril struggled to come to terms with his new comrade.

'And you. Cyril old chap. How many servants do you have in ah....Dewsbury? Is that what you call your estate?' It could have sounded a cruel remark in the hands of most others, but the innocent joy in Dan's voice made clear it was part of the intricate dance that he and Cyril had already started stepping together.

Cyril saw his chance and growled his response.

'When me Dad gets back from a shift at the pit, me Mam has a tin bath ready of water heated by fire. She washes his face, hands, chest, and legs like and that's it. Me Dad won't let her clean his back, except to rub it with a piece of old dry newspaper. He reckons that if he had his back washed proper like it'll weaken his spine like. I reckon its nonsense meself but he and few of the other older blokes at pit swear its true. So he goes to bed like that every night.

'After his bath, me Mam makes us all dinner as best she can and then we all sit for a bit and chat. Then we all go to bed. Me, me sister and brother in one room and me Mam and Dad in't t'other room with the youngest bairns like.'

Now it was Cyril's turn to be impassively amused. Dan looked at David with a quizzical gaze to check the possible truth or otherwise of Cyril's words. David merely raised an eyebrow and smiled slightly to indicate to Dan that he had better leave it there. David had many miners living in his town. He knew their trials and their living conditions. It was unlikely Cyril was exaggerating in any way.

Danuska Kissongsingh looked at Cyril, paused, and then said. 'My friend, your words may come from Momus, the Greek spirit of mockery and stinging criticism, but I suspect that you are in reality, Kratos, the true spirit of might, power, and strength!' The last three words were said slowly and carefully with great emphasis.

Cyril smiled. 'I ain't got a clue what tha bloody hell thee is talking about lad, but it sounds alrite to me. I take it tha did not study mining engineering at Oxford, tha way tha uses all them funny words?'

'I'm afraid a degree in classics does not get one along way in terms of understanding geology or much else other than language I am afraid, but I am sure you will be enlightening me in the future,' Dan replied. They both laughed together.

The mood after this exchange was bright and relaxed. Time had moved forward quickly, turbo charged by war, and bonds of friendship and respect that would last a lifetime had already been cast.

The relationship between Cyril and Dan continued to develop. The contrast between the wealthy Mauritian and the miner's son from West Yorkshire could not have been greater. It was the plot of good drama perhaps, and possible only because of the historical backdrop of a global war fused with the then reality of the British Empire and its Commonwealth and Dominions.

The relationship continued to entertain and amuse us throughout our weeks of training. Both parties grew to play their respective roles perfectly, each slightly exaggerating their backgrounds, accents, and misunderstandings for the benefit of their growing audience.

Nevertheless, the inherent contradictions of their backgrounds was marvellous to behold. One from a wealthy merchant class of empire, brought up in a large house with servants, with a lengthy and formal education; suave, sophisticated, and charming. The other, physically tough, direct, and from the poorest class imaginable, but self-made already at his young age. His destiny was in his hands alone.

Both were subjects of the King, though they came from different ends of colonial rule. Which man was which was hard to discern and in the end it mattered not. They were both greater than any label. In the strange magnificence of war they were reduced to being the same man. Both were sergeants in the RAF. They shared the same billet, the same food, the same clothes, and the same danger in the face of the enemy. The risk of death in the air created the perfect equality. As we found during our training (if we did not know it before), we simply had to work as a team or we might die. Status, title, or background was irrelevant when a German gunner was on your tail.

Two days later we were joined by an air engineer called Gordon Edwards, a 23-year-old New Zealander from a little town in the centre of the North Island of that country called Putaruru. "The place of the owl," he told us it meant in Maori. The son of a farmer, inevitably. Like most Kiwis who were small in number but large in heart, Gordon, or Don as he preferred, was incredibly practical. He and his family could build and fix anything. When the nearest town of any size was 40 miles or more away, you learnt how to keep things moving and in good working order. He was a natural engineer. Quiet, almost taciturn, but with a dry sense of humour, he fitted well into our little team and we all grew to respect his common sense and sound knowledge.

So there we were in early 1944, a truly international team readying ourselves for war: two Englishmen, a Scot, a New Zealander, a Mauritian and two Yorkshiremen. The ultimate war machine of the British Empire, perhaps, ready to defend our homes, our families, our lives, our ancient liberties, and our empire against the forces of fascism and dictatorship that threatened to overwhelm the world!

Well, perhaps some of those esoteric issues

might occasionally cross our minds, but not often. War is mainly viewed in hindsight by those who write the histories or mourn personal loss, or by those in later generations who look and read with wonder at the sacrifices and courage of those who actually serve and fight. To those of us who serve, however, it is real and survival is the instinct that drives us. We just wanted to get through it and go home, hopefully without letting any of our mates down. Not quite the bold martial spirit but pragmatic nonetheless.

We were young, vibrant, and alive – and we wanted to stay that way. We retained our ambition for the future and a life to be lived. At the commencement of our training, we were excited, however, in a way that only a young man can be. Life is an adventure at that age and war perhaps is the ultimate adventure and test of manhood. Roll the dice and survive and you perhaps you have the ultimate story to tell. A glorious warrior's death was not for us. We never wanted poems and eulogies written about us. We did want to fly in a large war machine. That thought was intoxicating. To live and to die was the choice. We always chose life and would leave the dying to the other man!

Now it all began.

Chapter 2

First Flight

Looking back from the distance of 50 years or so, I can honestly say that those next seven weeks in 1944 were the most intensive, tiring, and yet satisfying and enjoyable of my whole life. Only hindsight and my survival can provide that perspective.

Those weeks of 'heavy conversion', learning how to fly and fight with the latest RAF technology, were lived with every sense and sinew heightened and stretched. This was no drug-induced artificiality but the purest outpouring of human effort, emotion, intellect, and desire as we sought to weld ourselves into an effective team, capable of fighting a war.

We desired to succeed in our tasks as individuals. We desired never to let our chosen crewmates down and we desired, above all, to survive or at least to ensure that we had the skills to allow us the best chance to survive.

The rich mixture of youth, newly acquired

manhood, camaraderie, intellect, and humour, blended against the backdrop of global war and the imminent and perhaps ultimate challenge of death, was a heady mixture of emotion and even joy.

David led us through it all, down the carefully thought-out path he had planned to get us through the entire program. From the beginning he made it absolutely clear that we should prepare and train like no other crew for what lay ahead. His rationale was simple. If we trained to a point where virtually all action became routine and as near perfection as possible, we could rely on that in times of trouble and maximum stress, when the 'fog of war' and unknown terrors of battle came close. We must rely utterly on each other. No one could shirk or fail. He reasoned, as did the RAF, that if responses were almost automatic, fear itself might be eliminated or reduced.

That was the theory at least. It was simply taking the recognized military strategy to break down individuality and build up a machine-like team to its logical extent. My memories of those days are now only enhanced by the searing logic of the need to survive and by the hard work we all committed ourselves to.

The bond between the seven of us grew rapidly over those weeks. It remains to this day. I can say with utter honesty that there has never been a day, a waking hour, in my life these past 50 or so years when I have not thought about those weeks and the six men with whom I shared my life. The forge of war welded us together and before I sleep each night their faces drift across my ebbing consciousness. I will take them to my own death.

It began, however, rather badly!

The 'heavy conversion' unit at RAF Silverstone where we ended up (heavy as in heavy bomber) was equipped with the oldest, most threadbare clapped-out old kites one could ever have the misfortune to see. The war was on, very little could be spared, and the training crews got what was left. These birds had done maybe 60 to 80 trips over Germany. They had been shot at, hit, thrown around the sky, patched up, repaired, shot at again, and sent back time and again for more punishment.

As we stood in front of 'our' Stirling bomber for our very first training flight, little was said by the crew. Anticipation of our first flight together was now very much mixed with trepidation as to whether we would ever get into the air at all, let alone get back down. Even Johnny, who felt he could fly anything, looked suddenly underwhelmed.

Dan spoke first, but only to crisply observe, 'Ah!'

Cyril was more to the point. 'What the bloody hell does tha call this?'

Only our Kiwi engineer, Don, who claimed he could repair anything mechanical, seemed pleased. "Well, ain't she a beaut, boys. Just look at her!"

The Short Brothers Stirling was indeed a remarkable aircraft. She had four engines and was capable of taking off in just 500 feet of runway. She was originally based on a four-engine flying boat design which was the specialty of Short Brothers of Belfast. The trouble with this excellent specialism was that Short Brothers, until they designed the Stirling, had never before built anything with a retractable undercarriage to put down on the ground, so the spindly thing they built her with was, frankly, rubbish. A problem made worse by the fact that they actually lengthened the undercarriage during the war so she could get airborne even faster by angling the attack of her thick wings into the wind.

She was designed to span the Empire and be able to take off and land virtually anywhere, whilst carrying up to 24 men to far flung places, and return with any amount of cargo or to bomb cities from obscure jungle runways. They called her a 'jack of all trades' but in reality, she became the master of very little.

Worse still, some genius at the Air Ministry, who can only have been employable by Government, decided that she needed to have her original wing span of 108 feet reduced to 92 feet in order for her to fit into the pre-war specification of RAF hangar. Rather than alter the hangars they chose to reduce the performance of the aircraft, meaning that she could never get above 12,000 feet with a full bomb load.

As a result, she had to fly at a low level against the German flak gunners in the early stages of the war, and casualties were ridiculous. As the new Lancaster's and Halifax's came into service, the Stirling was taken out of the front line. She became a coastal reconnaissance plane and any that had survived were turned over for the training of youthful, wide-eyed bomber crews like us. Very pleasing!

As we gingerly climbed the ladder into her interior for the first time, led by our instructor, Pilot Officer Davis, a man with over 50 front line operations over Germany to his name, it was difficult to ignore the holes, tears, repairs, and loose rivets along her fuselage, wings, and control surfaces. She had been shot at and hunted by the enemy many times and now her lot was to be hurled around the skies by a load of inexperienced flyers who might be willing but had no experience and limited knowledge.

As we made our way along the tight narrow fuselage, clumsy and slow in our new and heavy flying suits, we had a good look at the concrete of the hard standing area below the aircraft through the various tears and rends in the fabric of the old girl.

Nervous anticipation now merged with a certain horror that she would not actually get us off the ground or would disintegrate in mid-air before we had even flown our first training flight as a crew! We were confident in ourselves as individuals but bemused to actually be sitting in a ropey old piece of engineering.

We took our places in our allotted crew stations. I was down in the bomb aimer's nose cone. Johnny of course was in the pilot's seat. In the Stirling, David as the navigator sat in a small cubicle directly below the pilot and connected by intercom. Don our engineer and Dan our wireless operator sat further back in the aircraft and separated from the pilot by an armoured bulkhead and hinged door. Further back still sat Geoff, our quiet young Midlander, high up in his mid-upper gunner's turret, directly above the bomb bay, with a set of servo motor fed ammunition boxes, and right away at the very back of the aircraft sat Cyril, our laconic Yorkshireman, in his rear gunner's turret. At the moment he was not feeling or sounding the least bit laconic. He was decidedly pugnacious with somewhat strongly worded views as to our chances of coming back alive. Up alongside Johnny in the second pilot's seat sat PO Davis, our instructor.

PO Davis had already given Johnny a thorough briefing on the many foibles and idiosyncrasies that the aircraft had built up over her 20,000 odd flying hours in the hour before take-off but the whole crew was forced to endure listening to them over the intercom as PO Davis went over the checklists again. It did not help morale greatly!

'Now remember, Sergeant Smith, the air speed indicator can get a bit sticky over 6000 feet. Not sure why exactly, so we will keep her below 5000 to start with. Also, number 3 engine has a carburettor problem in a climb of more than 35 degrees so watch your take-off angles and no sudden movements!

'Now it's vital we get these take-offs and landings right. This is a good old bird but she is an absolute bitch on take-off and not much better when landing! This high standing triangular wheel base we have with the main wheels under us and the smaller at the rear means she has a tendency to swing violently to the right on take-off before the ground speed gets up sufficiently for the rudder to have an effect, so what we are going to do is feed the revs in on the right engines for the first 20 seconds of the take-off run to try and avoid her swinging over too much. You got that?'

‘Yes sir,’ said Johnny confidently.

Apart from Johnny no one else felt the least bit confident. I knew that all four-engine bombers had a tendency to move to the right because that was the way the propellers rotated and the torque took it naturally that way. On the Stirling the high spindly undercarriage only exaggerated the problem and at low speeds before the control surfaces had sufficient air running over them to control the movement other things had to be done. In this case the aircraft’s two left engines would run at faster revs in an attempt to compensate for the problem. It was never an exact science however!

We sat in some trepidation listening to this endless list of problems and hazards which John had to avoid and were only slightly reassured by the knowledge that at the least PO Davis was to be with us as we faced the unknown. We had also located the escape hatches, and with four hatches for eight men, we thought we stood a chance. At last, the PO gave Johnny the all clear to start up. This was a complicated procedure in its own right, but somewhat to our amazement the four engines coughed and sheared into life one by one. Strangely, as the noise rose and the revs increased, we actually began to feel better. Maybe with four engines running she might get off the ground! The throbbing beat of the Bristol Hercules engines was reassuring as if the noise overwhelmed the nerves that we all felt.

Johnny released the brakes and we began to move forward slowly around the peripheral track towards the end of the runway. Sitting in the bomb aimer's bulb at the very front of the aircraft, it was my job to instruct Johnny if he was moving away from the centre of the paved track. The Stirling's steeply raking head up angle on the ground meant that John could not see the track ahead and needed my instructions to keep him centred. If we put a wheel on the sodden winter grass and mud on either side of the hard standing area, we would never have got out again and would likely be on a military charge for damaging one of the RAF's assets.

Finally, John had her lined up at the end of the runway, which stretched into the distance. He got clearance from the control tower to make his take-off and his calm voice came over the intercom. 'OK boys, here we go for the first time. Let's make it good.'

It did not feel to me like an historical occasion. I just wanted to get up and back down again in one piece.

I heard John and the instructor go through the final few checks of the instruments and then the throbbing of the engines began to rise and the vibrations of the air frame increased as the throttles were pushed forward and the power came on. Johnny was standing on the brakes as the power surged and the volume rose further. He released the brakes as the rev counter went past 2400 and we surged forward, gathering speed very quickly.

The Stirling could take off within 500 yards and we began to feel the aircraft lighten as the speed rose. The pitch of the propellers were altered as we reached take-off velocity and the throttles were "coarsened" to 1800 revs. Suddenly we were free of the ground and heading upwards rapidly. There were creaks and groans from the airframe, which could be heard above the roar of the engines, and the atmosphere was tense as we all held our breath. All except John, of course, and our experienced instructor. Both were too busy getting us off the ground and in any case John was in the air. This is what he was born to do. Gradually we climbed and John levelled her out at 3000 feet. The tension in the aircraft began to relax as we realised we were not immediately going to crash back to earth. We even began to enjoy the view. It was a great day for flying.

PO Davis instructed John to do a few simple banks and turns to get the feel of the aircraft and gradually he pulled the big bomber into a series of wide loops and arcs.

Confidence grew within the crew but none more so than within Johnny himself. As we came to know over the coming weeks, all reports about young Johnny being a natural pilot were true. His physical hand-eye co-ordination, his feel for the rhythms of the engines, the flow of air over the control surfaces of the big aircraft were natural and instinctive and his ability to anticipate wind shifts and air currents was almost supernatural.

We had all flown many times as part of our individual training regimes and with a variety of pilots in a variety of aircraft and you knew immediately who was on top of their game and who was merely mediocre or worse. The best pilots made it all look easy and had an inevitable air of self-confidence, even when both he and the aircraft were under maximum stress such as during take-offs and landings.

For some the clumsiness or slowness of actions on the landing approach ended with thumping onto the runway or even skipping off it. A couple of aborted take-offs not related to mechanical issues also did little for confidence. On these occasions no one said anything, but we all knew what any skipper was made of in those moments.

With John, he was like a top athlete or sportsman of sublime skill who always seemed to have more time than anyone else around him - team mates or opponents. Their minds worked faster, and as a result their actions and reactions were quicker and the outcomes were, therefore, always more certain and success easier to achieve.

In the air this shy, diffident boy became a true man. He seemed to grow taller and wider in his pilot's seat, his movements were smooth, almost liquid, and his voice became firmer, perhaps even a tone or two lower. His authority was clear cut. No one questioned how or what he should do, not even David, but then he had probably planned and wanted it this way.

On this, our first quick orientation flight together, we did a few short circuits of the airfield before PO Davis ordered Johnny to put us down, which he duly did, as light as a feather, barely a bump as the undercarriage hit the ground before a short taxi to our dispersal site and engines off! The silence was initially profound after being surrounded by the noise of the four thrashing engines for the last half hour or so. There was a release of tension from the crew in that our first trip together had gone without a hitch, mixed with a profound feeling of satisfaction and even anticipation that with Johnny as our skipper he would indeed bring us all back safely.

John stayed in his seat and discussed with PO Davis what issues he found with the aircraft and took on board some tips and ideas as to how things might be improved to overcome the undoubted problems with the old airframe of the Stirling. I listened to what was said but understood little. I took some comfort in the thought that things could only get better!

We climbed out of the aircraft to stretch our legs. The ground crew were topping up the fuel tanks ready for our next trip and a NAAFI truck had arrived with some tea and some rather aged and unsavoury looking sandwiches.

After our short break, we climbed back aboard our aged and creaking aircraft and were away again, this time to give ourselves a real test as a crew. John carried a few standard RAF manoeuvres known as "circuits and bumps" just to test the feel of the aircraft again and to see how she and he reacted under more sustained flying pressure.

This simply involved taking off, turning left away from the airfield whilst climbing to 1000 feet, turning left again and flying back parallel with the runway, and then turning left yet again to line up with the runway, dropping down to about 800 feet and then bringing her into land. That was the 'circuit'. The 'bump' involved setting her up so that whilst she was still rolling down the runway John would put the throttles full on and take her off again for another 'circuit'. Six or seven of these and John pronounced himself satisfied.

For the rest of us, there was not a great deal to do. Don kept an eye on engine temperatures. Dan had a quota of loop bearings and radio fixes to do as we circled. David prepared his charts and course fixings. The gunners and myself kept an eye out just in case we got a little too close to other aircraft doing the same circuits, but this was really about pilot skill and practice. John made it look easy and PO Davis rarely had to say a word.

After the last of the circuits we then headed off outside the airspace of the airfield for the first time to carry out what the RAF termed a "cross country" training flight. This was HCU (heavy conversion unit) training for real. A "cross country" was an essential part of any bomber crew training designed to simulate as far as possible the flying, navigation, and co-ordination skills of any crew. The term was quite loose as a great deal of flying was actually over the sea rather than country and was done at both day and night.

Each exercise might last around five to six hours to simulate a real raid and was usually made in a rough triangular shape. On this our first trip we had to fly northwest to a point on the

Isle of Man and then south to the coast of North Wales and then back over Lincolnshire to a spot just off the coast, where we had to drop a flare on a sea target after which our gunners got to shoot up said target and have a bit of fun before we returned to base and a cup of tea and a rest. This first trip was in daylight. There would be others later at night in an attempt to more closely replicate a trip over enemy territory!

This was now the point where David and all navigators came into their own. Dead reckoning navigation was what we had in those days. Fly on a compass setting at a set speed for a set time; keep a look out for all markers of progress: roads, railways, canals, bridges, towns, hills, and coastlines; mark your position, and start again. Teamwork and clever, calm mathematics by a navigator with a cool head and a fast brain were the main requirements.

No matter how good and skilful was your pilot, he was worthless if he was heading in the wrong direction! No computers or satellites for us in those days. A good man with a good compass and a set of instruments that gave you the best possible indication of speed through the air and, more importantly, over the ground was required. A good team should keep an eye out for expected marker points and feed information back to the nav, who would get them all to the correct position over a target to drop some bombs and then get the hell of there and back home before doing it all again the next night!

As we turned away from the airfield on a course of 278 degrees towards the Irish Sea, David gave us all instructions as the timings and marker points we had to look for. '5 minutes at 205 knots, summit of Mam Tor.' John had to maintain that air speed on that course and Don had to give the pilot enough revs to maintain that speed whilst keeping an eye on the fuel mixes and fuel utilisation to ensure we had fuel to get around our full circuit and back again with something to spare. The rest of us had to look out for those markers and make sure we stayed on track.

As the bombardier sitting up front in the nose, I had the best view and least to do. I could see most of Staffordshire and Derbyshire laid out before me, so it was not difficult to make out the upcoming Peak District and the summit of Mam Tor, its highest point. 'Tor dead ahead, Skip, estimate three minutes, I called out. We were on track and on time.

We passed slightly to the left of the summit and David recalculated our heading and timings. Manchester loomed huge and sprawling below us, but our next marker was the mouth of the River Ribble on the Irish Sea and the port of Fleetwood, and from there dead ahead across Morecambe Bay to Walney Island and the town of Barrow in Furness. All went well on this clear day and the Lake District lay off to our right. Its peaks and mountains over 3000 feet high looked benign enough on a day like this, but we all knew of training flights with inexperienced crews like us, way off course, lost at night in the fog coming down in those hills.

Meanwhile I for one in my special and unimpeded viewing position in the nose of the aircraft had the best view of the hills and fields and green land of Britain. This was why I flew. I had a perspective of my Country given to few and to none except the birds until just a few years ago as mankind learnt to fly. I felt alive and free and young. I sensed John felt the same way with the added joy that he controlled our soaring bird of sensory overload!

All seemed to be well, but what no one really knew, especially at night over areas with few markers such as the North Sea for example, was the precise effects of head winds or side winds on the aircraft. Whilst we might be following the correct compass heading, a stronger than anticipated head wind or tail wind might mean that we arrived at a designated weigh point late or early. Everything on the trip then had to be recalculated by the navigator, the engineer and the pilot to preserve fuel and time to target. Given that we would be bombing as part of a force of perhaps 500 or more aircraft, who all had to arrive over the correct target at the same time, or at least within 30 minutes of each other in order to overwhelm the air defences of the enemy, these calculations and ability to keep to them was vital.

A force arriving together as a swarm over the target meant that most would survive. Accuracy was, therefore, the key to survival. A lone aircraft lost over Germany rarely got back home.

The other, perhaps larger problem, amongst many, were the side winds, which could take the aircraft steadily left or right of its designated track. That is where the rest of the crew really came into their own, confirming David's landmarks to the left or right and how far we were out, with Cyril in the back confirming where we had been. It was vital we all worked together on this. We had to know exactly where we were over the earth in time and space.

For now, things remained steady. Weather conditions were good, clouds were high, and we could see exactly where we were and where we were going. But this was daylight. When going to our war we would have to do this at night, possibly in bad weather, with low cloud with Germans trying to kill us, whilst surrounded by several hundred of our own aircraft which we could not see, but whom we knew would be there.

We continued on and hit Barrow on time and then turned left on 171 degrees which should then bring us over the southern tip of the Isle of Man way out in the middle of the Irish Sea in 16 minutes' time. Cloud was down a little and there was mist over the surface of the sea. As we turned away from land, we could not see the Isle of Man, therefore we were flying over the sea on a compass course bearing only so this had to be right. There was a slight fission of nerves throughout the crew, or at least amongst the six of us who were facing forward. Cyril, in the rear gunner's seat, seemed to sense the change in atmosphere through his ear phones. 'It's all right, lads. If tha gets lost ah can still see England. I'll let thee all know how to get back.'

'Thanks for that, rear gunner. We'll let you know,' noted David and on we went. Ten minutes went by and those of us up front could still not see anything. 'Steady, lads,' said Johnny, 'keep a sharp look out.' Tension rose a little. Suddenly through the murk I could make out the shape of land slightly off to my right.

'Target ahead, Skipper.'

'OK bombardier, I see it too. Two degrees north, navigator.'

We were two degrees south of where we were supposed to be. Two degrees was maybe 50 miles out over that time and distance. Enough to miss a blacked out target over Germany. We had failed to allow for a northerly wind which had picked up and was blowing us south. It was good lesson. Our instructor, who had been sitting quietly beside John, made a few notes and suggested that maybe we could have used a drift flare. This was a flare which could be fired from underneath the aircraft which could have given Cyril watching out the back an indication of cross winds as it drifted down behind us.

At the very southern tip of the Isle of Man lay a small uninhabited island. This was the next jumping off point. We then had to turn due south and hit Holyhead on the Isle of Anglesey, 20 minutes' flying time away and all of it over the sea.

David made an allowance for the strong north wind that had taken us south of the Isle of Man and estimated that we should get there three minutes ahead of our original schedule. This we duly did and confidence amongst us grew. We then flew a big left turn over Anglesey south of Snowdon and then a direct track back over the Midlands and out over the North Sea. Five miles out somewhere off the Lincolnshire coast was a marker buoy which we were required to 'bomb' using a flare.

Again, tension rose as we left the coast over Cleethorpes. Our course had to be exact; our target was a speck in the ocean and we did not want to waste fuel looking for it as we had been in the air for almost four hours now.

'Target dead ahead.' I tried to keep my voice in neutral but I was pretty damned pleased to see a large buoy with a yellow flag flying from it. Now it was going to be my turn to control the aircraft on its bombing run.

We all had to practise our parts, and we were all vital to the mission, but the end goal of any Bomber Command mission was to release bombs over Nazi Germany. The sole objective of any mission and the only reason why Bomber Command existed during the war, was to drop high explosives on the enemy and destroy his factories, roads, railways and indeed houses, schools, and hospitals. There was no other purpose than the final action of releasing a bomb load with the ultimate aim of destroying the enemy's capability to wage war and in this way, to bring an end to this war.

At the distance of time after the war it was very difficult to explain to a younger generation born afterwards, that these bombs were for a number of years the only possible way that we British had to fight back against Nazi Germany after the clear cut defeat of our army in France and the withdrawal from Dunkirk. The British army had stood undefeated between 1914 and 1918 in the first war, but in 1940 we were utterly defeated within a few months and only the width of the Channel saved us.

Our allies, the French, were even more comprehensively defeated and humiliated and were forced to prostrate themselves at the feet of the Nazi victor. The Poles in whose interest we went to war were similarly eliminated and for the first two years of my war the Russians and the Americans took no part.

The German Army was quite literally all conquering! They were the most potent, successful and powerful military force on planet Earth. Nothing had been able to stand in its way for three years. After the war we were told and indeed we knew we had 'won'; but only those who lived through it knew that we had actually clearly 'lost' for almost four years. Only the coming of the Americans changed the balance.

In the meantime, all we had to annoy, harass, and irritate our German enemy was RAF Bomber Command and the very act of pressing a button and releasing a few thousand pounds of high explosives was the singular response the entire British empire was able to make in that bleak period. Here we were on our first major training run, on the verge of enacting that very response and that apex of action was my responsibility as the bomb aimer.

I was now in charge and calling out on the intercom to Johnny to follow course 78 degrees as we stalked the buoy with the bright yellow flag which was our target from 5000 feet. This was what I had been trained to do and I was calm but nervous adrenalin ensured that my heart was beating slightly faster. I had an overwhelming urge to show my new comrades that I was good at my job and that they could always trust me as I would trust them.

We came up alongside the target about three miles to port. I called to Johnny to come starboard 90 degrees and he banked the old Stirling on to our bombing run. The target was now dead ahead. I lined it up on my sight as I had been trained to do, having already programmed to take into account air speed, head winds, and bomb weight. I noticed that the aircraft was drifting right, driven by that north wind again. I called out to Johnny 'left, left' and he subtly adjusted the aircraft to bring it directly on track again.

There was renewed tension again throughout the aircraft. Apart from Johnny and I the rest of the crew could contribute nothing at this critical stage. Seconds went past and the target came into focus through my sight. As it neared the centre of the lens where the crosshairs met, I called out to Johnny again 'steady, steady'. He was perfect. The four engines were roaring. The noise saturated the air around us and seeped into my skin. Wind rushed over every edge of the aircraft, vibration, wind shear, and visual distraction all came at Johnny and yet he maintained the aircraft in perfect balance and stability.

The crosshairs of my sight hit the visual edge of my target and my right thumb hit the switch of my bomb release mechanism, releasing the single wooden 'dumb' bomb in the bomb bay. 'Bombs gone,' I shouted over the intercom as I continued to watch the falling wooden brick through my sight.

The laws of physics dictated the released

bomb continued to travel forward through the air at the same rate we were travelling whilst gravity urged it towards Earth. It was a strange sensation that I never really got over in all the missions that I flew, that the bombs seemed initially to want to stay with me before gravity took them in a perfect parabola toward their target which our bomb sights had been designed to allow for.

I watched as the dummy bomb seemed to travel across the surface of the sea, keeping pace with us perfectly before splashing down within perhaps 50 yards of the target. I was elated. 'We got her, boys,' I cried. A motley series of grunts and cheers over the intercom indicated that my colleagues seemed to approve. David's voice then came on. 'Good work, bomb aimer. Maintain discipline, everyone.' It was a terse and slightly sobering statement and an indicator of how he wanted things to be. Do our jobs, keep quiet, act professionally, return home, survive. We understood the requirement instantly.

Having closed the bomb bay doors, it was now our gunners' turn for a bit of fun. The drill was that they would now attack the buoy with bullets!

Johnny brought the aircraft down to 1000 feet and whilst rolling left and right alongside the buoy our two gunners blazed away at the target. The smell of cordite and the vibration of the guns filled the aircraft. The noise level was ratcheted up and the combination of gunfire, engines, and passing air – present in every training and mission flight we went on – was something I have never forgotten.

Johnny called out to the gunners to cease fire on our final pass and David called out the heading to take us back to base; just 25 minutes flying time away, he estimated. Dan took some radio fixes to confirm our heading and a safe flight path back home.

The taciturn PO Davis simply said, 'Well done boys, a good first effort.' I did think that our instructor with over 50 successful missions over enemy territory was actually more scared of flying with an inexperienced 'sprog' crew, as we were known, and was glad to survive a trip with us. At least over Germany you knew what to expect!

We all felt pretty good on the trip back. We had come through our first trip and had performed well together. We had hit our navigation targets and performed well as a team. We felt that with more training and greater experience we had it in us to become an excellent crew. Much flying and training was still to come, particularly at night, but we knew we could develop now as a close unit.

As we arrived back in the skies above Silverstone on that first run, Dan was calling out the radio fixes to take us in and John was on the radio to the control tower requesting permission to land.

The Tower told us to make another circuit of the airfield as a new training crew was preparing to take off in a two-engine Wellington bomber which I could see lining up at the end of the runway.

I had the best view of the events that followed, from my Perspex bubble up front, as we flew parallel to the main runway before turning to make a return to line up behind the main runway. I kept my eye on the Wellington as she prepared her take-off.

I saw the aircraft begin to roll forward on her run, slowly at first and then gathering speed.

She approached take-off velocity and her wheels left the ground, perhaps two thirds of the way along the runway. She began to climb and had just cleared the runway when suddenly her nose began to dip downwards. From only 150 feet in the air, the aircraft, at full take-off velocity with her throttles wide open, hurtled into the ground. I could hear the crack of her impact above the noise of our own engines.

There was a brief moment as she began to physically disintegrate and then a flash of flame as the air fuel in her wing tanks exploded and she burst into a fireball. Through that ball of hell her wings, engines, and tail separated in different directions. The moments of her disintegration appeared as if in slow motion to me. Suddenly emerging from the flames at the front of the aircraft I saw a man ejected. A human form cartwheeling through the air but surrounded and enveloped by flame.

I watched, transfixed, as the body hit the ground ahead of the flaming and fast evaporating aircraft and rolled on for perhaps another 20 or 30 yards. The flames enveloping the body began to subside but still covered the arms and legs and lower torso. As the body came to rest it continued to burn but the man was still alive! I saw him sit upright and begin to beat the flames with his ragged hands. He rolled from side to side over and over again in an effort to beat out the flames. This man was desperate to live!

Blood streaked down his flame-blackened face and on dark nights for the rest of my life I would wake with the dread image of his mouth without lips and the white of his teeth below stretched back in a silent scream of agony, of torture, of hellish indescribable pain as his very eyes evaporated in his skull and his skin sloughed off and fell in glutinous drops on the burning ground.

I turned away from the scene and cursed my position in the nose of our aircraft that had given me this view of the inferno and the end for these sons of unknowing mothers. My heart beat so hard I could feel the veins in my forehead thump against the hot sweat stained leather of my flying helmet. “Are you OK, Sergeant Astell?” came the call from John, who sitting in the pilot’s seat had seen events almost as well as I. “Roger Skipper, all OK,” I mumbled in return. David and Gordon sitting up in the cockpit with John were also witness to the terrible fate of our comrades.

As we drew away our gunners in their positions also had a view of the end of this small piece of the world. Only Dan, locked behind the banks of his wireless gear, had been spared.

The air was taut with tension yet again, our elation of minutes earlier at finishing our flight now forgotten. PO Davis said nothing. Our call sign came over the HF radio from the tower. 'E Echo please hold position over the airfield. We have an emergency situation and all aircraft are refused landing. Please advise your fuel status.'

John responded. 'Roger, tower. Understood. Fuel remaining for approximately 20, that is two zero, minutes.'

'Roger, E. Echo. Understood. We will prioritize your landing on Runway 2 east in 10 minutes. Stand by.'

This meant we would land on the slightly shorter cross-runway that ran at approximately 100 degrees to the main runway. In the meantime we continued to circuit the airfield at a low altitude, so we had a perfect view of the fire tenders and ambulance trucks arriving at the crash site. There was little that fire crews could do but keep the surrounding grass wet and put out the fire in the separated engines whilst the white heat of the aluminium and canvas in the airframe burnt itself out.

The Wellington Bomber had a lattice structure of aluminium which was a brilliant design driven by the necessities of war because of the shortage of the metal as the Germans closed down Britain's supply routes in their victorious triumphs of the first years of the war. The lattice of aluminium was covered by a canvas and fabric composite. It made the Wellington light, flexible, strong, easy to fly, and unfortunately, very quick to burn!

I noticed when an ambulance crew arrived at the location of the burning airman. I did not see them put out the flames that still adhered to the remains of his flying suit, but I did see the ambulance pull away from the location at speed. Was the boy still alive, I wondered.

Few words were said over the intercom as we waited for the call from the control tower to come in. Eventually we were told to approach from the east on Runway 2 across the wind. John put her down without much effort and we taxied to our designated dispersal stand. The engines spluttered to a halt and silence mostly reigned, apart from the pops and creaks of the old airframe and engines as they cooled down and reset themselves after the stress of flight.

We made our clumsy way to the tiny exit door in our bulky flying suits. A crew bus was waiting and we climbed in. I sat down facing David. I noted his ashen face. He caught no one's eye and said nothing. For once he was not part of the crew, it seemed. He was in his own world, in a different and distant place and no one was allowed to join him. Unusually I did not feel close to him and wondered what I could do or say to bring him back to us. I decided to keep quiet. This was his moment. The rest of the crew seemed to notice his need for isolation also and there was silence as the bus rumbled and rolled back to crew quarters, where we disembarked and stowed our flying gear into lockers and walked the yards to the adjacent hut for tea and debriefing with the designated Duty Officer who was accompanied by PO Davis. We came into the briefing room and sat at a table indicated by the Duty Officer, Flying Office Green, all the while saying nothing.

'Ok chaps, I understand you did well today,'

Flying Officer Green said, breaking the silence. 'Congratulations on your first trip together. Pilot Officer Davis informs me you have the makings of an excellent team. You are collectively strong, quick-witted, disciplined, receive instruction well and you have already begun to work together in the air very well. Your work was brisk, professional, and you hit all your weigh points and targets on time and in excellent condition. Well done.'

There was not much else to say. Each member of the crew went over their brief reports and Flying Officer Green made notes in a well-worn notebook.

'You are free to go,' he said. 'Operational training will recommence at 0930 tomorrow morning in the same aircraft, assuming all matters relating to the current problems on the airfield are cleared up. Any other questions?'

There was a moment's hesitation and then David spoke the question we all wanted to ask.

'What news of the Wimpey crew, sir?'

Flying Officer Green blew out his cheeks.

‘Not good, gentlemen. Four of the crew are dead, including Flight Sergeant Hughes, the pilot. The fifth man, the navigator, is very badly burnt indeed, but alive for now. He has 80% burns and he is not expected to live through the night. We are waiting to inspect the wreckage to ascertain the cause of the crash but between you and me we have seen this kind of thing on Wellingtons before. Hughes was a short chap, only 5 foot 3. He had to lean forward to reach the undercarriage retraction lever. Even experienced pilots on this aircraft sometimes look down to find the lever and in reaching down they allow the stick to move forward and that can send the kite straight into the ground! Let it be a lesson to us all: nothing can be taken for granted, gentlemen. Every flight, every action, every thought is hazardous in this business even before we get to grips with Jerry. Concentrate all the time. Eliminate risks and come home safe. Think about everything you do.’

He stood up and left us. We stood to attention briefly and then sat again, unwilling to catch each other’s eyes. David sat, lost in himself again. Somewhere far, far away.

Some minutes went by and the reverie was

broken by a couple of blokes coming into the room. I noticed that their faces and gear were sweat stained and blackened. They were obviously part of the fire crew that had attended the doomed aircraft.

Without saying a word, they grabbed their tea and sat down heavily in the corner of the room. They did not even acknowledge our presence; instead, they adopted an air that I had occasionally seen in pubs and church services and cinemas of my youth by men who had served in the First War. Men who had served at Ypres or on the Somme or another location of blood. Men who had seen, heard, and smelt terror and spilt blood; men who had experienced loss and utter inhumanity. It was called 'the thousand yard stare'. Black eyes looking into the abyss. They were present in bodily terms but their minds were elsewhere, attempting to process and reconcile what they seen in the recent past.

David sensed their distress, which seemed to chime with his own, and walked gently towards them. 'Are you alright, boys?'

Their reverie was broken. They turned

slowly to David. 'Not really, mate,' said the stockier of the two, 'but we'll survive, I guess.' There was a pause. David said nothing but the stocky one seemed to want to volunteer more information to assist his tortured mind.

'We've just pulled the last of those blokes out of the Wimpey. There's nothing left of them. Bare scraps of burnt flesh, a skull, burnt blood, burnt clothing and leather. My God, the stench! There is next to nothing to send back to their mothers, the poor bastards.'

'What about the navigator?' said David.

'At least the other guys were lucky, if you can say that, and just died. This bastard is still alive and screaming in agony. He is being tortured to death as his nerve endings die and every molecule in his body burns and decays. When we got to him he had no flesh on his face. His teeth and jaw bones stuck out like he had just come from hell. He was screaming, as I never thought any human ever could. I will die with the sound of his screams in my ears. The doc pumped him full of morphine through his arse cheeks, which were about the only part of him not burnt. That calmed him a little but when we tried to lift him onto a stretcher his flesh just evaporated in our hands, like trying to lift a pile of mud. I still have his blood and sloughed flesh under my fingernails. I'll never get rid of it. The noise and feeling of his skin and muscles dissolving from his bones as we tried to lift him is beyond me to describe.' His voice trailed away and he resumed his distant stare. His friend never said a word or looked up the entire time.

David turned back to us. 'Let's go, boys.'

Dan replied very quietly. 'Where to, old chap?'

'The pub, I think.'

And so, we left the base. A successful first training mission behind us, but our satisfaction long forgotten and our spirits slightly crushed by what we had just witnessed and heard. Although we knew men died in training, we had not expected death to come quite so directly to us at a training base in the middle of England. Our destiny lay elsewhere in the future, we felt, and yet death had sought us out here and now.

Thirty minutes later we were in The Bell in the village and our mood had begun to lighten ever so slightly. Our conversation as a crew turned back towards the events of our first flight together earlier in the day. We talked to each other and across each other about our feelings on take-off and what we had seen and experienced and how we might improve tomorrow.

As the beer flowed our mood lightened further and as the conversation between us moved and swirled between subjects, our mutual respect and understanding of each other grew and matured. It was a nurturing process I think, and a mostly unconscious part of our team building process.

David joined in the conversation, but it seemed to me it was a little mechanical and somewhat forced. He remained slightly on the edge of the group both psychologically and physically, which all of us found disconcerting, as we had grown used to his being at the centre of our little group even in the short time we had been together.

As time wore on it became a collective decision that our next pint would be the last for that night. Don went off to get the beers in and returned with a full tray and sat down to join us.

It was at that point that David decided to tell us his concerns and we learnt more about him in the next five minutes than we had in the previous few days or possibly than in the next few weeks we were together.

'Boys, I'm sorry I've been distracted over the past few hours. What we saw today with that Wellington got me down a bit and brought a few things home to me. That observer who was thrown clear and now lies dying even as we drink...'

He paused, searching for the right words.

'You see, I have, rather I had, a brother who was killed six months ago. He was an observer in a Wimpey also. He was with 26 Squadron in the South African Air Force, based out of Takoradi in the Gold Coast, chasing U Boats in the Gulf of Ghana. They were coming back to base after a routine op, apparently, when the pilot lost control on the final approach. No one knows if it was mechanical failure or pilot error.

'Anyway, the kite hit the runway at speed, careered off, turned over, and burst into flames. All the crew died instantly apart from the observer, who was thrown clear but covered in flames just like today. He was still alive when they picked him up and took him to the sick bay. It took him 20 hours to die. They buried him the next day with full military honours alongside the rest of the crew who had been buried the day before. He was my brother, Tom!

'I met the doctor who tried to save him a few weeks ago when I was home on leave. He came to my parents' house, which was kind of him. He tried to make it as easy as possible for my folks, which was really nice, but I took him to one side away from my parents and forced him to tell me the details. I needed to know and remember. His death was long, slow, and painful. The doctor could not really describe it but having seen that today I now know for sure and well...it hurts, boys. I am very sorry.'

There was silence around our little table and then Cyril spoke.

'Was tha close like, Sarge?'

'Aye Cyril lad, we were. Only two years apart. We shared a room growing up. We went to the same school, played cricket and rugby together in the same teams. Drank at the same pubs and went to the same chapel with the rest of the family. Real close, like.'

'How did your parents take it?' asked Don, our soft spoken Kiwi engineer, perhaps feeling the distance from home that he and his parents had to endure. He had left home two years before and no return was possible until the war was over, whenever that might be. Home was literally half a world away for him.

'Badly, as you might expect,' said David. 'My mum hid it quite well and she has five daughters to look after her, but my father has still not come to terms with it. Strange that, because he was always quite distant with his children when we were growing up, particularly his sons. I always thought of him as a bit cold. I had never heard of him crying until the day he learnt of Tom's death. I didn't know he had it in him, but now I think his heart is broken beyond repair. I find it harder to take Tom's loss because my old man cannot cope with the grief. It's hard to see a man you thought you knew break down mentally and physically. I think his inner fear is greater because both I and my brother Jack are away and serving and he knows as a father that he cannot perform a man's greatest role as a protector of his children. I guess he also sees something of his mortality in the premature death of a child.

'I worry most about my youngest brother, though. He is only 15 and has seen all of his four elder brothers go to war. He is left with just a few of his sisters and a family that must seem as if it has been suddenly scattered to the wind by the force of war. I am not sure how he will come to terms with it all.'

'How many are you exactly?' asked Dan in his perfectly trimmed voice.

'Ten, mate. Me mum and dad have been busy the last 30 or so years!'

'Same here,' said Don. 'I'm the 7th of 10. I don't think my folks had a lot to do on the long, cold nights on a farm at the end of the world. Not a great deal happens in the whole of New Zealand most days let alone in a tiny town in the middle of the North Island. My parents were quite strict Baptists, but I do think they took the commandment to "go forth and multiply" a little too seriously!'

We all laughed at that and the mood lightened ever so slightly again.

It was time to move on. It had been a long day, but as with most days to come the hectic nature of the war had its own logic which drove time and actions onward and there was little time to look back and reflect.

We retired from the pub and returned to a cold and rather barren Nissen hut where we all slept. Sleep was not that easy for any of us despite our exhaustion, but tomorrow would bring whatever it did.

Chapter 3

Johnny and Janie

The intensity of war drove everything on during this period. There was no time to brood, no time for contemplation or for much introspection. Train, train, and spend time together in the air and on the ground. Prepare for battle!

At this time over the winter of 1943–44, Bomber Command was undertaking major attacks on German industrial centres and Germany's capital Berlin. Loss rates were rising to around 5%. That may not sound too much but it meant maybe 15 to 30 bombers each night went down and perhaps 100 to 200 men died or became prisoners. That was virtually every night that the weather allowed.

These men left their airfields during those nights and never lived to see the light of the next day. They flew in darkness and stayed forever in the darkness of death. The average age at death was 22.

The training stations of which we were now a part could barely keep up with the pace of these losses. We were being fed into this machine and inevitably corners were cut and training had to proceed at a pace. Lessons might be learned, but often were not. We often had to make it up as we went along.

In these circumstances you come to rely and depend on your crewmates even more. The day after our traumatic first flight we were in the air for 5 hours and again as night drew in early at 5pm we were sent out for another ‘cross country’ through the depths of the surrounding darkness.

In these circumstances accurate instrument reading and close crew co-ordination for those of us who had a clear view outside were vital.

At night, even with relatively little cloud everything looked totally different. There was often no horizon. The blacked-out countryside merged into the blackened sky. The occasional glint of a river or lake or railway might help us, but accurate compass readings, timings of runs at precise rev counts, and a radio beam feed were usually what we had to rely on.

PO Davis was with us on our first two night runs out over the western isles of Scotland, but after our second run he announced in the bus returning us to the mess that we were now on our own. He reckoned we were good enough to survive without him and besides he had another six crews at various stages of training to bring along. Some were in need of a hard drilling and others were simply lacking in confidence and needed bringing along. One had severe disciplinary problems with a recalcitrant bomb aimer. We, on the other hand, had all the basics right and simply needed to spend more time in the air in a variety of testing conditions. Experience was what we needed and so he sent us on our way with his best wishes and the promise to keep an eye on our progress and read all our reports and logs and secure us a swift and clean passing out.

We did not, initially at least, quite share his confidence but our marvellous Stirling Bomber training machine was actually very comfortable to fly in and Johnny could throw it around a sky. It would respond almost instantly to any command he give it and for such a huge aircraft it was remarkably manoeuvrable. Johnny could pivot it virtually on one wing and head back in the direction we had just come.

After our initial hesitance, we actually grew to love the old girl. She was tough, strong, and for the most part very reliable, although that term was flexible.

On one occasion, returning from a long night cross country exercise, we were all exhausted although quite elated at our successful trip. Then our Stirling decided to act up.

Everything on the Stirling was electronically operated. An electrical switch would send a signal to a motor somewhere when you wanted to manoeuvre a wing flap or a gun turret or whatever. This was wonderful, when all worked well and the electrical motors, fuses, and solenoids were new.

Not so great when the aircraft had thousands of hours of flying time in the clouds and was parked outside in winter in every kind of weather. Eventually things started to fray, degenerate, and generally come apart.

On this occasion, about 35 minutes out from Silverstone and flying alone without an instructor, John instructed Don to put 15 degrees of flap on the wings to slow our speed and allow the aircraft to descend.

This should have been a routine operation as Don selected the correct switch, so he was somewhat dismayed, as we all were, to see and hear just one flap come into the correct position on the right wing, whilst on the left nothing happened at all other than a landing wheel on that side dropping down with a dirty big 'clonk'.

The uneven drag had the effect of skewing the aircraft to the right and John had the devil of a job bringing her back level with some swift movements of the throttle and ailerons to compensate.

A certain frisson ran around the crew.

'Everything alright up there, chaps, I trust?' came the perfectly modulated enquiry from Dan sitting behind his radios.

'What the bloody hell were that racket?' came the somewhat less modulated question from Cyril in the rear turret.

Don tried to calm nerves with a more

scientific approach.

'All's well, boys. Just a little negative earth leaking from the control valve console which is creating a cross directional current.'

A reply something akin to 'Bollocks' was all that was heard from the rear turret.

'Can you fix it, Engineer?' came John's polite enquiry.

'Not sure, Skip. Locating the valve responsible can only be done from the ground. Let's pull the flaps back in and try again.'

Don selected 'flaps in'. This had the desired effect of bringing the right flap back to level and the left wheel returned to its nacelle. Unfortunately, the right wheel decided it should then descend with a by now familiar 'clonk' sound.

This happened several times. Select your switch and down would come one wheel but no flap. Select your switch and up would go that wheel and down would come the other with the right flap following.

Most disconcerting! John had abandoned his

approach by now and had decided to fly away to what we hoped was a quiet piece of sky whilst we decided what to do.

There is no doubt that our all around lack of experience and general greenness was a major obstacle for us. No one had ever seen or heard of a problem like this before.

John came over the intercom after further consultation with Don.

'Right, boys, here is the situation. We have no means of setting and controlling the flaps to allow us to descend. I can exert some downward pressure using the rear flaps and we can bleed forward speed off by reducing throttle. The landing wheels will not come down together. We can have one but not the other. I'm going to call the tower and see if anyone on the ground can help.'

The rest of the crew including myself remained mute. What could we do?

There was a good deal of general chatter in the cockpit between John and Don as they ran through various options including one that involved a crash landing after most of us had bailed out, but fortunately that discussion did not last long.

Eventually, a technician from the ground staff was brought up to the tower. He had a solution but it was not particularly pleasant.

Apparently, no solution to the electrical problem was possible in flight. The only option was to get well back, say 20 miles back, from the runway and crank the wheels down by hand for which a series of crank handles had been supplied. The pilot would then have to carefully bleed speed and height away using the rear flaps, throttle speed, and the drag created by the early descent of the wheels.

Basically, John would have to fly the gigantic aircraft into the ground from a distance of 20 miles and hit the very beginning of the longest runway at the shallowest of angles in order to use the brakes and the reverse engine thrust to try and bring the beast to a halt before we ran out of road. All this in darkness!

The rest of the crew relocated to the centre of the aircraft and took up crash positions as best they could. Only John and Don, who had to control the revs and assist with the throttle, and

David remained up front. David had to call out the headings every 30 seconds as we could not actually see the runway lights as we began our approach so far back. There was too little room for adjustments left or right if we got the time to the runway wrong.

It took ten minutes of flying before the runway lights could be seen. This seemed an age to us sat back in our crash positions. We could hear David call out the headings and then repeat the altitude calls from John.

Time dragged on and with no view of the ground or ability to judge location and distance we felt utterly helpless with events completely beyond our control. We had to rely on our skipper and his skill and composure.

John brought us home as he promised he would. We hit the runway travelling at least 50 knots faster than was recommended and we began to smell rubber burning as the brakes burnt. John had to keep releasing them briefly to allow a slight cooling, but eventually the bird slowed sufficiently that he had control and was able to taxi to an emergency stop.

We tumbled out of the aircraft with much

puffing of cheeks and exhalations of nervous energy. Safe enough but very relieved, we shared polite, English congratulations to John and Don.

'Good effort'; 'Jolly good'; 'Splendid'; 'Well done'; 'Excellent, chaps' or words to that effect apart from Cyril who had a more direct pattern of speech, 'Ah almost shit myself ',which we all laughed at and we then all made the manifest effort to completely forget that the event had even happened.

As our training progressed there would be other close shaves and nerve shredding excitements such as on that night, but as this was the first emergency we handled on our own, it sticks in my mind more than any other.

In the days and nights that followed we spent much of the time in the air but also in the mess eating together, down the pub drinking together, in various training classes being educated together, at various dances and concerts, singing or being entertained together and in general growing closer in respect, understanding, and emotional attachment.

Relationships between us evolved not just as a group but also on an individual basis. Cyril and

Geoff, both gunners who had trained together, stuck closely to one another and more than any of us enjoyed a drink down the pub on any available occasion. The rest of us would often join them but not always. Don spent a good deal of time writing home and was the most fastidious of us in doing his laundry and keeping his belongings and kit in good condition. I presume in being so far from home, he had no one else to rely in this regard and never knew how long he would need this or that particular pair of socks or underwear!

Dan, our Oxford academic, read a great deal as you might expect and we discovered when a parcel arrived from home with various French works of literature and pamphlets that he was fluent and generally perfect in that language also.

John and I found we had a mutual interest in written history and historical biographies. We discussed much about Cromwell, the Glorious Revolution, and the characters of Napoleon and Wellington amongst others.

John and I grew quite close to David in particular, who we came to regard as something of an older brother. He would arrange trips on the nights we were not flying to dances and parties in

Buckingham. He always seemed to know when and where they were taking place and naive young country boys such as John and I were constantly amazed and embarrassed, in almost equal measure, as to his ability to secure a group of local or Women's Auxiliary Air Force (WAAF) girls to somehow bump into at these dances. David was simply the personification of sophistication and smooth self-confidence for us and I presume for the girls also. He seemed to be able to make them think he was interested in them alone and they flirted and fluttered around him. We simply lived in his reflected charm and were more than happy to be able to talk with real girls and perhaps dance very badly with the occasional one and even offer and receive the occasional chaste kiss.

One particular strategy that David introduced on a certain alcohol fuelled night out at the White Hart in Buckingham was to put himself and Danuska, our equally suave and elegant Mauritian, out in front of the group. No girls could resist them in combination. Dan would float out the odd phrase in French, affecting that he could not recall the precise phrase in English, David would assist in the correction to the appropriate English wording, at which point the WAAFs would melt!

It was John and my own delight to be in a position to offer introductions to this dynamic duo and to play up our close connections and general warrior-like camaraderie. Never before or since, I am afraid to confess, have I ever been able to meet and impress so many women. Some men have everything women look for, alas I was not one of them, but I could bask in the reflected glory of these two with no little effort.

John had a certain edge over me in these encounters; he was still a sergeant like the rest of us but he had the double-winged badge of a pilot on his chest, a badge no girl could ignore.

As the girls approached, attempting to get closer to the two supernovas of manhood whom we stood alongside, they might ask John, 'Are they with you, love?', indicating the object of their desires.

'Oh yes,' John would reply. 'They're part of my crew, actually. I chose them myself. Not bad chaps. Coming along nicely, in fact. I'll soon have them in shape.'

Normally this might have worked in building up John's status and sexual prowess, but the fact that he only looked about 16 years old and was normally blushing bright red and looking as far past the female questioner as possible, meant he wasn't quite convincing. The virginity was plain to see, although I suppose he did have the solace of knowing that if he ever needed an additional mother, many of the girls would happily help him out in that regard! Clark Gable he was not, however.

Despite his blushes, the system did in fact end up working for John. Within three weeks of starting training, John had fallen for a beautiful WAAF called Janie, who had a soft Edinburgh accent and auburn hair. She had the advantage of being the same age as John and an equal measure of youthful awkwardness. They had similar ages, backgrounds, interests and athletic prowess. They looked beautiful together and tender moments between them were many. Actually, they were perfect together!

In his lowland accent, he would refer to her as "Wee Janie", with a look of tender passion in his eyes as he said it. 'I'm taking wee Janie to the dance tonight.' 'I'm meeting wee Janie for a drink on the next night off,' or, in a moment of wistfulness, 'I think my wee Janie is absolutely beautiful.'

He would get some ribbing for that from the boys, but whatever his emotions on the ground, his skills in the air only grew. Possibly the male warrior instinct to protect his girl were inflamed, I do not know, but he was one hell of a pilot and he was my friend!

Janie's girlfriends, we learnt, were not that pleased with her as the relationship developed over those few weeks of training. There was an unwritten rule amongst the girls on most bases throughout England at the time, that you simply did not develop relationships with bomber crews. The death rate was too high! These boys did not come back to you. Hearts would be broken, emotions would be rendered, and relationships and memories that should last a lifetime would end in blood and hopeless loss.

"Don't go there, love," she was told.

Yet, still she went!

In the joy of her youth and the optimism of her love, still she went!

She loved his sparkling eyes, his warm soft skin, the rolling confidence of his walk and his open bashful smile as he greeted her. So, she went with him for those weeks and loved him.

We all loved young Johnny and his 'Wee Janie'. Their joy in each other's company was infectious. No one could deny them that. We all smiled and felt happier when they were together and we were with them. We couldn't know that the pitiless gods of war looked down on them both with ice in their hearts!

For the moment, however, our war and our training went on and our relationships continued to build. The relationship between Cyril and Dan remained a constant source of joy for us. Men from either ends of the world geographically, socially, educationally and as it turned out, linguistically.

The perfection of Dan's voice and grammar was endlessly fascinating to Cyril, who had never come across anything like it apart from on the BBC radio. Equally, Dan as a student of linguistics and a fluent speaker of at least six languages that I knew of (English, French, Hindi and Tamil, as well as ancient Greek and Latin), was equally fascinated by Cyril's dialect.

It began one evening in the cold night of an un-insulated Nissen hut. These purpose built huts could be thrown up in one day and were ubiquitous across the country in housing thousands upon thousands of men and materials. They were utterly devoid of warmth apart from one pathetic stove set in the middle of the hut almost as an afterthought.

This night Cyril and Geoff were trying to light it to give some impression of warmth, but with little success.

'The bloody problem with these things is that they got no decent assnook in 'em,' said Cyril.

Dan, who was lying on his bed reading a French novel, looked up.

'What did you say, old boy?'

'No bastard assnook on these things so there's no bloody draw,' replied Cyril.

'What on earth is an assnook my dear

chap?'

'Don't thee have 'em on fires on thee island?' said Cyril.

'It's a tropical paradise, my dear chap. We have fireplaces to cook on but what the devil is an assnook?'

'It's t'space between the top of the grate and the bottom of the bloody stove that allows air to draw, ain't it.'

'Is it?' replied an incredulous Dan. 'You have a name for the hollow space between a fire grate and the floor of a stove in Dewsbury? Why my dear chap, why? Why would you go to the trouble of naming it? Haven't you got anything better to do?'

'So thee don't learn thee about assnooks at Oxford then…old chap?' said Cyril scathingly. 'More's tha loss, I reckon.'

'It's like giving a name to... I don't know, the space between your toes or the space in the loft of the house. It's ridiculous.'

'Thee means tha underdrawing, does thee?' replied Cyril. 'Thee should get thee self an education, lad.'

'Yes, obviously I must mean the underdrawing,' said Dan. 'How ignorant of me. Give me some other words from 'thee' dialect that I should know.'

'I'll not be blethren with brussen like you, ah tell thee,' replied the mystical Cyril, which apparently meant he had no intention of speaking with a stubborn intellectual like Danuska.

'You really do have an effutiation of bambosh and flummery old chap. A fendangle of brimborion and bugaboo,' replied Dan.

'Bugger that,' came the equally effective response.

From then on, a little game developed between the two of them. Dan would ask Cyril the name of ridiculous or absurd objects or actions such as what the 'other side' of a pillow is called, or the name of the space between the prongs of a fork or what he called the fluff in the turn-up of his trousers, whilst Cyril would affect the most ridiculous sentences he could think of when speaking to Dan, such as 'Have you barconed your arrondissiments this morning, old chap?'

They actually got on splendidly and their humour and bonhomie rubbed off on all of us.

In the meantime, our training regime remained highly intensive. We added more and more night flying over greater and greater distances and often in awful weather conditions. Locating the isolated and appropriately named, "Rockall", 100 miles out into the Atlantic off the Scottish islands, was one of the more difficult assignments on a particularly dreadful night. We were glad to get back from that one.

Not all the exercises we did were in the air, however; our co-ordination as a team was tested to the limit by an exercise that took place in a hangar divided into separate cubicles. Each cubicle had workspaces for a crew with the pilot and myself as the bomb aimer on a raised dais.

Recorded engine noises filled the hangar so we could only communicate through the intercom. We were set an imaginary target and were tested with sudden information changes from instructors regarding weather conditions or mechanical problems or night fighter threats.

Over the work stations were placed two large clocks which were set to run slightly faster than real time and provided additional time pressure when calculations had to be reset due to changes in wind speed, loss of engine power, or changes to target destination.

It was a superb high-pressure exercise which left us all physically and mentally exhausted and showed how easily discipline and self-control could break down if set procedures were not followed. The procedures were there for a purpose and there were no shortcuts. Keep to your routines and you had a chance to survive!

After these ground exercises we would retire to the mess for some of the most godawful food ever designed by man, with the only grace being that we all had to eat it. Officers included. Following that we might retire to the pub in twos and threes or perhaps as an entire crew.

It was during this period that we came to know how each had made it into the RAF and what we all thought we were fighting this war for. This was an evolutionary process of constant discussion, assessment, consideration, and intellectual maturation. We came collectively to certain broad conclusions.

First and foremost, all of us just wanted to fly!

Men had only learnt to take to the air merely ten years before most of us were born (only three years in the case of the aged David!) and flight was something almost beyond excitement to the point of intoxication for all of us.

The RAF was the glamour service of the war and afterwards, at the very cutting edge of technology. To break the bonds of gravity and fly: what a thought; what an ambition for a 20-year-old who had grown up in the 1930s.

It was as if the war had been invented to allow us all to achieve these ambitions. Strange to think that we were all secretly grateful to Adolf Hitler, Germany, and Nazism for the opportunity to face our fears and fly.

'Now thank God who has given us this day,' Rupert Brooke wrote of the First War. This was precisely our collective vow of gratitude for this profound and glorious opportunity. None of us apart from, perhaps, Dan came from a background that would ever have allowed us the actuality of flying. Many thousands of our contemporaries volunteered to fly as we did, but only certain of us had the temperament, skill, and luck to achieve our goal, and we felt the privilege of it. This is what we wanted to do to help the war effort. Life during training and on operations was hectic, harsh, and yet wondrous, because virtually every day you had the opportunity to experience the heaven of powered flight.

In further discussion we also came to agree, albeit with a variety of opinion that lacked precision, that we simply could not abide the thought of being governed, ordered, and ruled by a foreign power such as Nazi Germany! One might call that patriotism if one wishes but more likely we saw it as a kind of British and Commonwealth cussedness not to be governed by anyone else that we had not agreed to or we had not had a say in putting in authority.

Dan and Don, although they were British subjects as opposed to British citizens, felt precisely the same way. Their homelands were not as yet directly under threat but they instinctively knew that should Nazism prevail then there was no place for them. It was quite a simple idea really. Germany and its political masters who drew their backing from the overwhelming will of the German people, or so it seemed to us, had to be defeated if we wanted to enjoy our futures. If this was patriotism or nationalism, we certainly never saw it that way.

'Sod the bastards. They ain't coming down my road. They can just bugger off,' was Geoff's rather succinct summary of the situation and there was a motley round of cheering as he said it. At which point someone ordered another round and the subject moved onto something equally profound such as when Johnny might ask Janie to marry him?

John would blush as usual and turn his gaze away.

'I'm not talking about that with you lot. She's too good for you – or me for that matter.'

David would often sit quietly during these exchanges with a slightly quizzical smile on his face. He would occasionally chip in to continue the conversation or to cleverly move it on in a subtle direction. I think he saw it as part of a team building exercise of equal importance to a "cross country" flight devised by our instructors. It probably was! It welded our consciences together and reinforced our collective belief systems and mutual respect.

Of course, we each had our own personal views on why we wanted to fly and fight.

Danuska had already made it clear when we first met that he regarded the art, literature, science, cultural heritage, and political systems of Britain and Europe as a civilisational peak in the sweep of history and worth defending with his time, effort, and blood, if necessary. Dan was an arch intellectual, a man of passion, and one of the most charming and sophisticated men I have ever had the privilege to know.

He had a clear view of the obvious outcome should the Nazis win. A global fascist victory could mean that someone of his skin colour, no matter how educated would have absolutely no place in the world. The global threat of Germany and Japan represented the slavery and subjugation of himself and his family.

He regarded Germany as having taken collective leave of its senses and now stood outside an ancient European artistic, cultural, and literary heritage.

'They burn books, for God's sake.'

To him Germany had become a barbarous cancer and the ideological basis of its current Government had to be utterly laid to waste in order to return a great people to their true path. In essence Germany had to be cauterised militarily in order to release it from the grip of the mutant disease that now held it.

Once that had been achieved, he then wanted to go further and put the entire world to rights. He felt it would only be a short matter of time before the British people would demand that all members of its empire would be released to chart their own course.

'You British will release us all to pursue our own destinies on the destruction of Germany and Japan,' he stated confidently. 'You will do it easily and peacefully because that is your nature and the essence of your democracy. The British Empire was only ever designed to exist for a short period of time. Just sufficient time to allow you to transfer advanced technologies, legal systems, and democratic ideals around the globe. A democracy cannot run an empire for long, the inherent contradictions of your personal freedoms and your common law system will not allow it.

'In this regard it is the most unique ideological and technical experiment constructed on a global scale that history has ever witnessed. I salute the British people in this regard. You will leave roads, railways, schools, hospitals, law courts, organisational structures, and democratic ideals in some of the most obscure and isolated areas of the world. They will be left to us free to mature and grow. It is the greatest transfer of assets, wealth, and knowledge that the world has ever seen.'

'Are you sure that will actually happen?' asked a somewhat bemused David. 'Why will we do that, please tell?'

'Of course you will, my dear chap. Once Germany is defeated and Japan also, there can be no possible justification for you British to stay in India, Africa, or Mauritius for that matter. You cannot win a victory for liberty, freedom, democracy, and civilisational good and then not grant those very things to countries and peoples that are now colonies. It would be absurd and ridiculous and the greatest hypocrisy. This war will free Europe and the rest of the world from fascism and end colonialism everywhere for good!

'The most magnificent thing about this war is that it has a clear enemy in the form of Germanic fascism and Japanese militarism. The very darkness of the enemy will make the victory over them all the more brilliant. The brightness of the cleansing process that victory will bring will sweep away all the inherent obstacles to peace and freedom for all the peoples of the world. All the forces of current darkness and ignorance will disappear in the sun-kissed beauty of our victory. The forces of good will triumph over evil on such a global scale that the world will surely be cleansed. Our peace that we fight for today will be of absolute purity and the British people and those, such as I, that support you around the world will share your joy and the fruits of your victory.'

Dan was inspiring. At 22 years old he was a passionate visionary and a revolutionary. I believe he saw the world in a way that no one else I have known ever could. He was not held down by the norms of political and social structures. He spoke multiple languages and his mind was, as a result, simply wired differently. He was no philosopher, although he understood philosophic structures, but he was a deep and wondrous original thinker and the angles of his thought processes lit up the darkest depths of any problem. I miss him to this day. What would the world be like today if he had risen to prominence?

My world was simpler and much more orientated to England and its land, fields, woods, and hills. I simply loved it for what it was. The smell of it in the spring, the beauty of its contrasts through the seasons. I fought because I literally loved my country. Its landscapes seeped into my very soul and gave me quiet, unrelenting joy. From a boy, I walked it lanes, learnt its bird calls, and the names of its flowers and trees. I smelt its grass and heather, studied its history, and marvelled at its utter beauty.

I can think of no more enchanting view than that seen whilst walking across the landscape on a warm sunlit day in late spring or early summer, when you spy at a distance, the perfection of a church spire or tower emerging as a perfect note from a symphony, set within the rolling beauty an English county. God himself could have placed it there and surrounded it with the joy of an English village, a garden, a wood, a hill, all set in a glade of paradise.

I worshipped the poets and writers who worshipped it! I endlessly speculated as to the energy and prescience of the people who had created this garden of perfection over 10,000 years from the time when the ice that covered it had rolled away and in doing so had created the curves and gracious beauty that allowed man and nature to join together to create a cradle of perfection on earth. I cannot imagine that paradise itself could be more green or well-watered. From my position as bomb aimer in the very tip of the aircraft I had the best view of country and my love for it only grew as a result. No one was going to take it from me.

David had already explained that he was fighting for his family as much as anything. One of his younger brothers was already dead, and another even younger had been called up in the conscription of 1939 of the then 20-year-old males. This brother had no choice in the matter but David did, and he chose to volunteer so that his younger brother did not have to serve alone. More than that, he expressed on a number of occasions his love for his large family. As the oldest boy, I think he regarded it as his duty to protect all of his family, particularly his five sisters and his youngest brother still at home.

That being said, I felt that he was also glad to be away from his job and his career back in his home town. He was successful and well-established, highly regarded and set for higher things – and I suspect that was precisely the problem!

He came from a modest background. His father was a skilled printer by trade and was not wealthy in the Britain of the 1930s. David had achieved almost everything that a man of his education and background would ever be allowed to achieve. He had done this with almost effortless ease. He was intelligent, charming, and warm-hearted. He had become the Assistant Borough Treasurer of his modest little northern town at the age of just 27. He could have taken over the most senior position in the department within the next five or six years. But then what?

He knew that his life was already set in

place and his career path certain. Comfortable, organised, warm, and secure, with a good pension at the end of it. But then the war came and suddenly he could see a way out and a way forward. An opportunity to travel, to move outside his comfortable social circle and enjoy risk, adventure, and love that had never been the place previously of an Assistant Borough Treasurer.

David sought a warrior's life for a few years before returning to the easy security of his life in his cosy northern town. The RAF represented joy and exhilaration on a level he could never have known without this conflict. It was again one of the glorious ironies of this war with fascism that it freed so many young men to explore opportunities, trades, friendships, and loves that they could never have had in a period of extended peace. Only war, or perhaps revolution, has this ability to accelerate and magnify individual lives and social trends. Perhaps it is why mankind fights? Peace is welcome and wonderful, but for young men throughout history conformism and submission to authority and traditions can be tedious. David's life of peace, security, family love, and safety gave him no room to explore ambition, as he saw it.

Excited as he was for this adventure, he was determined nonetheless to live through this conflict; peace, in the end, was for the benefit of his middle age. How much more fulfilling was a life that involved at least some element of desperate risk and the defeat of odds against living to that age?

Old men love to sit with their children and grandchildren and tell of lives of derring-do and survival. The glory of their youth ensures their respect in the years ahead and a place, no matter how small, in history. All men crave it and David was no different.

Although we never quite acknowledged it out loud, we all knew that war was an exciting, creative, and dynamic force that would shape our lives to the end of our days. To make it work, however, we had to survive. We knew that outcome was not completely in our own hands, but that – in the strangest of ways and strictly in hindsight – was the joy of it!

In the meantime, after five weeks of the most intensive period of training, it was now time for us to all make our acquaintance with what for us was the greatest war machine of all time. The Lancaster bomber!

We had all seen one and heard her fly but our first encounter with her was when we were transferred to RAF Swinderby up in Lincolnshire for the last two weeks of training on Lancaster familiarisation.

We cadged a lift in the back of an old Wellington, although David and Don mysteriously stayed behind with their kit and told us they were going "overland" and would meet us that evening.

It was not the most comfortable trip we had ever made, wedged into odd bits of the old "Wimpey" but it only took an hour across country before landing in the bomber county of Lincolnshire: flat, windy, close to Germany, and now operating with over 60 bases, both British and American. The air was thick with bombers and the ground shook throughout the day and night with the noise. I felt somewhat sorry for the mainly rural inhabitants of this county. Although they were not directly in the front line, the war surrounded them and their towns and villages and they could never escape it.

We came onto the base at Swinderby in the early afternoon of a day late in March 1944. We checked in with the Adjutant's office and were allocated a Nissen hut just outside the perimeter of the base. A covered truck took us there and we stashed our kit and settled in. Every Nissen hut I ever stayed in looked, felt, and smelt the same and appeared to be maintained at a constant temperature only slightly above freezing no matter what the season.

We hiked back to the base after stowing our kit, looking for a cup of tea and something to eat. John was keen to get to know a 'Lanc' as soon as possible and sought out the Flight Office to check that his crew had been allocated a slot and instructor. As it happened one new crew had not yet arrived as expected, due to illness of one member.

Pilot Officer Burrows, a senior instructor, told Johnny he was happy to take him up then and there and get a head start.

'Just a couple of bumps and circuits, young man. Not much, just you and I. We don't need a crew for this. Orientation only.'

So it was that the four of us – Dan, Cyril,

Geoff, and myself – got to sit on a bank just off the end of the main runway and watch our Skipper take his first flight in a Lancaster Bomber.

As Johnny brought her around the peripheral track near our position, we all cheered and put our thumbs up. Johnny returned the signal with a huge grin on his face. PO Burrows sat beside him on the co-pilots slot with dual control levers.

We watched Johnny line her up at the end of the runway and then felt the power and heard the noise of her magnificent Rolls Royce engines began to rise. She swung gently from side to side on her brakes as the power rose and suddenly Johnny was off and running; the crescendo of the engines on full power drummed through our very bones.

Smooth as you like she was off and banking to begin her circuit parallel to the runway. She was a beauty. I hold that image of her in flight and sweeping over us in my mind to this day. What a sight and sound she was: elegant and sleek, but with the menace of a huge bull roaring in anger.

Twenty-five minutes after take-off, Johnny

was back down and taxiing to his dispersal site half way down the secondary runway.

We ambled back to the crew room in time to see Johnny step out of his crew bus and walk towards us alongside PO Burrows.

His face bore the marks of something close to ecstasy, I think. He was grinning from ear to ear, his face was flushed with pleasure.

'How was it then, mate?' inquired Cyril.

'Absolutely bloody marvellous,' was all Johnny could say.

'Congratulations, Sergeant,' said PO Burrows. 'You're one of the most natural pilots I've ever seen. You've got the hang of her already. You don't need me anymore. Just load your crew up tomorrow, take it easy, feel your way into it, but she will tell you what to do. She's the most responsive aircraft I have ever flown. The two of you will get on perfectly. Do a couple of long cross country runs tomorrow and you'll be more than ready, I assure you. I need you and your boys to be ready for war in two weeks. Do you understand?'

‘I do, sir.’

Burrows then looked at all of us. ‘You’ve got a great skipper here, boys. Look after him and he will look after you. Good luck.’

He turned and walked away as we were left to shake hands with our superstar skipper and to wonder yet again how he made flying look so easy.

Once Johnny had stowed his flying gear we walked back to our billet. As we approached the entrance to the base a little car swung onto the base driven by none other than Don with David smiling alongside him.

They drew to a halt and stepped out too much cheering, clapping, and general back slapping.

‘So, this is what you’ve been up to,’ said Geoff. ‘Where did this come from?’

‘Oh, I had a little deal with a chap in a pub who was being transferred to Canada on training duties,’ said our suave navigator. ‘She needed a bit of work on her but our genius Kiwi engineer here made light work of that. So here we are. We now have a crew, a car and can explore this wonderful county in comparative ease and comfort.'

Getting seven of us in it and on it was a little tight to say the least, but who cared. Off we went to find a pub.

Over the next two weeks the intensity of our training went up a further notch. The Lancaster proved to be everything that we had heard: tough, resilient, magnificent in the air. In the hands of a pilot like Johnny she was as smooth and clever and as powerful as any aircraft built to that date.

Johnny took her up to her ceiling at 25,000 feet and down to 50 feet. He pulled her left and right and stood her on her elegant wing tips. There was seemingly nothing it could not do.

We only had one complaint: The escape hatch for the crew up front – pilot, navigator, engineer, and bomb aimer – was pathetically small and was actually located under my bomb aimer couch. In any emergency we knew that we were not all likely to get out in time. There was nothing we could about that, however.

In the meantime, we worked hard night and

day refining our skills, improving our teamwork, and co-ordinating our efficiency in the air.

The four days' continuous assessment at the end of the two-week 'conversion' course were particularly satisfying for myself. Using twelve pound smoke bombs and working closely over the intercom with Johnny to get our approach to the range targets just right, we passed out top of our particular HCU for accuracy.

We were tight, we were tough, and even though I say it myself, after seven weeks of "heavy" training we were bloody good! We knew it, our instructors knew it, and the RAF knew it!

2 days before the end of our official training period, Johnny received a message from the Adjutant's Office to report to the Commanding Officer at 14.00 hours on a beautiful early spring day. We all guessed what it was about, but sat nervously for 30 minutes in the NAAFI waiting for the return of our young skipper.

In he walked as shy and bashful as ever, with a sheepish grin spread across his smooth features. 'Well, Skip. Tell us all?' Don spoke for all of us.

Johnny paused and looked away and then back to us. 'Alright, chaps. You will have to address me as sir from now on. You got that?' There were heartfelt handshakes and congratulations from all of us. Our skipper had just been made into an officer and a gentleman. He was now officially Flying Officer John Smith and entitled to all the rights and privileges associated with his rank.

We were all delighted for him. No one deserved that promotion more. We were only sorry to know that he would now be assigned to billets in the Officers' mess and would no longer spend time alongside the rest of us.

John left the six of us to go and find a new uniform indicating his rank at the Officers' mess and be allocated a new billet and generally to carry out all the administrative requirements of someone holding the King's Commission.

As he left there was much exaggerated standing to attention, saluting and sharp calls of 'yes sah' from the rest of us. 'My first order as an officer, gentlemen,' he said, 'is that you all meet me outside the Officers' mess at 18.00 sharp. A big night in Lincoln is in order, I think. I leave the precise location to you. Oh, and the first round is on me.'

'I should bloody well hope so,' said Cyril. 'On tha pay grade tha's on now it's going to be more than one, ah tell thee...sir, he said as an afterthought followed by a crisp salute.

A heavily loaded little car made its way into Lincoln that night with Geoff and Cyril standing carefully on the tiny running board whilst clinging to the door handles.

This was the first time any of us had been into the beautiful city of Lincoln. Its cathedral was a thing of immense grandeur and beauty and after a quick walk around its interior and a promise to myself to spend more time there we all shuffled into the Saracens Head pub. The place was a sea of blue RAF uniforms. With so many men stationed in the county this was inevitable and the beer and noise flowed freely in a permanent fug of cigarette smoke that grew ever more dense as the night wore on.

As we settled in for a long night, it was a time of genuine satisfaction with our achievements as a crew and of some nervous anticipation of what might lie ahead.

Tomorrow we would learn which operational squadron we were to be assigned to. We were all conscious that within a week we would probably be flying over Germany. It was a strange sensation. Anticipation, hope, expectation, and excitement blended with nervousness and frankly fear. Not necessarily fear of death but certainly fear of the unknown and of not performing our job as required and letting the boys down. What would the next few weeks and months hold for us? We were a single moulded unit and would face it together. That fact gave us all strength and emboldened the spirit.

That night was long and possibly the most enjoyable of my life. With hindsight it was also the most poignant. Our last chance before entering the front line of the war to spend time in each other's company and to savour our own skill, camaraderie, and the purest enjoyment of friendship. It was as if it was our last supper together.

The next day we were declared ready for war and ordered to join 876 Squadron at RAF Sawston Manor in the bomber county of Lincolnshire.

Chapter 4

The Death of Youth

The day after receiving our operational orders we packed our kit and some of us using our crew car and others travelling by train or cadging lifts in RAF trucks, we departed for the frontline base of RAF Sawston Manor 40 miles to the east of Lincoln out towards the coast at the foot of the Lincolnshire Wolds.

We arrived on the afternoon of April 23rd 1944. It was a glorious spring day. There was a glow in the air. The trees and hedgerows of my England were showing the first blush of growth and new life. The daffodils were still out, if just past their best. I heard a great tit shrilling 'teacher, teacher' and watched as sparrows twittered around the houses we passed on the way to the base.

Sawston Manor had been a frontline operational base for over 2 years now. Driving into the main gate with David and Johnny for the first time, I could immediately sense the change in atmosphere from the training bases I had been on.

The noise was greater, with the sound of heavy engines being run up and tested around the airfield. The energy levels of all personnel seemed to be at a higher level. Everyone moved a touch faster and the focus and concentration levels of active service personnel seemed that much greater. Flying crews, ground crews, WAAFs, civilian operatives – they all seemed to have a greater gravity and purpose. We may have been several hundred miles from Germany but this was the front line of the war effort.

We entered the Adjutant's Office to 'check in' so to speak. Johnny, as our officer, led the way and after he presented his papers the warrant officer gave us a curt welcome. No time or need for pleasantries it seemed. We sensed the mood.

'Flying Officer Smith, please report to the Officers' mess immediately. Your crew are assigned to Hut 7 off the base near Winton Church about a mile away. My orderly will direct you. Please make yourself known to the

Squadrons Flight Office and good luck to you all.'

To be truthful our arrival on the front line was something of an anti-climax. I have no idea what I was expecting – bunting, marching bands, and heroic cheering perhaps? Instead, we were all but ignored. We were to learn that this was the case with all "sprog" crews, as inexperienced newcomers were known. Why bother to get to know anyone, why build friendships or relationships when you could be dead the next morning? We had to rely on each other because, frankly, no one else expected you to live!

This fact was brought home to us as we exited the Adjutant's office and noticed on the edge of the parade ground a huge pack of what appeared to be feral dogs. All breeds, shapes, and sizes. Dirty, scruffy, and hungry. No one cared for them! Maybe 30 or 40 animals, including two bitches with puppies.

There was little in the war up to that moment that discomforted me more than learning that these were formerly the pets of crew members who never returned!

It was the British eccentricity that our love

of animals translated, in this case, into a desire to bring them along with us, wherever that may be. Although pets were against regulations, boys would bring their beloved dogs with them onto the base and sneak them into Nissen huts. The authorities would look the other way, thinking they might be good for morale.

Owners would swear various mates to look after their dogs if they failed to return. Frequently this occurred but within days the new owner too might also be lost. The poor animals were now alone, unloved, unknowing, and whimpering in their own sadness and bewilderment. Packs would form and grow and every month or two, gun shots could be heard across most bases in England as they were culled.

Was it beyond tragedy that these previously beloved animals would die in gross anonymity and forlorn neglect? Was their death a metaphor across the bomber bases of England for the death of their masters in the benighted skies over Germany?

My blood runs cold at that thought and I still shiver to this day when I think of it. Every living creature was surely forsaken at that time. Death was everywhere and nowhere. Men disappeared into the night air never to return, leaving only their pets, who, in turn, received a bullet to the head and a heave into a ditch beside a road to rot and be forgotten.

Our hut was in quite a lovely spot. There was a small church at the end of the field where the huts stood and a farmhouse the other side of the lane. We got to know the farmer over the next few weeks and he would usually save us some fresh milk if he could.

After settling in we drove back down to the base as we had promised to catch up with Johnny in the NAAFI. Before we met him, we took time to have a stroll around and get to know the layout of the place. The sound of Merlin engines running up was everywhere. Aircraft being tested for mechanical efficiency and airworthiness filled the skies.

We returned to the NAAFI building where we found Johnny pacing outside. His face was slightly drawn and his skin paler than normal. He did not smile his big-hearted, shy grin as he greeted us. He looked suddenly older and more serious and slightly drawn.

David sensed the change. 'Are you alright, Skip?'

'I'll tell you when we get inside,' was the curt and unusual response.

We grabbed a cup of tea and some appalling hard tack biscuits and all seven of us sat down either side of a large table with Johnny in the middle. There were few others around at that time of day, a few aircraftsmen in the corner having a quick break before heading back to work on their particular Lancaster.

There was a strained silence as we waited for John to find his words.

'Boys,' his voice was low and nervous, 'Boys, I've been ordered to fly on second dickey op tomorrow night. It's going to be quite a big show apparently. I'm to fly with Squadron Leader Doyle who will head up B flight and act as Master Bomber over the target.'

We remained quiet as John sought to find further words.

'What do you think, boys?'

It was a question, but I felt he was looking for a statement of permission to go from all of us and was hoping we might refuse. There was more silence as he looked at each of us in turn. We were all a little perplexed by his question and unsettled by his nervousness.

A “second dickey” was a perfectly normal way for a Bomber Command pilot to begin his operational tour. A new pilot arriving at a squadron was expected to fly in the second seat alongside a senior and experienced pilot on an operational raid over enemy territory in order to gain knowledge of actual conditions under fire. No amount of training could prepare one for the actuality of war in the air over Germany. The fear, the flak, and the fire below scrambled nerves and had to be faced.

Most new pilots with certain normal reservations welcomed the idea of getting some first-hand experience with a veteran crew who knew what they were facing. It usually enabled the skipper to lead his own crew with greater authority when they themselves had to face the ordeal together. The crews themselves felt more confident if their skipper had at least seen some action and had come through it.

David spoke for all of us.

'It sounds good to us, Johnny. Flying with Doyle, he's done 26 ops with his crew hasn't he, eight of them over Berlin. Never had a scratch, has he?'

John nodded rather miserably and scanned the floor searching for more words.

'I don't need this, boys. I'm already one of the best pilots around. I don't need this experience. I promised I will bring you all back home and that I will, but I have to be in charge of the kite when I fly. Doyle will be flying and calling the shots. I will just be there to watch. What if we get into trouble? I can get us out of anything. I don't know this crew.'

'John, we think you will be fine. Doyle must be a good pilot and a good skipper; he's a Squadron Leader for a reason. You'll be fine, mate!' David's words were soothing and said with authority, but John's anxiety was clear to see.

'Boys, I'm your skipper. You are my crew. We fly together and we survive anything. If we are apart, I cannot see it working.'

John's face was stricken now, his voice cracking with anxiety. We had never seen or heard him like this. We were unnerved now and worried for both him and ourselves. Our quiet Kiwi engineer now spoke up from the other side of the table. He looked directly into John's eyes as he spoke.

'Skip, please! You have to go. You have your orders and you cannot disobey a direct order in the face of the enemy. You know that, but more than that, Skip, you must go for all of our sakes. We need you to get that experience. You will be a better pilot for it and we will be even better in supporting you when we fly together again knowing that you have already been through it. You owe it to yourself and to us to go. We will always stand behind you and you must know that. You cannot let us down as we will never let you or each other down.'

The calmness and directness of Don's words only enhanced their power. John looked at him for many seconds. He blew out his cheeks, scanned the floor again, and drew in himself as he spoke.

'I'm sorry boys, I apologise. Of course, of

course you are right, Don. It is my duty to go. For King and Country and all that, but you are right, I must go for all of us.' He paused. 'Besides, when I met Squadron Leader Doyle just now, I knew immediately that he was a bloody good bloke and a superb pilot. He told me that he has every intention of completing his 30 ops as soon as possible and then taking a rest. He actually used the words to me. "I will bring you back, Smith!"'

There were strained smiles amongst the crew now.

'I'll be alright, boys. As soon as I get back the beers will be on me. Right?'

We broke up but the atmosphere remained taut. We were mystified as to John's behaviour. We knew the nerves and fears he must have when facing the enemy for the first time but we expected him to carry it through to cement the bonds of comradeship and enhance his skills.

We drifted off to different parts of the base to read, write, drink, eat, or talk and by the time we returned to our hut some equilibrium had returned and we all slept well that night.

I can't say for certain, but I believe that John

had a hard time sleeping that night. He was still quite subdued when he left us for the night. Whether he got any sleep or no, the rising sun hours later must have warmed his soul as well as his body, and helped him see reason and regain his resolve to do his best by himself and his crew.

Walking up to the runway, he must have been invigorated by the "Lanc' engines running up. He saw the aircraft as living things. He knew his destiny was to fly them and their size and power gave him a strange comfort now.

And of course, there was the image of wee Janie, smiling at him, that must have given him the greatest boost in strength of all.

When Johnny joined us in the Sergeants' mess for a cup of tea before his flight, we were glad to see his usual shy smile had returned.

'Morning, boys. How are you all?' We were delighted to see our skipper returned to normal.

'Tha's alright, Skip?'

‘I’m well, thanks, Cyril old boy. Never better. Weather looks clear. I’m on Ops tonight. I will see you all tomorrow morning with a story to tell, I think!’

‘That’s the spirit, old chap,’ came Dan’s encouraging words. ‘Excellent thought.’ Our world appeared to be tilting back to equilibrium as we left the Sergeants mess that morning, or so we thought.

As we walked from the building an orderly approached John and saluted smartly. “Flying Officer Smith. Would yourself and Sergeant Patterson present yourself to Squadron Leader Doyle in the Flight Office immediately?” He saluted again and turned and walked away in the direction he had come. There was a brief silence as we all exchanged quizzical glances and raised eyebrows. Having two of the seven of us called in didn’t sound good. We all walked over to the Flight Office together, and five of us smoked nervously outside while we waited for John and Geoff to find out what this was all about.

John and Geoff exited the building, their faces set in grimaces that foretold bad news and of a future suddenly less certain. The gods of our war were enjoying this moment. Geoff spoke first and in typical forthright manner.

'The bastards want me to fly tonight on the big op. I've got to fill in on PO Sharp's crew whose mid upper was wounded two nights ago and no replacement is around. I don't know what to say boys, this is a fucking disaster!'

David looked to John. 'What did you say, Skip?' The question was neutral but the implication was clear. This had to be stopped. 'Not enough, clearly,' was all John could say, shocked as he was with his new orders.

It was an operational requirement, a strategic imperative, an unwritten rule, and a superstitious action that you never split up a good crew. Nothing good would ever come of it. A Lancaster crew of seven must work and think and act as one unit. You could not simply drop a new member into a tightly bonded and highly trained team.

Except!

We all knew it happened all the time. The vagaries of war, death, injury, and illness all deemed that it could and would occur.

For us, however, it meant our world had just turned upside down. An untested crew could be broken up quickly to make up for losses elsewhere, but this change felt like someone had removed a brick from a wall or a strut from a roof. Everything had the potential now to weaken and collapse. Worse still, the risk of error in the air due to miscommunication or misunderstanding was all the greater. Geoff had never flown with this crew. No matter how good and how experienced they were, Geoff was a potential danger to them and therefore, to himself.

'Fuck 'em! I'm not going,' Geoff was very eloquent when riled.

'Skip, let's go back in and see what we can do,' suggested David.

John nodded. 'Alright, let's give it another go.'

Once more, we milled around outside in nervous anticipation of what our Skip and Nav would be able to do.

When John and David returned from their second attempt, they were shaking their heads. ‘Nothing doing, I’m afraid, boys,’ said John. ‘Squadron Leader Doyle has made it clear that this is a very difficult mission and he needs every aircraft in the air, so this is how it is. Geoff, you’re flying tonight. I suggest you go and find Flying Officer Sharp and get to know your new crewmates as quickly as possible. Bobby,’ he turned to address me, ‘you are duty bomb aimer tonight. It’s a big responsibility ensuring all your fellow bombardiers are fully prepared and kitted out. The briefing is at 14.00 hours.’

Resignation, bewilderment, and some anger fuelled our little group. This was not meant to happen. We had never, in all the weeks of training, considered the possibility that we might be split up before we had flown our first operational mission.

We were not prepared psychologically for this eventuality and we felt the world spinning out of our control. Our training had prepared us for whatever combat could bring, which is where we drew our confidence and courage as a team but now our world was being torn asunder before we had even started!

Geoff moved off the find his new crewmates and the remaining 6 of us stood in rough circle trying to find words to comfort each other.

Cyril and Dan expressed the same sentiment in their respective vocabularies. 'Bugger the bastards,' from Cyril and 'This is a jolly bad show' was Dan's slightly less eloquent response.

'Nothing doing, boys,' said David. 'We are in the hands of the war now and all I can say is that we did get a promise from the Squadron Leader that once tonight's show was over, we will be reunited as crew and fly together. So Skip, you have a good trip tonight and I'm sure Geoff will be fine with Sharp; he's good, I hear. We will be together in the morning and we'll take it from there.'

We broke up at that point, John to go and check out his flying gear and the other four to places I knew not where, but they had time to kill and bad thoughts to come to terms with. We agreed to meet in the NAAFI an hour before the briefing time of 14.00.

As "duty bomb aimer" for that day and night

I knew I was in for a long, tiring period, although not quite as stressful as the raid itself. I was to attend the initial intelligence briefing and hand out and ensure that all my fellow bombardiers were given the correct flight maps, aiming points, fuse settings, and every other detail they would need to fly their mission. I had to ensure they signed for every piece of information and on their return, I was to collect all the data and reports to ensure that the full information on the success or otherwise of the raid was recorded and logged. I was also on standby to fly up to the very point of departure if for any reason any bomb aimer dropped out at the last moment.

I bade farewell to my four comrades who were not flying that night just prior to the mission briefing. The base would be on lockdown and they would not be allowed on the site for security reasons. I joined the throng of blue uniforms heading towards the largest hut on the base – the briefing room designed to hold over 250 men at a squeeze with a small raised dais at one end behind which was a large red curtain concealing a huge map of western Europe.

I took a seat towards the back with my papers and charts at the ready. There was a buzz of conversation in the air mixing with the fug of cigarette smoke and palpable tension.

The Commanding Officer entered with his Operational team and the room stood to attention. As he took his seat on the dais, he asked everyone to stand easy and there was a brief surge of noise as chairs were scraped back and breath exhaled.

I looked along the length of the room and spotted Geoff sitting alongside his new crew. He looked tense and distracted, continually smoothing his hair, scratching an imaginary itch on his ear or nose, and puffing his cheeks out to relieve the nervous energy. He was facing the enemy for the first time without the men around him whom he knew and trusted; it must have been difficult.

John sat near the front with his crew for this evening's run. Skipper Doyle sat on the main dais ready to give his briefing. He was to be the lead bomber that night. The Master of Ceremonies over the target. He would direct the force in over the target; liaise with the pathfinders who would lay the marker flares and call the waves of bombers in on the VHF radio;

alter the placing of those target flares if necessary and co-ordinate all actions over the target. He and his aircraft would spend the longest time over the target area and would be amongst the first in and the last out. To the master bomber went all the honour and glory and the greater part of all the danger.

I looked at John. His youthful features remained impassive.

The CO addressed the room. 'Gentlemen, the target for tonight is of crucial strategic significance to the enemy. An industrial site upon which almost the entire enemy war effort is dependent! Knock this out tonight and you will have gone a long way to ending the enemy's capability to wage this war. I leave it to Wing Commander Redmond to give you the details.'

The large curtain was drawn back and many pairs of eyes stared quickly at the red tape laid carefully over the map which led to the target. The tape travelled over the North Sea, across Holland, and ever deeper into the heart of the Nazi Reich.

There was an audible sigh as we realised that the target was Schweinfurt; almost 1000 miles inside Germany and home to three factories that produced over 40% of the enemy's ball bearings. It is not well known today, but low horse power radial engines used in the trucks, tanks, and aircraft engines of the Second World War needed thousands upon thousands of ball bearings to run smoothly through their gears in order to achieve high energy ratios and output speeds.

Schweinfurt was therefore strategically vital and as a result the narrow valley that held these high value targets was heavily defended with anti-aircraft batteries on the surrounding ridges. Being so deep inside the Reich, Schweinfurt required four hours of flying there and another four hours back whilst exposed to aggressive and motivated night fighter activity.

The briefing proceeded with details of timings, course settings, bomb loads, aiming point, and intelligence on flak positions both into and out of the target. All this to discover we were actually part of a diversionary force of 225 aircraft, whilst the main force of 500 bombers attacked the industrial centre of Essen in the Ruhr valley. By splitting such a large force, it was hoped the bombers would confuse the German defences. At least that was the theory.

The briefing broke up into small groups of specialists within each crew and this is where I came in to ensure that every bomb aimer going out that night had exactly the right set of maps, coordinates, and every detail he would require for his mission.

After that it was two hours to take-off and the crews went off for a meal and to prepare as well as they could for their ordeal. The base was locked down and no one was allowed in or out. All phone lines were cut to prevent any talk getting out about the fact that an operation was actually on and what the target might be.

I had no crew and no one to talk to. I headed for the library to try and scrounge some paper and returned to the Flight Office to write a letter home in the event that I was actually called to fly at the last moment. I wanted my mother to know my thoughts and feelings in the event that I did not make it back.

I sat in the corner to write, but words did not come easily. I signed off an hour later having written no more than a page and half about the weather, the food and how I was doing "quite well". I mentioned that I might be on "ops" tonight and would write again once I returned. I said nothing of note and never came near to what I really wanted to say. Thousands of similarly frustrating and bland letters were probably being written on bases all over England at the same time I was writing.

Time drew on and no word came of my need to fly. I began to relax, but the rest of the base did not. The level of intensity and noise rose across the acres of the airfield. Riggers continued to work on their aircraft. Engines were tested and retested. Armourers drove trucks loaded with bullets and trailers loaded with bombs out to each Lancaster. Guns and bomb bays were loaded and checked. Noise, actions, and emotions began to run high.

Finally with an hour to go until take-off the crews began to arrive and gear up in the locker rooms, stowing their day gear and getting into clumsy flying suits before waddling to the buses and trucks waiting to take them out to their aircraft.

I watched the crews intently. Men beheld the coming action and their possible deaths in different ways. Most said little and would not make eye contact with their fellow flyers. Some went too far the other way, being excessively garrulous or laughing a little too loudly in too high a pitch. Their outward energy almost certainly hid a soul in some turmoil and perhaps encased in dark premonition. Still others simply looked cool and professional with jobs to do.

I waited outside the Flights Office as the crews made their way to their transport. I was suddenly aware of Johnny walking toward me. He had a red line running across his forehead, which looked raw and strange.

'You alright, Skip?'

'Not really, Bobby. Someone has stolen my flying helmet. I've had to borrow one but it's too bloody small. I've only had this one on a couple of minutes,' he held up the offending item, 'and it's like having my head in a vice. This thing will give me an eight-hour headache. I cannot fly like this.'

'I'm sorry, Skip, let me get mine as we're closer in size.'

I ran to the locker room and brought mine

back for Johnny, who stood nervously on the tarmac edging towards his bus.

'Thanks, Bobby,' he said. 'You will have it back – hot, sweaty, and out of shape – in the morning.'

'I'm sure I will, Skip. Don't worry about it.'

We stared at each other for a minute. So much could have been said, but little was.

'Good luck, John,' I said. 'Go well, Skip.'

'Thanks, Bob. Give my best to the boys, will you?'

'I shall, Skip.'

He paused again.

'Bob, if by chance I don't make it back, will you see Janie for me and tell her ... tell her... tell her that I love her?'

He held my eye for another second and turned away. I called after him.

'Skip, I'm sorry but you will have to do that for yourself. That's too messy a business for me to do.'

He turned to face me again. 'You're right, Bob, I must tell her properly when I get back.' He smiled gently.

He ran to catch his crew and disappeared into the melee.

I hoped to catch Geoff but the buses and trucks were pulling away now in a hail of revving engines and crashing gears. I stood alone. No flying for me tonight!

I was still officially on duty, however, and would be so until the crews came back in the early morning and were debriefed and dismissed. What to do? I decided to head out to the perimeter track and took up a station on a grassy bank near to the main buildings to watch an operational bomber squadron prepare to depart.

Dusk was on its way and the early spring air of Lincolnshire was beginning to chill. A Lancaster was about 50 to 60 yards away on its dispersal pan. The crew were climbing aboard. I watched them go!

PG-B was cast in large white letters on its side. I kept my eye on the mid upper turret to see who was to man it. I hoped it might be Geoff, but the face in the Perspex bubble making himself comfortable was not my crewmate. I watched as he checked his ammunition feeds, the intercom connection, and the electrical circuits.

With 20 minutes to go to the first scheduled lift-off time, a flare went up from the control tower as an indication to start engines. The time taken to start all four engines of Lancaster was less than five minutes. Across the airfield the noise of 15 Lancasters starting up 60 Rolls Royce engines was startling, uplifting, and magnificent. A symphony of radial purity. The roar of a mechanical pride of lions!

As PG-B came to life it drowned out the noise from the rest of the airfield for a moment. I looked back to my gunner friend. He looked at me and slowly raised his thumb in acknowledgement. I returned his signal. He nodded imperceptibly and swung his turret away to check the hydraulics. He never caught my eye again and finally the pilot pulled her away onto the peripheral track and headed her to the end of the main runway to join the rest of the squadron in a haze of noise, engine smoke, and whirling props.

A green flare went up from the control tower and the lead Lancaster began to roll down the runway in a blast of noise as the engines rose to full power. Every two minutes another Lancaster took off, passing a waving crowd of WAAFs at the end of the runway. Sixteen aircraft left Sawston Manor that evening and suddenly all was quiet. The contrast with the cacophony of noise over the previous 20 minutes of hectic activity was profound.

The last aircraft lifted off at 21.30 and they were due back in just over 8 hours. It was to be a long night and I had to remain on duty the whole time. It was an assignment I found difficult. I thought of Johnny and Geoff and my new gunner friend frequently through that long night, but having no means of knowing what they were truly facing or feeling fed my fear for them. Having no control over any given situation and having to accept fate and destiny without the power to alter it created monsters in my consciousness. I felt very alone and far from my crew as my mind roiled.

Conversation with WAAF, NAAFI staff, and various ground crew who crossed my path was perfunctory and impersonal. My heart ached for news but there could be none for hours yet. Time was a merciless torturer. I paced, I walked, I scanned the sky now and then, I tried to read the odd faded magazine lying around, I tried to nap, I prayed, but nothing would speed time or ease my mind and increasingly racing heart.

Around 01.00 when I knew they would be approaching the target, my anxiety increased even further and my imagination became feverish. I drank tepid, weak tea and paced some more. What was going on those skies above Germany? I tried to rewrite my letter to my mother to get closer to the real emotions I felt, but words would not come as thoughts remained half formed in my mind and constantly, constantly I tried to imagine what was going on over Schweinfurt.

I returned in the cold night air to my place on the grassy bank and sat there in full endurance mode for two hours or more gazing at the night sky and straining to hear the noise of returning engines, all the time hoping with the ridiculous superstition that held all bomber crews, that if I maintained this position in which I had seen them all leave, I would somehow guarantee that they would all return.

Time inched forward. Around 0400, I decided to return to the flights area and make my way to the control tower to await the return. I wanted to be the first to hear over the RT radio if any aircraft were in the vicinity.

I climbed the stairs to the operations room. Three WAAF radio operators and numerous male officers were cramped into the stale room. There were no windows and the poor quality of wartime lights and the cigarette smoke intensified the atmosphere and made the room appear smaller.

I found a space at the back near the door. No one took any notice of me as they concentrated on their jobs and readied to bring their Squadron home, knowing that some returning aircraft might be damaged or carrying wounded crew.

Little was said. We just waited. Fidgeting, adjusting clothing, and checking switches and dials needlessly. According to the large clock on the wall it was 04.22 when the first voice was heard from a returning aircraft. We knew the main force had crossed the coast ten minutes earlier so we expected this news.

'D Dog calling Silksheen, on approach now. Request clearance to land. All is well.'

The radio operator in front of me repeated the code sign of the base.

'Silksheen calling D Dog. Understood. Approach is clear on Runway 2. Lights will be on; wind direction is south by south west. Proceed to dispersal immediately.'

It was as clinical and professional as any wartime conversation could be. I exhaled a breath of pure relief. D Dog was Geoff's call sign! He and his crew were on their way back in and all sounded well from his skipper.

I stayed for another 15 minutes or so to listen as another ten aircraft called in with timings and approach headings and arrangements were made to bring them in. There was however no call from A Apple, the call sign for Doyle and Johnny!

Time went on and I heard the surge of engine noise as the first Lancaster touched down, which I presumed was Geoff and D Dog. The noise faded quickly through the brick of the control tower as she taxied away to her dispersal point on the other side of the field.

Geoff and his crew would be disembarking

soon and heading to debriefing for tea, coffee, and an hour of searching questions from intelligence officers on all aspects of their trip. All information, no matter how trivial, was valuable. I also had to be there as part of my duties to meet all my fellow bomb aimers and collect their maps and reports and ensure that everything required by Intelligence was present and correct.

The noise of returning aircraft continued and code letters, captains' names, and landing times of each Lancaster was chalked up on a large board on one wall. A Apple and J Jig remained conspicuous by their absence. My stomach began to churn, both with post-midnight hunger and concern for Johnny.

I left the control room to go and take my place at the entrance to the debriefing hut to meet my fellow bombardiers. The night was cold after the heat and smoke of the control room. Lights from the runway were still on, beckoning the crews' home and the base was again a cacophony of noise and action. Just as the sudden switch from noise to silence at the start of the night had been remarkable, so too was the contrast now to the stillness of just 30 minutes before.

I stood outside the briefing room as the lights from the first returning crew bus swept off the airfield and halted 20 yards from me. I now witnessed the return of an operational bomber crew from its front line and the heart of their battle. Although technically I was one of them, these men had crossed an invisible line that I had yet to experience. They had been into battle combat and had seen and tasted fear and death. It was and remains a very secret place and it is the reason few who see it really want to talk about it afterwards.

The first men exited from their bus. They were slow and stiff and not just because of their cumbersome flying gear. They moved without ease or confidence. Having no control of one's own destiny can remove that from a man. Confidence is fragile and facile. No matter how skilful, well-trained, and experienced they might be all bomber crew knew it counted for little if a night fighter lay in your path or if a flak shell intersected precisely with your aircraft. Their faces were dirty and sweat stained and their eyes and foreheads etched with tiredness. Physical and mental fatigue seemed to radiate from them.

There was something else overlaying this,

however. A tangible sense of euphoria! It was extraordinarily strange to observe this contrast. They had survived. They were home to comparative safety and security. They had tested destiny and the gods of war and had come through. Such was their lot. Could they do it again?

Ten men passed me in their slow waddling state of fatigue and quiet resolve. Then I saw Geoff emerge from the bus. He was a changed man. Physically the same, but now altered in his very soul and spirit by a new experience that I could not, as yet, comprehend. He carried the by now familiar expression of his comrades, tiredness and a realisation of survival.

He looked up only once and caught my eye. I smiled but his expression did not alter. He looked at me firmly and then almost imperceptibly he faintly shook his head. It was the slightest of movements but it chilled me to the core. He looked away, determined not to acknowledge me, and disappeared into the briefing room.

I stared after him, feeling confused, fearful, and ignorant. What did that shake of the head mean? Was he acknowledging his own fear and distaste of what he had just seen and done or was it something else?

I had to carry out my own duties now, meeting my bomb aimer colleagues as they arrived back and collecting all their maps, settings, reports, and aiming results. My clipboard held the names and checklists of 15 names, each bomb aimer from every crew that had gone out. Over the next hour the names of two were conspicuous by their absence: Sergeant Goodhue, the bombardier of J Jig, and Sergeant Broad, the aimer of A Apple. Johnny's crew.

I learnt that the raid had been hard and difficult with, as expected, heavy flak over the target, a large night fighter presence and as a result, considerable losses. I was dismissed at 05.30 and walked outside. I had not seen Geoff leave.

I decided to return to flight control to see if I could find out any news about Doyle and John. As I arrived, I could hear the gentle but persistent voice of the WAAF radio operator. 'A Apple, please acknowledge. This is Silksheen. J Jig, please come in' They were still searching the airwaves for them in hope and fear, and quietly praying with each message they sent out.

The WAAF operator's voice was carried on the radio waves radiating from the tower. The electromagnetic wave that carried her clear and distinct voice travelled at the speed of light seeking and hunting through the night air for a compatible receiver set to that exact wavelength. The wave continued outward incessantly but could find no respondent. Her voice theoretically still carries outward to this day into the eternity of the universe seeking its long-lost recipient. Eternity beckons her ever onwards.

Fifteen mens lives were unaccounted for on those two planes. The lights of the runway were still on, beckoning their crews home as false dawn started to brighten the sky. 'Come on in, boys.' Silence! An unstated beseeching scream seemed to echo across the base. "Come on home boys" Silence!

I listened to the nullity with mounting trepidation. Time was now approaching when hope must die. The time when we all knew that the aircraft would be out of fuel and the certainty of loss would be upon us. If we heard nothing in the next four minutes, either on the radio or by telephone from another airfield where a damaged A Apple or J Jig might have put down, then they must have gone for good.

I went outside again, praying, hoping, urging them to return. The first rays of sunlight were breaking from the east, coming from the place where they had flown into the distant night. I stood trying to breath slowly, but my heart was racing.

Dawn raged onwards. The sun itself began to appear as a sliver on the flat Lincolnshire horizon. In the three minutes that the sun took to appear fully above the long horizon, our Johnny was gone!

I can never forget that moment and the vision of the light coming forth. The sun of our life-giving Earth appeared and in so doing heralded the darkness of death and the loss of John. The contrast is unbearable to this day.

He was my friend and my skipper. He was so very young and beautiful. Those months we spent together as a crew in 1944 welded an unbreakable bond between us. All seven of us. The bond was now broken and torn and the pain seeps into my soul with every sunrise I have witnessed.

I now felt alone and adrift in the world. The only others who would understand my pain were David, Dan, Cyril, Don, and Geoff – the crew Johnny left behind. I turned to find them, for solace and companionship.

Chapter 5

Upon Daisy Hill

I was extremely tired after that terrible night as I hitched a lift back to our billet. The early morning light was bright and the air was fresh but my soul was dark. It was 06.30 as I approached our hut beside the church with some trepidation, not sure what to say to the boys.

They were up and in various stages of dress preparing to go down to the Sergeants' mess for breakfast.

David was the nearest to the door. He looked up and smiled at me but I saw his face change immediately as he looked into my eyes. The darkness within me must have shown on my face.

'Bobby,' he said slowly. 'How went the night?'

The other boys had stopped what they were doing. Dan was brushing his hair with an ivory handled brush. Cyril was attempting to locate his tie and was distracted, but he turned briefly.

'Bobby, boy. Tha looks knackered,' he said cheerfully enough, but then stopped himself as he too noted the look on my face. 'Fuck! What's up with thee?'

'Have you seen Geoff yet?' I asked. The room was silent and tense now.

'No,' said David cautiously.

'I expect he will be along soon' I said.

'You've seen him, then,' said David. 'Is he alright?'

'He looks OK,' I said 'but I did not get the chance to speak to him before his debrief.'

'Did you see John?' David insisted.

I hesitated and looked away.

'No boys, I have not. He is listed as missing together with all the crew of A Apple. He's not back and nothing has been heard from his aircraft.'

The silence in the room was solid and

palpable. Nothing was said for perhaps 30 seconds.

'Nothing at all?' asked Dan.

'Nothing,' I replied.

'Officially missing then?' was Dan's question.

'If not already listed then I think he is about to be,' was all I could say. There was extended silence as reality rushed in to the small, cold hut.

'Oh Christ, does that mean we are going to be split up?' Don's voice cracked a little with his concern.

'Let's hold tight with that thought,' said David. 'We cannot be certain yet and besides Squadron Leader Doyle gave us his word we would be sticking together.'

'Absolutely understood, old boy,' replied Dan crisply. 'The slight buggeration, however, is that he presumably is dead or missing along with John. Did he leave any instruction to that effect in the event of his failure to return?'

'Don't worry, Dan. I'll make sure the senior

officers know of that promise. I'll make sure we stay together no matter what happens.' David's voice was calm and authoritative as always. We wanted to believe him.

We returned to silence; lost in our thoughts as we attempted to come to terms with the loss of our joyful young skipper. I had had a few more hours to contemplate his death than the rest of his crew, but I was not much further along in accepting it!

The noise of an arriving truck and the sound of men disembarking it shook us a little from our reverie. Cyril checked the window.

'It's Geoff, lads. He looks bloody awful.'

Cyril opened the door as Geoff approached and stepped inside. Five pairs of eyes were on him. He did indeed look terrible. His hair was matted to his head by ten hours in a sweat-stained flying helmet. His eyes were bloodshot and the skin below them was dark and sagging with tiredness. He moved slowly, as if he had aged ten years.

He could not look at us. His eyes remained downcast as he walked slowly over to his bed, dropped his kit, and threw himself down on it, turning over to face the ceiling as we all moved towards him.

We gathered in an unruly circle around his bed as he continued to stare past us, fixing his gaze on the corrugations of the roof above. We waited. He spoke at last.

'I can't see myself doing that 29 more times and surviving, boys!' His voice was calm but carried a hint of aggression and despair. 'My god, what a thing is this fucking war! The bastards are trying to kill you all the way there and all the way back. They don't know me, I don't know them, but still, they want you dead. I never thought of it quite that way before, but everything they do over there is designed to kill you as quickly and as terribly as possible. Night fighters coming in at all angles! Bloody hell they are fast; that is assuming you actually get to see them. Tracer bullets screaming past you! Search lights everywhere, flak! Fuck the flak! I never want to see or hear or smell that stuff ever again. You cannot hear yourself think as you go through it. You just pray and feel utterly helpless. The kite is getting thrown all over the place. I was sick twice into my mask over the target. You just have to suck it back up and swallow it. The stench is unbelievable. I thought my head was going to explode. All the time shouts and instructions are coming through over the intercom. I didn't know where I was or what I was doing half the time. Fucking hell! Fucking hell! Fucking hell!'

His voice trailed off and he continued to stare at the ceiling. He was a long way from us mentally! There was silence again and then David spoke gently.

'Geoff, lad. Are you going to be OK?'

There was a pause. Geoff's voice relaxed.

'I expect so! The crew I was with were pretty good. I'm glad I was with them. They got me through and they are the reason I am back.'

'Geoff. Do you know John is missing?'

David's enquiry was gentle and yet urgent. Geoff finally looked at us from his prone position. He spoke slowly.

'He's not missing boys! He's dead! I saw him go down with Doyle. I am sure it was them. I know it was them.' The statement hung in the air for a moment.

'What do you mean, you know?' I asked.

'We were in the first wave. Doyle was the master bomber as you know. We could hear him over the VHF giving instructions as the pathfinders put their markers down. When he was happy, he called the first wave in to follow him on his heading. We were just back of his aircraft on the starboard heading. There was another 'Lanc' on the port side and just above and behind him. I could see them all from my turret what with the flak and the searchlights.

'We were two minutes into our bomb run with another minute or so to go when the 'Lanc' on his port side got hit by the flak or something else. Whatever it was, it veered across to starboard all of a sudden and took out Doyle. There was a massive flash and I saw the two of them began to fall. I think they took another one of us out as they went down. God it was awful. I didn't see any parachutes. The radio instructions went dead.

'We made our run and dropped our bombs and turned away north. I heard the "2 i.c" come over the radio saying that Master had gone and that he was taking over and calling the shots.

'John is dead, boys. I'm sorry, he went down with Doyle. I don't want to think what he suffered as he felt the impact and realised that he was a goner. I hope it was quick, that's all. I cannot believe I am having to tell you all this. A couple of other crews confirmed at the debrief that they had seen the same thing and that Doyle had gone off the air instantly. These crews are experienced. They know death when they see it. There is no hope, I'm afraid. We're on our own, boys!'

His voice changed to a plaintive cry. 'What are we going to do without him?'

Silence resumed. We looked at each other for several minutes and then down to Geoff, who had resumed his gaze at the ceiling. Finally, David spoke.

'Geoff, Bobby. You stay here and try and get some sleep. You both must be knackered. The rest of us will go down to the Flights Office and see what more details we can find out and try and see what they plan to do with us. I'll try and get a meeting with the CO even if I have to wait in his office all day. We're staying together, boys!'

David was calm and reassuring and we dutifully did what our leader suggested, the rest of the guys piling into the car outside and leaving Geoff and I alone.

'How are you feeling, Geoff?' I asked tentatively.

'Tired, fed up, and bloody scared, mate. I never imagined it could be that bad. I don't know what I was expecting really, but that was as bad as it could be. We'll never get through this Bob. I just cannot see it. Poor John! My God, what must have gone through his mind. He fell fifteen odd thousand feet. How much did he know? Did he try to get out? When did realise he was going to die? How did he face it? I keep thinking about it. What if had been me?'

He paused and could say no more.

'We all wonder what it will be like if we have to face it. We'll be alright, Geoff.'

That last sentence I said without any conviction and more as a method to calm my own frayed nerves.

'Oh , I suppose so!' said Geoff trying to

reassure me I think. 'God, I'm buggered. I've got to get some sleep. Let's hope that David and the boys find out what's going on.'

We agreed on that and both took to our beds. Strangely I slept almost immediately. Perhaps it was the body's way of helping me to come to terms with the loss of John and the uncertainty we all felt. It simply switched off.

When I awoke, I glanced at my watch. It was 3pm. Geoff was still fast asleep, fully clothed on the bed two over from mine. I climbed out of the stiff bunk and walked to the ablutions hut, 100 yards away. I had a good wash in the cold water and brushed my teeth. I felt vaguely human again, but my guts still gnawed and ached with loss and anxiety about our future.

As I returned to our hut, I saw our little car returning up the gravel road. The boys were all there. David, Dan, Don, and Cyril. They looked solemn but relaxed.

I walked over to them. 'Geoff is still sleeping. What's the news?'

David spoke. 'Johnny is confirmed missing believed dead along with one other aircraft from the squadron. No one is holding any hope. Doyle is confirmed being hit by another aircraft from another squadron. I saw the CO, which was good of him. He was sympathetic but reminded me that there was a war on. I told him that we wanted to stick together: morale, experience, co-ordination, and all that. He agreed with the principle but needs time to work out his rosters. Anyway, no promises, but we have 72 hours' leave whilst he works out his options. He warned me there was a strong possibility we would be used to replace losses in other crews, but there was a pilot returning from a long illness and he has a mind to see how we might all work with him.

'Anyway, boys, there is nothing more we can do for the moment, we have three days to wait and then take our chances.' He paused for a moment. 'I will let Geoff know when he wakes. Just now I am going to take a moment at the Church to remember John and then I will help the Adjutant's office to sort out his affairs.'

We looked in various directions and at each other as we began to ponder our options for the next few days.

I thought I might return home to see my mother, but quickly remembered that she had told me in a recent letter that she had to go to Aberystwyth to visit an ageing and unwell aunt. It was an arduous journey involving several trains and many hours there and back.

I must have looked lost.

'What are you planning to do with your leave?' asked David.

'I'm not sure, to be honest. I cannot go home as my mother is away. Maybe I will just stay around here and go into Lincoln for a bit. There are also the remains of Bolingbroke Castle down the road where Henry IV was born which I'd like to explore. Perhaps I will take a bike and go over there.'

'Why not come with me?' said David. 'I'm going to call options on the car and go back to Silverstone if I can rustle up enough petrol coupons. I need to see Janie, for her own and John's sake. We can see how she is and tell her what went on. God knows how she will be feeling. Then I thought I might head back home to see my mother. I did not tell you, but my father is very seriously ill. We have a big house.

Two of my sisters are married and away. One brother is serving as you know and one other is, well, dead as you also know. We will have plenty of room. Come along and meet what is left of my family. I could do with someone to share the drive with.'

I thought for a moment and felt that it was my duty also to see Janie as I had been the last one to see John alive. I was also partly intrigued to see inside the life of my sophisticated older comrade. To be honest I felt somewhat flattered to be asked along. I agreed to accompany him.

We packed a few things and following a failure to secure the necessary fuel coupons we decided to take the train instead. Three changes, five hours, and a cadged lift in an RAF truck for the 100-mile journey.

David had phoned ahead and left a message with one of Janie's WAAF girlfriends that we were heading down to Silverstone. We arrived in Buckingham just after 18.00 and went straight to the Black Horse to meet them. Janie was sitting at the back of the smoking lounge in a small cosy corner with two of her friends, Alice and Audrey.

Janie stood to greet us and moved towards

David. She appeared calm at first, strong even, but as she approached David her soul disintegrated and her strength deserted her. She collapsed into his arms and simply sobbed deep, heavy cries of loss and pain. Cries of dreams and hopes destroyed, of a future now uncertain. She dared not look up from his shoulder. Her body shook as if in the deepest fever. It seemed endless.

Her two girlfriends could only stand behind her as their own tears flowed. We were all helpless to assist her and offer her comfort. Only David's arms around her seemed to hold her physical body together.

It was a cry heard on a million occasions during this war. No words could comfort bereavement like this; the profundity of the emotional amputation and death of someone so young and full of energy and ambition as Johnny could not be cauterized.

I and Janie's two friends stared into the middle distance, our faces set and our minds in turmoil with concern for Janie and our own loss.

David held Janie and did not move. He locked himself into her embrace and allowed her pain and suffering to flow from her. Eventually the cries and tears eased. She dared to raise her face. Her eyes were red and bloodshot and her cheeks wet with tears. She finally stood back. David indicated that we should all sit down. He produced a clean handkerchief for her, which I suspect he must have known he would need, but said nothing as she tried to clean herself up and regain some composure.

We were now sitting in a warm and safe pub in the heart of England, but we had just witnessed the pity of war as surely as if we were standing in a frontline trench. A life of a comrade, a friend, and a lover had been taken in an instant and now those of us left had to pick up the pieces and attempt to carry on.

Janie, undoubtedly, had in her mind made all her plans for her future with John. She had met the man she wanted to spend her life with. She had probably planned her wedding and her honeymoon. Her first home would have been pictured in her imagination; the colour of the curtains and layout of the lounge and kitchen. In Johnny's face she would have seen the vision of her children and her grandchildren. Her dreams were welded into her love of John.

Now all lay in ruins. The entrails of her love and hopes and dreams now spewed like rotting flesh over the putrid future days of her life. She could see nothing good in her time to come!

Women throughout the ages must have felt like this as the news arrived of the death of a husband, a father or son in the ugliness of war. Janie was adrift in a sea of pain and agony and there was as yet no safe harbour.

Her face remained streaked with tears as she sat down. David sat to her right and Alice and Audrey to her left. I pulled up a stool facing them all.

Janie spoke first.

'Do you know how he died?'

David looked at me and back to Janie.

'Yes, we do. One of our crew was on the mission and witnessed it. You don't need the details, Janie.'

'Yes, I do,' she shot back. 'I have to live the rest of my life. I must close this.'

‘They were hit by flak, Janie. The plane blew up over the target. He cannot have known anything. Geoff was in an aircraft flying behind them. His crew had to take over as lead bomber. That is how we knew it was Johnny. He was with the Squadron Leader. We thought he would be fine with him. We were more worried about Geoff.’

David had oversimplified the story, but only slightly, I consoled myself. Johnny had died over the target, that was true enough. Janie did not need to know that John might have had time enough to contemplate his own death for several minutes as he fell from the skies.

‘No one got out, then?’

‘No Janie, there were no parachutes. All crews died I am afraid, including our boy Johnny. We’re all so sorry. He was our Skipper.’

Her tears returned.

‘But what about the rest of you now?’ she stammered. ‘What will you all do?’

‘We’re going to work with a new pilot, I’m afraid, and carry on with our tour,’ David sounded confident for her. 'Don't worry about us. We will be fine.'

'Oh no! Oh no!' she said and her soft Edinburgh accent which emphasized and flattened and elongated the "o" sound made her voice all the more plaintive and forlorn. 'You are all so good together. John used to tell me how wonderful it was to fly with a crew that were so clever, and who were such great friends.'

She started to choke up as she spoke.

'He loved you all, you know. He told me that as long as he lived, he would always love you all and would never have such great pals, and now, and now he has gone from us all. What will we all do, what can we do?'

She broke down again into wracking tears. No one could help her as another spasm of grief rolled over her. We sat quietly waiting for her poise to return as best it could. When it did, she spoke again.

'Do you know he told me so often that he loved you all, but he never once said it to me! I know he did, but he just never said it. I know he was shy and nervous sometimes, but I wish more than anything I could have heard it from him just once.'

Time stood still. No one could look at her or at anyone else. Her wishes and desires were scrawled across her tear-streaked face and it was too much to see.

Dare I speak? I felt I must.

I looked up towards her from my downcast position. Everyone sensed the movement, including Janie, and immediately looked to me. I barely knew what words to say. I needed to speak but until the very second that I found the first syllable on my tongue, I had no ideas in my head of the tone or timbre, let alone the actual words I would say.

'Janie,' I spoke very slowly, trying to find the words.

'Janie.' My voice sounded strangely imploring, as if willing her to understand.

'Janie, I saw John as he boarded his dispersal bus. He had mislaid his flying helmet and the one he had was too small. I gave him mine, as it was a better fit. I wished him good luck of course as he went to leave me for that last time. He paused and came back to me. He told me to tell you, Janie, that if he did not come back, I was to tell you that he loved you and that he always would.

'He meant it Janie, with all his heart and with his soul. He did love you to the very end and I saw it in his eyes, he loves you still. Please have no doubt about that. I am just so sorry it required me to tell you this in these circumstances.'

There was silence and I felt Janie's eyes searching deep into mine. I sat still and returned her gaze. I wanted her to find the truth of my words in my eyes. I saw her pupils widen slightly and even a very soft smile form at the corners of her mouth as she found that she was indeed loved!

Her tears returned but this time they were different. Tears of relief, perhaps even tears of slight pleasure. Tears of comfort, tears that still stung and hurt and stained, but tears that nevertheless held warm, life-sustaining memories, tears that would allow life to continue.

She came toward me and embraced me so tenderly that I myself was almost moved to tears.

'Thank you, Bobby. I love you as he did,' and then she kissed my check and resumed her seat next to David. He in turn nodded slightly to me, in thanks and perhaps admiration.

We left Janie that night and made our way back to our old base at Silverstone. We cadged a bed for the night in a cold damp Nissen hut and left before breakfast to catch the first train north. David had phoned home from the base telephone the night before we left and had sketched out rough plans and arrival times to his family.

It was a long and rather sombre trip after the previous night's events, but we did catch some good sleep during our various train rides. The spring weather that day was utterly perfect; one of those bright English days of transition from spring to summer!

It was a day which was fresh and warm with only the slightest zephyrs of air that seemed to waft the pleasures of spring towards you. The crispness of the air was refinement itself. With seemingly no convection currents or breezes to distort them, sounds seemed to become more distinctive and individualistic. The noise of a train rumbling in the distance or the far-off roar of an aircraft, a bird calling nearby or even a person clearing their throat; all seemed to sit for a moment in the crisp, calm air. Just as the sounds were clear in the calmness of the air, the light seemed to crystallize each moment with a perfection which simply does not exist on the mundane days of wind, rain, or even the rare day of extreme heat, which distort the world and reduce perceptions and senses. Such was the day we set out upon that morning in late April 1944.

We travelled via Buckingham to Leicester, to Nottingham and onto Leeds before taking the local train to Huddersfield whose second stop was Morley.

We clanked and rumbled into the little station deeply cut into one side of a hill just before the line headed into a tunnel under Morley. As we exited the train the heat of the day radiated off the extensive Victorian stonework which seemed to climb all around us and seemingly held the hill in place rather than letting it crumble onto the line.

The world at that moment seemed to be confined to this small station in the deep cut with only the blue sky above reminding us of a wider vista. We were the only passengers to alight from the train and as we got our gear together on the platform the train clanked off into the tunnel and with, an ever-reducing rumble, disappeared into the darkness.

Suddenly there was perfect silence and then I heard them in the crispness of the air. Skylarks, singing high and higher somewhere above us. The stillness and heat of the day only served to amplify the ecstatic beauty of their wittering. It was impossible to see them but also impossible to ignore their presence. They flew high in the sunlight and they flew to announce their love and their life. I could only contemplate the contrast with David and I and Johnny. We flew in darkness to bring death either to ourselves or those below us.

David indicated that we cross the wrought iron pedestrian bridge and then climb the long ramp and steep stairway up and out of the cut towards the blue sky where the skylarks sang. The climb left me a little out of breath, with my heart gently pounding as we emerged onto the cobbled street above.

'That, my dear boy was Morley Bottoms

station! I hope you enjoyed it? Welcome to my little town, built on seven hills don't you know. Just like Rome but without the grandeur, or the gold, or the circuses!'

He swept his hand around to encapsulate the surrounding area. I could not make out seven hills. A row of terraced houses on the road opposite and a dark soot blackened street heading back down the hill to my left was all I could discern of David's grand vision!

'We go this way,' he indicated to our right. We walked past the row of terraced houses and suddenly the town was at an end and behind us and we were in the countryside. Fields were on either side with blackened dry stonewalls reflecting the proximity to an industrial township. The land sloped up to the left and a stile was built through the wall up the hill and away from the railway cutting.

David indicated that we should climb over the wall using the three steps on either side of the stile. As I climbed down the other side, I noted the ground becoming steeper up through four fields, each surrounded by its guardian stone wall. The grass smelt fresh and new. A few sheep grazed slowly on the sweet new growth.

Looking up beyond the fields at the brow of the hill stood a small group of solid stone, soot blackened houses which were clustered around the low summit. A dirt gravel road led from the hamlet back down the hill to the smoky town. Standing slightly apart from the group of solid homes was another slightly more imposing dwelling. Not large but with a wide frontage and a couple of attic rooms set out from the slate roof.

'Now then, Bobby, this is my hill all on its own. Daisy Hill this is! See that bigger house up there? That is my parent's home. All ten of us grew up there and a small touch of paradise it is to me. Daisy Hill House, no less.'

He did not expect a response from me. Simply naming his home and being here was enough for him. The larks meanwhile sang on, twittering their agreement as it was their home also and they sang of their joy at the beauty of the day.

Whist we were still three fields away from the big house on the hill there was movement in the lane outside the house. A teenaged boy appeared, followed eagerly by a bouncing German shepherd.

The boy ran quickly to the nearest stile and scrambled over it, whilst the dog materialised on top of the wall and jumped down to join him. They both ran across the field and over and through the next stile.

As the boy emerged into the field that we were toiling up he slowed and put his hands deeply into the pockets of his trousers and adopted an insouciant walk towards us. He threw his head back a little as he approached us and began to smile a wide, warm-hearted grin.

David returned the smile. They stopped short of each other and continued to just grin. The boy, although clearly younger, was almost as tall as David and certainly would be taller than him within a year or two. He was skinny but with the broadening shoulders and the drawn cheek bones of youth. His hair was dark brown, thick and wild, and his green eyes sparkled.

'Now then, our kid,' said David, his voice carrying a warm emotional lilt that one only uses for someone close to you.

'You alright, olden?' said the boy, the smile widening on his lips.

'It's good to be home, kid,' he said and the two embraced. No awkwardness, no shyness, just genuine affection.

David turned towards me with one arm still around the boy's shoulder.

'Bobby, I'd like to introduce you to my baby brother....' he paused and smiled as he looked at his brother 'Walter!'

The boy shook himself from his brother's grip. 'Oi, watch it. I don't care if you are in His Majesty's service or not,' his eyes blazed.

'Sorry, sorry, mate! Bobby, this is my brother. You call him Stevie as everyone else does. Steve, this Bob.'

I proffered my hand. 'Stevie. I'm really pleased to meet you. I fly with your brother. He shows me where to drop our bombs.'

'Hey Bob, good to meet you too,' he said in the soft Yorkshire voice that I now recognised was a family trait. 'Is he any good with his directions?'

‘He’s not bad,’ I replied slowly. ‘Why did he call you Walter?’

David stepped in. ‘It’s his real name. My Father called him that because a rather distant Uncle who was something important in the temperance movement had died the week before he was born and he wanted to honour him, I think. Only trouble was that my old dad hated the name and only ever called him Stevie from the day he was born. No one in the family knows why and we may never know now, but all of us only ever call him Stevie or Steve and if any of us ever forget we get into trouble as you just saw!’

‘Got that?’ said Steve as he winked at me. ‘This is King, by the way,’ pointing at the large excited German shepherd who drooled his way around my legs.

‘Come on,’ said David. ‘Let’s go home. How’s Dad doing, by the way?’ He looked seriously at this brother who hesitated and returned his questioning gaze.

‘Not too good, Davy. I don’t think he knows where he is. He cannot move. Mum has to try and feed him through a straw and clean up the bed as he cannot control his movements. I don't like to go into his room, you know. I did the other day. He tried to speak but it was gibberish. All I saw in his eyes was the indignity of it all. Honestly, I don't want to see my dad like that! I wish it were all over in some ways. It's so hard on Mum, she is tired and upset most of the time, what with Tom gone last year, Jack overseas, you not around... and now this....'

His voice trailed away. The youthful spirit had gone for a moment and David put his arm around his brother's shoulders again.

'I know, mate. I feel it too. We'll just have to get through this together. Come on, let's get up to the house.'

They turned and walked upward arm in arm. I followed unsure how I was going to fit into this family trauma. I need not have worried I was to find.

We walked into the large kitchen at the rear of the house. It was cool on a warm day, but I could imagine it being equally warm and welcoming on a long, cold winter's night.

A large window looked out onto a cobbled

rear yard. A huge table with assorted chairs and benches lay off to one side covered with a jumble of clothing, place mats, old letters and papers, and the general jumble of family life. Pictures of family adorned the wall behind the table. A large single light hung from ceiling with the odd upward wall lamp giving it some support in lighting the large room.

A big fireplace, unlit for the moment, recessed into another wall. The room had a sense of permanence, warmth, and soft joy. Clearly it was the beating heart of this house and the place where many conversations had taken place and many plans had been hatched over the years.

We put our gear in one corner and young Stevie went to put the large kettle on the gas stove. We sat at the table.

'Where's Mother?' asked David.

'She'll be with Dad, I presume.'

'Does she know we are here?'

'Not yet. But I will go and get her, shall I?'

It was as bland a piece of question and answer between two brothers who were 15 years apart in age could be, but I could not help but notice the ease and tenderness and the softness of the tone with which the words were spoken. It told of something higher and closer.

Steve disappeared through the far door into the hallway and I heard the rapid climb of a flight of wooden stairs. I looked at David.

'You said your father had a stroke?'

'Yes, a few months before we all met. It's not good. I don't think he has long to live. I'm sorry for my mother, my sisters, and Stevie in particular. Everyone's away from home or working. He has no one to talk to. He is the baby of the family and all he's ever known is the daily whirl of huge family. Noise, dirt, laughter, warmth. I think he feels it has all been taken away from him and it must be difficult to come to terms with. He's having to grow up quickly, much more quickly than the rest of us ever had to.'

Steve returned with a short grey-haired lady in a flower-patterned apron. Her face was slightly drawn and tired. Her green eyes were fringed with dark lines of worry and emotion. David turned to greet her. She was surprisingly short next to him.

‘Hello, Mother. How are you?’

‘Oh David, love. It’s so good to see you.’

She reached up to pull her eldest son towards her as David reached around her shoulders to hold her close and kiss her.

‘Oh, David lad, David lad. I cannot believe you are here,’ she murmured, her voice soft and emotional.

She held him close and kissed each cheek and then stepped back but continued to brush his hair back behind his left ear. It was a gesture only mothers can do. A gentle sign of maternal love and joy. A sign of protection and of concern.

‘Mother, I have brought someone to meet you,’ David pulled away. ‘This is Bobby. He’s the bomb aimer of our crew and not a bad bloke even if he is from Cheshire!’

I stepped forward to hold her proffered hand.

‘It’s lovely to meet you, Mrs Lumb. Thank you for allowing me to visit your home.’

She grasped my hand in both of hers and pulled me forward to kiss me.

'It's lovely to have all you boys here. I have three sons away at war as you know, one of whom I will never see again. I love having you all around me, even if it is for a short time. Are you well? Is my David looking after you?' She held my gaze and my hand for a little longer.

'Mrs Lumb, your son is the finest man I know. It is a privilege to serve with him.'

'Oh thank you Bobby. I know he will take care of you all, but just make sure you bring him back to me.'

I smiled carefully at her, but could think no words of reply. I thought of her lost son and of John. She seemed to understand the uncertainty of the future with a flutter of her eyelids and a short intake of breath.

'You will be well, Bobby. I can see it in your eyes.'

Again, I was mute, trying to think of reassuring words. David interjected.

'Now then, Mother. Let's leave the

young'un alone.'

'Yes of course, dear! Dinner tonight, shall we say 7. Your favourite; rabbit stew. Two of your sisters will be here and Steve of course and yourselves so it will be a bit like old times,' I caught the sound of slight regret in her voice. The old times would never return for her. There were no 'old times' for any of us now, just the grinding need to get through the present and see what the future might hold.

'I'm taking Bob down to the pub, Mother. I guess Stevie will tag along. Don't worry, he won't be drinking,' he winked at his brother as he said this, "but I'm going up to see Dad first.' With that he took himself into the hallway and up the stairs.

'Tea, dear?' asked his mother.

'Of course. Thank you,' I replied.

She indicated that I should sit at the large oak table. Stevie came to sit alongside me whilst his mother busied herself at the stove with a large pot of tea.

'So,what's it like then?' asked Steve. 'Does

my brother know what he is doing?' he smiled knowingly to himself as he said this.

'Actually Steve, I think we are pretty good together as an entire crew. We passed out near the top of our class you know. Your brother is brilliant as a leader and as a friend. He keeps us all together and is so calm and relaxed in the air and on the ground. I thought we were all going to be fine and get through this war until yesterday.'

Steve looked suddenly concerned. 'Why, what happened?'

'Steve, I should let your brother tell you.'

'No, go on. What happened?'

I took a deep breath and told him.

'Our skipper, Johnny, went on his first mission the other night. He didn't get back. It was a kind of real time training mission for him with the Squadron Leader to give him the experience of a real raid, so he could lead us on the next one. We all felt pretty confident as the CO had done 26 Ops and always came back. I saw Johnny before he left on the mission. He was in a bad way. He didn't think he would make it back and sure enough he got the chop. I had to wait up all night praying for his return.

'We all feel pretty bad, Stevie. It's why we are here today, your brother and I. They gave us leave at short notice whilst they try and work out what to do with us now that our skipper has gone. We are really scared that they might try and spilt us up after all we have been through together in training. Your brother is trying to persuade the new CO to let us stay together and find us a new skipper. It's really unsettling I'm afraid. We are all relying on your brother to get us through.'

Steve listened in silence, his face impassive at first, but then becoming emotional.

'Oh God,' he said in a resigned manner, 'don't tell my mother, will you? She is so afraid at the moment, what with Tom gone, my Father being so ill and David and Jack being on the front line. She is a bag of nerves.'

He paused.

'My family have given so much, you know. I will do my bit too when the time comes as soon as I get to 16, but my Mother suffers the pain of the sacrifice of her sons, I think. I try and help her and keep cheerful, but every time the post arrives or the phone rings, she gets so tense and afraid. I don't know how much more she can take. My eldest sister has a small baby and lives nearby so that helps to take her mind off things a bit, but I know it is very difficult for her.'

'I'm sorry, Steve. I won't say a word, I promise you. I guess it's the same for my mother also as I am her only child and my father is dead. I try and keep things light when I write home so as not to worry her. There are families up and down the country waiting and hoping and fearing, I know. In some ways we chaps have it easier. We have each other and in a small way we have control over what happens to us. At least we can try and reduce the risk by training hard, although that didn't help poor John, I'm afraid.'

We sat in silence for a moment, alone in our thoughts and with our unstated dread for ourselves and our future. That was how it was back then. No one in any place was unaffected by total war. Death could come to any of us at any time. Quiet, unrelenting courage was all anyone had to get them through, whether on the front line or at home.

David returned from visiting with his father. He looked grim but the old wry smile soon returned.

'A quiet trip to the pub I think, chaps?' He addressed his young brother in this comment also. 'Catch up on the gossip!'

We tumbled down the gravel road off Daisy Hill and down to Morley Bottoms, as it was called. The appropriately named Black Horse pub stood on the corner of the street as the by now cobbled road began to climb away from the base of Daisy Hill and up Scatcherd Hill, the next of Morleys' famed seven hills.

The three of us went into the taproom. Gas-fired light and cigarette smoke filled the room, whose walls were dank with the smoke and the soot of ages.

'David Lumb! Well, I'll be. How are you, young fella?' said a bearded, balding man behind the bar. He was large and square-set, and the glass he was drying looked small in his giant hands.

'Sydney. I'm very well, thanks. Yourself?'

‘Well enough, well enough. Welcome home, my boy. It is wonderful to see you, it really is.’ The man’s words were said with genuine affection.

‘Sydney. Let me introduce you to a member of our crew. This is our bomb aimer Bob, and you know young Steve here. I hope you don’t mind him joining us. Bob, this our local landlord, friend, confidant, shoulder to lean on, and the puller of the best pint in Yorkshire, Syd Miller.’

I reached out my slim hand and found it gripped by a huge claw, rough-hewn but warm and welcoming.

‘Always pleased to see our Bomber boys,’ said Syd. ‘Only bloody way to get back at Jerry for the time being. Look after each other, won’t you lads.’ He withdrew his giant hand whilst I might have flexed my own behind my back to check the circulation.

We sat in a corner and over the course of the next hour various punters would make their way over to the table and shake hands with David and Stevie and ask how they were and enquire about their parents. They would make apologies and polite enquiries about their father and ask after their brothers and sisters and generally bring themselves up to date with the Lumb family of Morley. Clearly the family was well-known, popular, and held in high regard.

David would reply politely and ask a few questions in return on the health, well-being and whereabouts of various friends and extended family members. The pub was a clearing house of information and local news.

I listened with growing sentimentality to the to and fro. I found that I was attaching myself to this family and this community. Life here seemed harsh from the stories that I heard, but there was a genuine spirit and collective bonhomie. David was regarded locally, as he was with our crew, as a leader and a man to share a pint and a confidence with. He was their man and they were his people. It was a genuine and a life affecting moment for me to witness this.

We left the pub and wandered back up Daisy Hill in the sweet air of dusk. When we arrived back at the house there was a flurry and clatter of talk, movement, laughter, and hugging and kissing as David greeted several of his sisters. Joy was quite unconstrained and the noise level rose as voices cut across each other enquiring, laughing, calling, and teasing. Old stories were embellished and polished and the bright mood I had felt in the pub earlier continued through the night behind the blackout curtains as the rabbit stew was consumed with homemade elderflower cordial.

Later that evening everyone stopped briefly to listen to the BBC news, and hear the latest developments from the war and the reality of life outside the cosy kitchen. One sister left to join the fire warden crew, which she had volunteered to serve in, and shortly after that it was time for bed.

David, Steve, and I shared ‘the boys’ room’ as it was called. The walls and sideboards were littered with pictures and trophies and memories of boys growing to maturity and manhood. Sporting trophies and times of innocence and excitement lay all around. Records of a time that was never to return.

The next morning, we were all up early to leave: David and I to begin our return journey to Sawston Manor on the first train to Leeds, and Steve to ready himself for school.

David's mother made us a simple breakfast of leftover rabbit stew and a little toast with some weak tea. Talk around the breakfast table was light but the strain and tension of departure was in the air.

David went upstairs briefly to say goodbye to his father. Whether his father even realized that his oldest son was about to leave him and his home could not be known. I was not present, so could not know how poignant was that last embrace of his dying father. In the depths of his stroke-damaged brain was his father's flickering consciousness; lying in the recesses of crushed synaptic chords and arteries crying to be heard by his son? The imprisonment on the darkest of isles that brain damage inflicts on the human mind is the cruellest of punishments. Surrounded as he was by the love and joy of his own home, he could not make his agony heard. To hold your son as he leaves for war and to follow one already dead, without the ability to acknowledge it must be the most heartless of torments!

As David returned to us downstairs, I thought I caught a glimpse of his own distress and his own concern. The demons I saw in his face that morning and the thoughts they created in my own mind as he took his leave from his family haunt me to this day.

David's emotional torture was far from over as he joined us in the kitchen. Now he had to say goodbye to his mother in her own parlour. She looked small beside him as she reached up to hug his neck. I sensed that she did not want to let him go, but wanted to hold him and feel him and smell him forever. Her firstborn son. How many times over the millennia had this leave-taking of a son from his mother as he goes to war taken place? This was made all the harder for her by the death of one son whilst a third was in unknown danger in the Far East. A tiny mother of sons, with no control of her own or their lives and of the circumstances of their possible death.

David's mother finally released him. Tears moistened the corner of her eyes. She looked older and more forlorn. She turned to busy herself at the stove, more as a distraction than out of any need. David seemed to slump a little more and turned to me and his brother.

'I think we had better be going.'

'I'll come down to the station with you,' said Stevie, who was dressed in his rather smart grammar school uniform with scarlet piping on his blazer.

'Good idea,' I replied. 'I think we may need the company.'

We picked up our kit bags and Stevie his school satchel and we moved towards the door. David looked towards his mother, who seemed to have recovered a little of her poise. 'I'll see you off at the door, love,' she said gently. 'Now off you go and look after each other, won't you.' It was a plea and not a statement.

We shuffled out the door and down the short garden path into the back yard. David's mother waved weakly and somewhat tiredly at us as we turned the corner and trudged back down Daisy Hill and over the fields and stiles, retracing our steps of the day before down towards the station.

The weather matched our mood. A dull sky, threatening rain. The breeze was cool and removed what warmth we may have felt from the previous evening. There was not much birdsong; perhaps the birds were busy searching for food or keeping warm or carrying out some other task for survival, and had little time for singing. The Lumb brothers and I didn't speak. The focus was simply to reach the station. Steve walked closely beside his brother but seemed distracted.

We crossed the last stile and landed in the road above the steps that led down to the station in the deep cutting. This was where Steve had to turn down the road into town and walk towards his school day.

There was a pause. Nothing was said and no one moved. Suddenly Steve came towards his brother. His face was drawn and tight, his lips bloodless. He reached his arms around his brother's shoulders and held him tightly to him. His eyes were firmly closed and corners of his mouth were drawn down.

Slowly he pushed himself back and opened his eyes, whilst still holding the tips of David's shoulders. His eyes were moist and imploring as he looked into the face of his brother. His voice was hoarse and his breath came quickly although he spoke slowly.

'You have to promise to come back to us. You have to promise to come back to me! You must! You must! You have to come back.'

He drew back fully and looked to the

ground, the tears now real on his cheeks. He wanted to say more, I think, but the words would not come nor did he trust his own voice. David looked momentarily overwhelmed. His brother turned away from him facing down the street, his hands balled into fists and slight thumping movements indicated his frustration and anger.

'Stevie Boy, David called after him, but he did not turn.

'Stevie Boy.'

Steve turned slowly back to face him. David moved quickly towards him and now it was his turn to hold his brother in his arms. He pulled him back to face him and looked squarely into his eyes.

'Stevie, I promise you on the life of our parents that I will always come back to you. You must be strong for all of us. I know you are young and it is so hard for you and all of us right now, but there are thousands of people up and down the country suffering loss and desolation just as we are. We must be strong, you and I, and pull together. Look after yourself, Stevie, look after our parents. Love our family always and I will come back, I promise you.'

They stepped apart. One brief look into each other's eyes and then Stevie turned and walked down the hill and out of my life.

David stood for a few moments and watched him go. His back was towards me. I saw him brace his shoulders as he prepared to face his life again. The last 20 minutes of farewells to his father, his mother, and his youngest brother had been a pitiless battle of pure emotion and sadness. I was exhausted simply as a witness to it. What could it have been like for the man himself?

Coming after the loss of Johnny and the thought of a return to active duty without our skipper with us was trauma enough, but to have to bear the tearing, wrenching departure from his beloved family was a compounded misery.

'Sorry about that, Bobby! Not meant for your eyes, I'm afraid.' David paused. 'We're all going to be well, you know.'

Was that a question or a statement, I wondered again. I merely nodded as we turned to the station and even in the gloom of the grey day, the larks began to sing again over Daisy Hill.

Chapter 6

On the Wings of War

David and I returned to Sawston Manor that morning, eager to find how our crewmates had got on during their leave. We checked in at the Adjutant's office and met up with the rest of the boys in the NAAFI.

It appeared that Cyril and Geoff had never actually left! They had simply gone into Lincoln and Cleethorpes on successive nights and had undertaken a heroic attempt to drink the whole of the county of Lincolnshire dry. They looked much the worse for wear and in need of sleep, but in a post drunken haze of general bonhomie.

Dan and Don, our intrepid colonial cousins, had taken themselves off to London to do something of a tourist trip, which wartime London could still offer in amongst the rubble. Old churches and cathedrals together with the British Library seemed favourite locations for our erudite pair, with a trip to Highgate Cemetery thrown in to see the grave of Karl Marx!

‘Getting to know the enemy’ was Don’s somewhat enigmatic comment on the matter, whilst Dan added, equally mysteriously, ‘Not sure how long them Ruskies will be friends after we’ve seen off this Hitler chap.’

We received a message that we were to report to the CO’s office at 16.00 hours, presumably so we could hear his decision as to our future as crew.

We returned to our hut and killed the time in different ways, trying not to dwell on what life might be like if the CO decided to split us up. A few of us caught up on a little sleep. A few more decided that we might spruce ourselves up and shine a few boots and buttons to impress the CO if we could.

As the hour neared, we made our way to the CO’s office in the main administrative area of the base. In the large anteroom an adjutant greeted us and told us that the Commander would be ready to see us in five minutes.

We heard the sounds of voices within, but could make out nothing else. The air was thick with nervous anticipation. We shuffled around a little, brushed back hair, checked buckles and belts, and waited. The phone on the adjutant's desk rang and he indicated that we should go in.

The six of us walked into the CO's office, saluted as best we could in the slightly confined space of his office and removed our brevets as we were told to stand easy. The CO looked up.

'Good leave, gentlemen?'

He expected no reply and none was given. We noted that sitting to his left in the corner of the room was a short stocky Flying Officer with words "Australia" on his shoulder lapel. He had dark unruly hair and a thin pencil moustache. He was regarding us all with some intensity but no emotion on his face.

He radiated an aura of aggression and aloofness.

'Gentlemen, can I introduce you to Flying Officer MacRae from Brisbane. He is a top pilot and will be your new skipper. He has been with the squadron some time, but has been quite ill for the last month or two. I am pleased to say he has made a full recovery and is keen to get back in the air with a new crew. He is fully aware of your recent loss, he himself lost his own crew whilst he was incapacitated so it seems you were made for each other, so to speak. Any questions?'

There were many of course but none to be spoken in front of the CO as our eyes swivelled back and forth to our new skipper.

'Just one sir, if I may,' said David. 'How long do we have to get to know each other, so to speak?' as he mirrored the CO's statement.

'Yes, we will give you a week of training I think, depending on the weather of course. You're all fully trained airmen and it's simply a matter of getting used to each and co-ordinating together. Anything else? Good! Why don't you adjourn to the briefing room and get to know each other? Over to you Mr MacRae, and good luck.'

MacRae stood. The aura of aggression remained. 'OK boys, you heard the Commander. Let's go. Thank you, sir.' He put his cap on, saluted, and walked to the door without looking as we were expected to follow.

Nothing was said as we followed him at a distance to the large cold and drafty briefing room. There was no raid on tonight so the room was empty. He turned to face us and removed his officer's hat.

'Sit down boys, will you.'

We drew up a variety of chairs in a loose circle around him. He paused; the aggression was still there but subtly altered. Initially I had thought his bristling manner was directed against us but now it seemed directed more at the circumstance of our situation rather than towards any individuals.

He looked at each of us in turn and seemed in no hurry to speak, which gave him an air of self-confidence.

'Right, boys. It's bloody good to meet you. I've heard nothing but good things about your training record. I am sorry about your skipper. I know how hard it is to lose the team around you.'

As with all Aussie accents, his had a timbre that was down to earth but friendly and relaxed. We began to warm just a little towards him.

'My name is Frank MacRae and I come from a small town about an hour outside Brisbane. I've been here 18 months but I've been flying for over six years now.'

He paused again. We were intrigued. How could he have been flying for that long? Before the war? He answered our unspoken question.

'I was a pilot with the Queensland and Northern Territory Air Service before the war, transporting anything that was needed from medicines to children's clothes to Outback farm stations. I did a lot of hours on my own, so don't worry boys, I know my stuff.'

We did not doubt it. The aggression returned to his voice this time mixed with anger.

'I flew three missions over the Ruhr with my last crew. We were bloody good. Then I go and get glandular fever which puts me out of action for six weeks, by which time my boys have gone and got the bloody chop during that raid over Nuremberg along with all the rest of the poor bastards. What did we lose that night? 97 crews was it 700 men? You all know what it feels like to lose close mates, but let's not go there. We'll mourn them after this bloody war is over.'

Another pause. No words from he or us; how could there be! 'Right, that is all in the past.

Now we have to get together and work bloody hard so let's not bugger around. Tomorrow at 0700 let's get up there. The weather looks set so we'll do a big cross country and back for lunch at 1300. We should know each other pretty well by the end of that. Any questions?'

David looked directly at our new skipper.

'What have you heard about us exactly, sir?'

'Call me Frank when we are alone and on the ground, Nav, will you; and only call me Skipper when we are in the air. I hate this bloody ranking stuff. It makes no difference when we are up there, just make sure we keep intercom discipline, that's all.'

We all nodded in agreement.

'I'll tell you what I've heard. You're all bloody good both individually and as crew. You're tough, tight, and together and that, gentlemen, is my problem for the moment. I've got to fit with you and not the other way around. I'm not Flying Officer Smith, but if we're going to get through this together and not go the same way as Smith and my old boys then we are going to have to find a way of working together and fucking fast. Do you agree?'

His tone remained hard but somehow still open and welcoming. We knew it was his invitation to stand alongside him and fight with him. David spoke for us.

'Skip, thanks for those words. We understand and I can assure you that we are your crew now. We belong together and we will come through together.'

That was it. We had a new skipper!

We all went down to the pub and swapped life stories and recent history as well as a few useful anecdotes as to how we might work together. We warmed to our tough new skipper from Brisbane who was brash, assertive, self-confident, and very opposite in character to our beloved John!

The next few days and nights we flew together. It was a repetition in some ways of the last couple of weeks of training with John. Frank MacRae was a good flyer. Not a natural like John, more mechanical and a reactionary type of airman, watching his instruments constantly. He could not 'feel' the aircraft the way that John was able to and as a result we learnt to give him more information on external landmarks and conditions and Don would feed him more data on engine settings.

We adapted to each other. It was different and daunting and slightly unreal to begin with but the anvil of war shaped us quickly enough. Ten days after meeting we were officially signed off training and returned to active service, and two days later we flew our first mission.

It was early May 1944 and our target was Wesseling, Germany. Our Squadron lost three aircraft that night including one on its 29th mission. It was the ultimate baptism of fire for all of us, aside from Geoff of course. MacRae at least had seen it before on his three trips over the Ruhr and that was a major benefit to all of us. He kept up a constant dialogue of reassurance and instruction over the intercom as he noted that the flaming area below, the smell and the sound of the flak, the burning aircraft going down around us, were all normal.

'Standard procedure, boys,' he kept saying. 'Ignore it. Let's stick with this. The bastards aren't taking us.'

They were strangely comforting words, I found, and our training did the rest. We did indeed find our responses sharpened and focused purely on doing the job we were assigned. We could and did tune out the reality of the noise and smell and the death around us. That in itself was reassuring. I found it curious that I could analyse my thoughts and actions rationally as if existing outside myself and looking inwards. I could do this even as adrenalin rose in my veins as we approached the target and I took control of the aircraft just prior to calmly calling "bombs gone" as I pressed the bomb release mechanism. I surprised even myself with my sangfroid.

For us it turned out to be a relatively smooth trip, and as we landed back at Sawston Manor, I was still somewhat in a 'zone' and reacted to the questions thrown at me by the interrogators of the intelligence team at the debrief in a mechanical and almost perfunctory tone.

'Timing of your bomb release, Sergeant?'

'01.26 sir. No hangups.'

All standard responses. Nothing emotional. Nothing over stated. All calm.

It was only when I left the debrief with the rest of the boys and was sitting in the back of the bus on the way back to the billet that the restraint I had imposed on my emotions in the face of overwhelming danger came to unravel.

The vision of the boys around me and the sound of their tired voices as they discussed the mission seemed to shrink and shrivel into a narrow space. The very air around me seemed slurred and displaced. Time was distorted and the colour of the world retreated into a frozen sort of monochrome sepia drabness. My breath seemed to freeze in my chest and indeed the very act of breathing became superfluous.

In my restricted aspect, with all my senses seemingly in a catatonic state, I sat. I was as a primitive single cell life form, merely existing in a primeval stew of fear and intellectual and emotional overload. I must have remained that way for some time. My senses began to return as if from the deepest of slumber as we approached the billet by the church.

I recall David and Dan calling me through the mist! My sight expanded and their faces swam into view as in close up but still blurred and softened. I felt their hands on my shoulders and under my arms. They were hauling me up from my seat. I found I could not walk. I was suspended between them and incapable of putting one foot in front of the other. It was frightening! I simply could not recall how it was to walk.

I was dragged off the bus and fresh early morning air hit my face and forced its way into my paralysed lungs. I felt my chest draw breath and return to life.

'Are you there, Bobby old boy?' I heard Dan's crisp tones in my brain and life returned a little more. I felt hands on my shoulders still and they were shaking and rocking me gently back and forth. Suddenly I was back!

'Bobby, you had us worried. Are you alright?' David's concerned voice worried me.

'Yes, I think so. Not sure where I went there,' I stammered a little groggily. I was as a piper at the gates of dawn. Had it really happened?

I was dragged somewhat unceremoniously into our hut and lowered onto my bed as awareness continued to return to me. I heard the mutterings of the boys' voices and I felt their gazes watching over me with concern and gentleness.

I recovered from my initial trauma during a long sleep through the day after our return and I awoke to an empty hut with the boys probably out looking for something to eat. There were no operations tonight or they would have woken me. A look outside confirmed that as the weather had locked in with low thick cloud and drizzle.

My head felt heavy as if I could sleep forever. Muscle movements were sluggish and other motor functions were clumsy and impaired. I splashed some water on my face and dressed and grabbed a bike out the front of one of the huts and cycled onto the base.

I went to the medical centre and sought out a doctor. The centre was quiet. We had not suffered many wounded on last night's raid -- just death, with 21 men going down with the three lost aircraft! A pretty RAF nurse was on reception. I was non- committal with her as to my reasons for being there, merely saying that I was "under the weather" and needed to see a doctor. I was directed to wait and was eventually called in to see a medical Officer maybe around David's age of 30 or so.

'Flight Sergeant, how are you?' he greeted me with a certain degree of introspection and asked me to take a seat.

Strangely his white coat, stethoscope and various drawings, posters, books, and accoutrements of the medical trade that surrounded him seemed to reassure me. I felt that I could be on neutral ground here with a pure personal problem and a sympathetic hearing from a relatively youthful officer.

'I'm Lieutenant Cartwright, by the way. Let me take a few details from you, Flight Sergeant.'

We undertook the usual introductions. Name, age, rank, and serial number were all noted down and then the formal statement that every doctor in the world uses when meeting someone for the first time in their surgery.

'So! What appears to be the problem?'

I waited for a moment as I was not sure what to say, precisely. Finally, I found some words.

'It was my first op last night, Doc. I arrived back OK, but then I began to feel somewhat lightheaded and even without a degree of physical control. I have slept it off today but I do feel rather strange right now. Heavy in the head and leg!'

The young doctor now paused as he chose the right words to respond.

'Flight Sergeant, I can prescribe a few aspirin for the nausea that you feel. Is that what we shall call it?' He paused again and looked directly at me. 'You're not alone, you know!' It was a strange beginning, I felt -- what did it presage? 'Your body will have reacted to the stress of combat in a certain way. Huge excess volumes of adrenalin and other chemicals will have been produced by your body to help you get through the mental and physical strain of your mission. The body together with its brain is a remarkable organ for assessing risk and then producing and releasing the necessary doses of chemicals to give it the best chance of survival. Like any overdose, however, whether it be alcohol or sunlight or adrenalin it has to clear itself of the excess which is why you may have lost control of certain bodily functions. Next time you will know what to expect and I am sure you will find that you can exert your mind to control the adrenal excess.'

I nodded. It did seem logical although I remained sceptical as to the level of control I might be able to exert on myself. The doctor went on speaking, however, as much as a means of reassuring me as providing a diagnosis.

'You know, last year I was the medical officer at RAF Holme when Leonard Cheshire was the CO. He is in charge of the old Dambuster boys down at 617 Squadron now, as you know. He once said to me when we had a spate of nervous breakdown cases (not that I am saying that applies from you Sergeant, far from it), that he had the utmost sympathy with these men. He said that he had been blessed with an ability from whence he knew not where, to block out all emotion on a raid. It was simply a job that needed to be done to the best of his ability and he could focus purely on the mechanics of flying and carrying out the necessary actions to achieve it. He knew, however, that most human beings were not like him and that they were programmed throughout millennia to avoid risk and harm. To live in terror of death every time you get into bomber and to know that there is a very high chance that you will not return to your family and friends and to all that is familiar...to know that and still do it he said; now that is true courage. Courage of the type I do not possess.'

I left the doctor's office in a somewhat strange but more enlightened mood.

Years later I was to read of post-traumatic stress, the concept of which simply did not exist in this war! With hindsight that description seems right for what I went through that night, and something like what that young doctor was trying to describe to me.

Our training had produced a state of virtual automation under stress over the target, which it had been designed to achieve. The mind took over and directed the body to carry out its programmed tasks, but pure humanity had not deserted me and the fear, the noise, and hysteria of combat still remained and it was as if these raw emotions were drained into a separate compartment buried deep within the brain. It was the mind's protective mechanism and it worked! But these emotions still had to resurface at some time and excrete themselves from the body and mind in order that it could purify itself and ready itself for the next contact with the fight or flight necessity.

In my case I think that during this first operation, the stinking, fetid corruption of initial fear, self-loathing, and cowardice that I felt over the target were held in a sub-section of my mind and enabled me to carry out the job I was trained for. When the time was right, however, and when the mind deemed it was no longer in danger, it regurgitated this corruption and in so doing it shut down the main elements of the body's functions and left me without motor functions as it flushed itself clean of the explicit horror and terror that it witnessed.

As I carried out more operations I learnt to understand and control this element of my psychic make-up, but to this day the residue of horror still exists and I can wake sweating, held in a vice of roaring emotion and absolute terror. It does not last long, but it never leaves me.

As the years went by and I attended Squadron reunions and dinners I learnt that I was not alone and to a degree all those who served suffer from this delayed stress. Only family, friends and love have saved us.

During the war itself I witnessed men who could never overcome this trauma. Often, they died over the target in screaming agony having forced themselves by a pure act of self-will to climb into an aircraft and in their last terrible moments they found themselves face to face with their ultimate torment. They went to their oblivion having made no peace with themselves. A special purgatory must have awaited them. I grew to know the distracted distant look on the faces of these condemned men during meals or briefings. I began to recognize the men who would not come back and would die in hell.

Occasionally, just occasionally, they would simply disappear from the base. Their minds would collapse completely and they would enter a particular world of tormented hysteria and hyper terror. Authorities would act and remove them to a world of incarceration, indifference, and contempt. In their own way, although they might physically survive the war, thereafter they were the walking dead!

Mental destruction is the most terrible burning legacy of any war and ours was no different, made worse by the strategic and mechanical inevitability of raids over enemy territory night after night.

Within the next eight nights we had flown three more missions over Germany. I became accustomed to the tortuous wait after each briefing as the minutes and hours to take-off ticked by. I decided to try and close my mind to the thoughts of death and focused on the myriad of details and checks I had to make during the mission. I tried not to let my mind wander away from the task at hand and worked closely with David to ensure we both knew the track to the target and back and all the markers and weigh points we needed to look out for to ensure we were always on course.

I wondered how Cyril and Geoff coped with it all. Their intellectual stimulation prior to any operation was perhaps not as great as mine. As gunners they had to sit and wait and observe and scan the dark skies. Moments of action were brief and rare. They must have had more than enough time to contemplate their fate and I marvelled at their composure through it all.

As May of 1944 drew onward, we became quite an experienced crew, with nine missions behind us. The crews with an even greater number of missions than ourselves began to show us a hint of respect. Nothing in particular, just a look into your eyes as you passed in the NAAFI or the walkways between the huts rather than a gaze into the blank middle distance as when we first arrived. An acknowledgement perhaps of shared knowledge, skill, and possibly luck!

Towards the end of the month with the fields of Lincolnshire at their most glorious and the May blossom in the hedgerows like rolling gun smoke of colour, we were called to briefing for a mission which we discovered was to be over France rather than Germany. It was an initial relief when the curtain drew back and we noted a rather shorter route and fuel usage than was normal when flying to Germany. Two and a half hours flying time was all it was, which pleased all present.

Also pleasing was the nature of the target: a former French military base now used by Panzer Divisions as a formal training ground. Barracks, garages, repair shops, fuel depots, as well as the tanks themselves all stood in our flight path. A real military target that might help to end the war earlier and save some of our army boys their lives in the upcoming invasion which we all knew was coming.

The mission involved some new tactics, however, and I noted that MacRae in particular became agitated as details of the mission were explained by senior officers.

A new short wave radio system was to be used with the master bomber and the pathfinder crews laying flares over the target in the form of a roadway of flares back to a main datum flare some 50 miles back from the target, over which the main force were to circle. The master bomber would then call the waves of bombers into attack along the "roadway" of light on the new radio system. The timeline was tight and there would be a large number of bombers, over 400 of them, passing over the target very quickly in order to obliterate it.

We were told it would be straightforward. In and out quickly with few night fighters likely to be around and little flak. Back home in just over two hours.

As the details of the mission were relayed to

us and notes were carefully taken, one man at least was not happy!

Our Skipper MacRae began to swear in fluent Aussie under his breath as the flare signals and timings were read out. I was sitting next to him and could feel and hear his rising irritation. At the end the intelligence officer asked the normal and perfunctory 'Any questions?' The normal queries and clarifications at this point duly came, but then MacRae decided to make his point. He stood and paused for a moment and all eyes swung towards him.

'Sir, I just need to be clear on our mission tactics here. You are asking us to circle for a period of time over a brightly lit flare marking the beginning of a pathway of marker flares to a target marked by further flares. Over 400 aircraft will orbit in an airspace of just 4000 vertical feet awaiting a call from the master bomber to come on in after he and his team have successfully marked the target and all this is going on within easy flying distance of four known German night fighter stations and all whilst under a full moon? You expect, sir, that nothing can go wrong with this plan and there are no alternative arrangements that need to be put in place in the event that some element of this plan breaks down?'

MacRae's voice was reasonable and well-modulated but the contempt was clear. The senior officer present responded the only way possible in the circumstances as he could not allow for error. 'It is a well thought out and innovative plan, gentlemen. The speed of the operation will ensure that there will be little time for the Germans to respond with night fighters and provided we all stick to the timings, little will go wrong. Good luck to you all!'

MacRae said nothing more, but we could feel the rage emanating from him. He walked out of the briefing with his eyes and shoulders fixed firmly forward. We all followed of course, uncertain as to what would come next. Three hundred yards from the briefing room he appeared to decide what he wanted to do and around the corner of a Nissen hut he turned back towards us. We formed a ragged circle around him.

His voice dripped with sarcasm.

'My father lost a brother in the last war on the western front with some bullshit plan like this one, boys. I'm not having it. Too much can go wrong here. Too many aircraft circling over a brightly lit flare in a full moon is asking for trouble. The Germans will see everything. If there is the slightest delay in the Pathfinders marking the target, we are sitting fucking ducks and all that assumes that we can all hear those bastards telling us to come in. We're not doing it the way they want, boys! I have a bad feeling about this.'

'Navigator,' he said, 'find me a course and location south of that datum flare which is as far away from those night fighter bases as we can get. I'm not circling that bastard flare. We can still hear any call and we can watch to see if the target is marked correctly.'

And so it was that we took off that night for this raid. We formed up as required and flew for 2 hours and found ourselves heading toward the target as required. Off to port and exactly on time we saw a large yellow flare going down and burning on the ground, marking the datum point. Presumably the Pathfinders were off over the target now marking as the mission required. MacRae saw the flare go down and called over the intercom.

'Let's stay away from that death trap, boys.'

We flew further south west for five minutes and then began our own solitary circuit. As we turned, we could still see the yellow flare on the horizon and knew that was where our comrades were now locked. Shortly afterwards we also saw a red flare go down 20 miles to the west of our position. We knew that was the aiming point as set by the master bomber.

It was at that point that the raid was due to commence with a call from the master bomber over the shortwave RT. We knew the call should come but all we could hear ourselves was a remarkable cacophony of noise. Heavy static, a type of clapping as if a large bird was flapping its wings followed by the unmistakable sound of an American voice announcing that the band would now play "The Yellow Rose of Texas." It was surreal and deeply unsettling.

The red target marker remained burning in the distance and we knew we should be bombing but no call came through instructing us or anyone else in the main force to begin bombing.

The moon shone, the flares burned, the target waited, and the ridiculous tumult on the

RT only grew! Cyril called up from the rear turret.

'What the fuck is going on up there, Skip? Can't we go in?'

MacRae said nothing and then suddenly from back over the datum flare we began to see bright orange flashes and explosions. Lancasters were being hit and were falling. We could feel the concussion of a fully loaded bomber exploding in mid-air from our position miles away. Aircraft began to burn and left a trail of sparks and flames as they were shot to the ground and burned there in a terrible rage of red and green.

Now we began to hear words over the RT, but not the call to come in and bomb. Instead, we heard the sounds of confusion and death as the main force were attacked by a swarm of angry German night fighters. We were listening to the chaos and fog of war in real time and were witnesses to a well thought out plan of attack falling to pieces and destroying lives.

There was supposed to be strict radio silence from the main force and the order was clear to all crews. Other than the master bomber and his code words, broadcasting to other aircraft in the group was forbidden as everyone on that frequency including any Germans listening in would hear you. You could give away your position or your tactics. But as the timings of the original operating plan slipped by, tensions amongst the crews circling in the full moon whilst tethered to the bright yellow flare on the ground began to grow.

The German fighters were now within the bomber stream itself and making hay. It was like shooting ducks in a barrel. The faster fighters could not miss the endless target of Lancaster bombers which were constantly in range.

Still, we heard only the static and the incongruous noise of American big band music coming over the frequency. Tracer bullets lit the sky, fully loaded bombers exploded with percussive bursts that rattled our aircraft. Other burning aircraft were falling to the ground and then suddenly the screams of fearful and dying men came over the blasted air.

Discipline disintegrated as skippers and crews realised that the plan to orbit this datum point whilst awaiting their turn to bomb the target had collapsed and they were virtually defenceless. Anonymous voices filled with fear and concern began to fill the frequency.

'Fucking hell, master bomber, we're being slaughtered here. Pull your bloody finger out. When should we bomb?'

'Let's get in there and then fuck off.'

'This is hopeless. Let's go, boys.'

Occasionally, after stating his rank over the air a senior voice could be heard trying to order silence and discipline, but the violence all around us was echoed in the chaos on the frequency. From our position removed from the carnage we could see at least a dozen red and green bonfires of crashed aircraft on the ground. Inside them our friends were incinerated corpses. Next morning a charred flying helmet or glove along with pieces of flesh, a finger, an ear might be found to mark their graves. A death in war like this was hellish.

Suddenly over the open frequency came a voice that chilled us all to the bone. A young pilot, possibly on his first mission, was trying to fly his aircraft whilst attempting to maintain poise and control as the world collapsed around him and he could take it no longer. The certain knowledge of imminent death ripped his courage to pieces. His voice was shrill and high and at the edge of reason; calling for help, for escape from the darkness drawing around him. It pleaded for physical and moral support where, in his despair, he knew none could come.

'Oh God, Oh God, I'm burning, I'm burning, I'm on fire. Oh God help me, please help me. Two of my men are dead. I'm falling, I'm falling. I have no control. Oh God, Oh Mother, Mother, Mother please help me, save me, please save me.'

The voice trailed off into incomprehensible screaming and sobbing which seemed to go on forever.

MacRae, who had predicted this debacle and watched and heard it unfold, finally cracked himself. I don't know what caused him to do what he did next, but to this day I regard it as unforgivable. We were all on edge, surrounded as we were by the sights, the sounds, and the overwhelming paranoia of war, but the Aussie accent was clear and as strong as ever!

'For fucks sake, go away and die like a man,

you yellow bastard. We don't want to hear you screaming. Take it and shut the fuck up.'

MacRae's voice was steely and left no room for argument. Everyone in the circling aircraft heard it. Whatever others thought about the callousness of the words, they had the desired effect. Silence froze our own aircraft and presumably the rest of what was left of the raiding force who heard it.

MacRae's voice came back over the intercom.

'Right boys, no more waiting. We go in and bomb now. Bomb aimer, give me a course. Let's go...now!'

We flew in over the clearly marked target at 8000 feet and dropped our bomb load perfectly. David gave MacRae a course for home and away we went, saying nothing the whole two hours back. Over Sawston Manor the landing was carried out as if on a training run. No banter, no congratulations. Professional, well-trained silence other than necessary exchanges of information.

We were the first back as we had been one

of the first to bomb. Little was said in the bus. Cigarettes and lights were proffered, and received with the odd 'Thanks,' followed by a long exhalation which was designed to cover to a degree for the ice-cold atmosphere.

Intelligence officers awaited to debrief us. In normal terms it had been a highly successful and straightforward raid for us. We had bombed our target with great accuracy from the correct height. Our photographic record showed a perfect hit. Our gunners had not had to fire a single shot in anger. We were spotless with not a mark on the aircraft.

And yet! We had witnessed something of a massacre of our force and the taste and sting of the callousness of war was bitter in our mouths, made personal and multiplied many times by the knowledge that it was our own skipper who had waved a man to his death.

MacRae was unrepentant. He gave his version of the operation to the young intelligence officer, who took copious notes, and then he could not help giving a final sign-off.

'I told you bastards this was a crap fucking plan. I hope someone at the very highest level pays for the death of those boys tonight. Next time, listen to us before you send us out on that kind of bullshit operation again!'

He walked out into the night. He never spoke about the incident again. Years later at various reunions there was often mention of 'the voice of that Aussie bastard' by those who had been on the mission, but I never identified him.

It only became clear after the war that our master bomber had for some reason been attempting to broadcast the bomb code on a frequency set 30 cycles out of line with what the main force was listening on and the US services radio was presenting a big band concert on the same frequency as ourselves, hence the Yellow Rose of Texas!

Despite all other elements of the raid working well, this one error had proved disastrous and the main force spent 12 long minutes circling in vain at a time when perhaps 40 German fighters were free to attack them at will. In those 12 minutes of delay over 200 men died. The force only attacked after we and several other crews decided to wait no longer. It was a footnote in a war in which millions died.

After MacRae left us to make his way to the Officers' mess the rest of us attempted very briefly to discuss the morality of the night. Comments were to the point!

'Hard bastard,' said Cyril, indicating our retreating skipper.

'Slightly uncivilised tonight, perhaps?' offered Dan.

'Who gives a damn what he did or said. We're still here, aren't we, and besides he was exactly right about the problems with that op,' was Don's practical observation.

'At least we were bang on target,' was my own banal contribution.

Everyone looked to David for a final comment. 'You are all correct, boys. We did well tonight but I fear that this night will be remembered in history for all the wrong reasons.'

We turned for bed.

Chapter 7

The Wounds of War

May ran into June and we flew another nine missions over France and Germany. On June 5, 1944 we were briefed for a mission to bomb the French city of Caen in Normandy in order to isolate the German garrison there. The next day we heard that the, much anticipated, invasion of Europe was underway and that raid had been our small contribution.

By the end of June, we had flown 19 intense missions and were a knowledgeable and experienced crew who were looked upon as one of the most professional and reliable in the Squadron. We now found ourselves in the first wave of most attacks.

As July arrived, we reverted to bombing targets in Germany. Our twentieth mission was on the night of July 10th. We were briefed for a heavy raid over a target in the Ruhr, or "Happy Valley" as it was widely known amongst the crews with a mixture of sarcasm, irony, and fear.

That night as we approached the target and went into our, by now familiar routine, the flak was intense. Perhaps amongst the worst we had seen. The smell of cordite rent the air even through our oxygen masks and the aircraft bounced and rumbled in the unstable air. Everyone was suffering with elevated stress levels, just trying to get through this job, get over the target, release, and get home.

I was concentrating on the bomb run, instructing MacRae to hold steady on course as the crosshairs of my sight came over the red target marker. I pressed the release button and the Lancaster lurched upward as it expelled its ten tonne cargo. In that moment I was aware that the noise and the awful thump and concussion of the flak shaking our plane seemed to grow in greater intensity. The aircraft was rocking from side to side in the percussive waves as we turned for home.

Suddenly, there was a blinding flash and a crash of dreadful noise followed by darkness and a fearful pain in my forehead and over my eyes. Simultaneously, I felt my oxygen mask ripped away and a froth of foul-tasting liquid entered my mouth. Oil, hydraulic fluid, burning cordite, and cold thin air entered my lungs as I fought to breathe. I gagged and rolled on my back, coughing deeply. The pain in my chest and head was compounded by my fear that my death was imminent.

I felt the plane lurch downward suddenly and then over to the left. I was flung onto the roof of the bombing compartment and then just as suddenly I was flung back to the floor as the aircraft jumped upwards. Even as the movements made me dizzy, I was vaguely aware that the Skipper was attempting evasive manoeuvres.

Suddenly we were level and although blind and struggling for breath and with a vicious pain over my forehead and through my nose, I was considering the fact that I still felt alive! Don's voice came to me through the air that seemed to be rushing through the cockpit.

'Bobby, Bobby. Listen to me, mate. We're still over the target trying to make our way home. Things are pretty bad. The Perspex bubble has been shot away with you in it. Stay still or you're going to fall out the front. I've clipped you into the front gun turret which should hold you. You will have to stay still as you can and I will get to you as soon as we are out of this. Hang on, for Christ's sake."

My head throbbed in the overwhelming noise of the rushing, freezing air. I could barely think. My hands brushed across my eyes and suddenly I could see a little. I realised that blood was coming from a large cut on my forehead which was flooding into my eyes and blinding me. I blinked away more blood and could see a little more but only seemed to see the broken and torn remains of my bombing position through a bloody haze. Now nausea and shortness of breath began to overwhelm me and I began to black out. The little light there was began to shrink and dizziness and darkness rose around me. I passed into oblivion!

I have no idea how long it was before I came around, but I felt warmer although the throbbing pain over my eyes felt, if anything worse, as if my skull had been split in two. My nose was blocked with blood and terribly swollen. I came to slowly and realised from the noise we were still in the air. Dan was looking down at me.

'It's alright, old chap. You are back in the emergency area behind my position. We've been shot up quite badly up front. The Skipper and Don are trying to get us back. She is not handling well, what with her nose virtually gone. You're in a bit of a mess, I'm afraid. Big flap of skin cut away over your forehead. Your nose might be broken also. A fragment of something must have shot away your face mask and ripped your face up. You're a lucky boy, though. If that shell had been half an inch closer you would not be here now. Well done, old boy!

'We're about 30 minutes from home. The Skipper had to come down to 5000 feet to get you home. You blacked out with no oxygen. It's been a terrible bloody trip Bobby, but I think we will make it. Now I've got to get back to my station to help talk us in.'

Morphine must have been in my system. I felt distant and sleepy. I was vaguely aware of a landing and then I felt hands lifting me through the aircraft and down into an ambulance and then blackness again. I awoke and was aware of clean crisp sheets and a face mask over my nose and mouth with oxygen I presume flowing through it. I drifted back to sleep for I knew not how long.

The next thing I knew I was being gently shaken awake. The mask had gone. 'Bobby, Bobby, let's be having you. We haven't got long.'

It was David, Dan, and Don standing on either side of my bed. 'Hello, boys,' I said but I could barely force the air from lungs to speak. My breath rasped in my chest and throat. 'How do I look?'

'Not good at all, my dear boy,' said Dan. 'Try not to speak. Your lungs have been badly damaged apparently and you may need them drained. You have an awful cut across your forehead with 30 stitches. Two black eyes and the most obnoxious nose imaginable. We hardly recognize you. But apart from all that you are still with us.'

David spoke.

'We got hit over the target, Bob, just as you completed the bomb run. The doors had closed and we were turning away when a piece of flak must have torn the nose away with you in it. God knows how it missed you, presumably you were just turning around to check the bomb doors had closed. Either way you are a bloody lucky boy. Your mask was torn off and you must have been breathing something pretty nasty for a while at 20,000 feet, you had vomited some pretty awful stuff by the time Don got to you.

'It was a nightmare trip back. We had to take evasive manoeuvres a few times to avoid night fighters. You must have been really thrown around and it's a good job you were still clipped in. The Skipper took a hit in the neck from a fragment of the canopy that was taken out by the flak. It looked worse than it was. There was a fair bit of blood, but he stayed calm, held us steady, and Geoff and Cyril finally drove the bastards off. He's been put forward for a DFC we hear, and he deserves it, quite frankly.

'After we got out of trouble the Skipper stayed down at 5000 feet so you could get some oxygen into your system. Our speed was down a bit but the engines were OK and the Skipper brought her home with Don's help. We don't know how the fighters never found us on the two hours over the Reich on the way back. The force lost over 20 we hear but you're here and we're all here!'

There was silence as I tried to smile at my friends but it was too painful and I must have looked like some gargoyle in trying it.

There was more silence and an unspoken

question hung in the air which David must have sensed.

'You're in here for a couple of weeks, mate. Your lungs and nose won't stand up to breathing oxygen through a mask at 20,000 feet. We've whistled up a new bomb aimer for the next few weeks until you get yourself right.'

I felt a cold dread in my stomach. The thought of the boys flying without me was too awful to contemplate. We were one team. How could we look after each other if we were separated? It was an irrational thought but we all knew it. Bomber crews were fiercely superstitious and we had already lost Johnny. To split us further was to court fate, although we all knew that an unconscious bomb aimer, unable to breathe through his mask over a flak covered target, was out of the question.

Nevertheless, my stomach was in knots and my head pounded with fear and worry for the boys if we were not together. Nothing more was actually said but we all knew how each felt. The war mechanically chewed its combatants up and spat them out, no matter their desires.

Through my mashed up nose and flattened

vocal cords I spoke.

'Hopefully the weather will close in and no one will fly for two or three weeks whilst I get myself right!'

'I hope you are right, Bobby. I only hope you are right,' David responded without enthusiasm.

'What's he like, this replacement of mine?' I asked.

Don took up the response.

'Seems a good sort. An engineer before the war, so my kind of guy is Jimmy. From Southampton, I believe. Flew two missions with a Canadian skipper who got himself really badly shot up a few weeks ago. He got his boys back but collapsed with blood loss and without three of his fingers on his left hand. He cannot fly again so they split his crew up and now Jimmy is with us for a short while until you get yourself right.'

'Sounds like he'll do alright.' Now it was my turn to be less than enthusiastic.

Conversation moved on and we talked

around nothing of consequence. I grew tired and a nurse arrived to usher the boys out. They left me and went to continue their war.

My hospital bed was located in one of a couple of huts that made up the medical centre, a mile from the main base, but I could hear and indeed feel the time when an operation was on. From experience I recognized when the atmosphere of the base changed and the engines started their roar.

Two nights after my warding in I sensed and heard a raid getting underway. I felt helpless and useless. I listened to the roar of each take-off and thought that perhaps I counted 14 aircraft going out. I slept listlessly and a few hours later I listened as they came back in.

My heart was beating hard. Did I hear just 12 or was it 13 come back? I felt more nervous in some ways than when I was actually flying. Now I knew how the ground crews felt awaiting the return of their aircraft.

I asked a night medical orderly who was in the lit anteroom if there was any news on the raid. It was unlikely he would know anything but I asked anyway.

'Any idea who's back, Fred? MacRae's crew?'

Glad of the excuse to relieve the boredom of his night shift, he volunteered to cycle down to the flights office to see what was going on.

'I'll go and check if you want, Sarge. Give me 20 minutes or so.'

He was back shortly after the promised time which I had spent in a fruitless and frustrating stand-off trying to read whilst all the time praying and bargaining with God for the safe return of my friends.

Fred arrived by my bed.

'2 FTR Sarge. MacRae and his boys are back OK though.'

Thank God, I thought, putting aside the fact that two crews had "failed to return" and ignoring the agonies and heartache of those that loved those 14 men.

'They are debriefing now, Sarge, and will be

turning in for bed shortly, I think. It's 0430. Maybe you should be thinking of doing the same?'

I agreed with my new guardian angel and did indeed finally drift off knowing that the boys were safe for another day.

The next few days dragged by. I read a lot but would often be interrupted by medication usually followed by a prolonged coughing session during which copious amounts of blood and mucus seemed to come forth and which caused the cut across my forehead to throb as I exerted myself to bring up the corruption! It brought to mind the hours after my first combat flight, when my body had tried to rid itself of the overdose of adrenalin. I marvelled at how the body worked so hard to expel anything – chemical or physical – that upset its equilibrium.

The boys would drop by now and then in ones or twos. Dan and I might talk about literature while Cyril and Geoff mainly talked beer and cigarettes. The Skipper dropped in for a brief and slightly strained check as to the state of my health. Aussies like MacRae did not tend to do emotion and certainly not in Bomber

Command when death was ever present. He did mention, however, that the invasion of Europe seemed to be going well enough and that he was looking forward to finishing off Hitler so he could get back to Australia and 'give the Japs some hell!'

In the 12 days since my hospitalisation the crew flew three missions without me and I was beginning to feel that they would finish their tour and that I would have to make up ten missions with another crew. It was a depressing thought.

Very early on the morning of July 18th 1944 whilst it was still dark, I was awoken from my sleep by the sound of the airfield coming to life. Engines were being run up and tested. I could feel the life and energy of an approaching operation being readied.

The timing was unusual with this activity and readiness starting at 02.00 in the morning. This could only mean that it was going to be a daylight raid somewhere over northern France as the Allies tried to break out after D Day. The news was telling us that Montgomery was held up in front of Caen

I slept fitfully through the preparations and

at 04.00 just as light was appearing I heard the roar of the squadron as Lancasters took to the air. I counted them out: 14.

I slept on the edge again and awaited their return. I was up for breakfast at 07.00. My appetite was returning as my lungs healed and my metabolism returned to normal. I was feeling much better, although the view in the mirror of my now purplish/yellow visage was still not in the least pleasant.

Around 08.30 I heard the roar of bombers again as the squadron returned. I lost count but I thought 13 or 14 were back. It had clearly been a short mission, five hours at most, meaning northern France almost certainly.

I was sitting in the small lounge area of the hospital hut a little later reading Dickens when in walked David and Dan. They both looked very tired but I noted that Dan's hair had been perfectly groomed and brushed into place.

Dan spoke first as David looked almost unable to do so through sheer weariness. 'Just on our way back to the billet old boy, but thought that we would drop by to see how you are. You look to be healing up steadily?'

'Thanks, boys. It's great to see you both. How was the mission? Is everyone safe?'

'Very well. No problems,' Dan continued. 'Just back from a trip over Caen. The Germans are very well dug in there and are holding up Monty, so the high-ups asked us to flatten the northern suburbs of that beautiful ancient city, I'm afraid. I trust God will forgive us.'

David spoke up but his voice sounded distant and lethargic.

'Perfect trip, Bob. No fighters, little flak. I think we took them by surprise. I hope Montgomery can do his thing now and get on the way to Berlin.'

'I hope so too, boys,' I replied. 'I'll be back with you soon. I'm so bored here right now. As you say, it's healing up but I doubt I could put a flying mask on quite yet.' My concern was for them, however, and not for myself.

'Take your time, dear boy,' said Dan, 'the war will still be here waiting for you.'

There was a pause in the banter and Dan looked at me. I sensed he wanted to say something of importance but he remained silent.

'Are you alright, Dan?'

'Well enough, old boy. Just tired, I think. Up all night you know. It eventually takes it out of you. Looking forward to some shut-eye, before I get too nervous! We'd best be off.'

I found it a strange comment from my normally eloquent and rational friend. David in the meantime simply stared into the middle distance in his exhaustion and said nothing, which I found equally disconcerting.

They both stood to go and shuffled towards the door. David was the last out and at the last moment he turned back towards me.

'Look after yourself,' he said simply. He smiled his familiar wry smile, his brown eyes twinkling again, but he looked older and his usual self-confident aura seemed to be missing. Gone to some other place only self-sacrificing warriors know.

I wondered then and I wonder still what he knew and what he was thinking about on that day that he turned away and left me!

I turned back to *Edwin Drood* but I could not shake the feeling of discomfort and uncertainty that David and Dan had left me with. The routine of the hospital day dragged on. I was fed and examined and injected and given certain pills. I read some more.

I was actually preparing for bed when I heard and felt the base seemingly begin preparing for another raid! What on earth was going on, I thought. They cannot be going back out tonight! They would barely have had any sleep, both aircrew and ground crew. Perhaps a few hours in the afternoon! Neither the aircraft nor the men would be in any condition to fly. This could not be right. But the noise of engines being run up and tested was unmistakable.

I was very disturbed and seeing my new medical orderly friend, Fred, was back on duty again, I asked. 'Are we on again tonight Fred, do you think?' I was seeking reassurance, as Fred could not possibly know.

'I don't know, Sarge, but it certainly sounds like it, doesn't it? That's going to be a tough assignment. They only got back around midday today from the last one, didn't they?'

At 21.45 I heard the first of the queueing Lancasters go to maximum boost and take off. 12 others followed shortly afterwards. I offered a short prayer that wherever they were going, they would return safely.

I could not sleep through that long night. I sat awaiting the droning noise of their return. Possibly just after 0300 I thought I heard the first sound of a lone Lancaster over the base, quickly followed by three more. I got up and went to the window, the better to hear rather than see, as all was dark in the Lincolnshire countryside. There was quiet for another 10 minutes and then the sound of two or three more landings in quick succession and then, nothing!

This did not sound or feel right. I could swear I only heard six or seven return. There must be more to come. I waited in the semi-darkness, willing myself to hear something more. Nothing!

Time went by. Had I fallen asleep and actually missed the first of them returning? Was my mind playing tricks on me? I ran over the last 20 minutes in my head but I could not work out why so few of my comrades seemed to have returned.

I was anxious now and alone. Fred had gone to the canteen, expecting all his patients to be asleep. I stood and paced and sat and paced and sat and stood again. I tried to convince myself that all was well. Even if only a few were back perhaps the boys were not actually on the raid given their exertions of the morning before. In any case, I reasoned, they were so knowledgeable and experienced that they would come through no matter how rough things were. As usual it would be the other "chap" who went for the chop.

There was little point in trying to go down to the base. It would still be on operational lockdown until all debriefing had taken place and the crews were released from further duty. The agony was to be forced to endure this without news. It was the story of the war for service and civilian personnel on all sides and all locations.

I heard Fred come back and called him to ask if he had heard any news.

'Nothing I'm afraid, Sarge. It does seem a little quiet I agree. You really should not be out of bed, however. Your lungs are still not right.' I cut him off.

‘I’m fine, Fred, thanks. I’m worried about my crew. You understand that, don’t you?’

‘Yes, of course, Sarge. I will leave a message with the Adjutant’s office to advise me as soon as the all-clear sounds so to speak, then we can decide what to do.”

‘Yes, thanks, Fred that would be helpful,’ I replied.

I went back to bed and tried to read by the light of low wattage bulb behind the blackout curtain but sleep and concentration on anything other than the nagging uncertainty of the moment was futile.

An hour later Fred crept into my room.

‘Sarge, the base is now off operational alert. I cannot leave the hospital but I understand your concern and as I will be busy for the next hour I may not notice if you leave your bed for a while. It so happens that my bike is just outside by the door, by the way.’

His meaning was clear. If I went AWOL from the hospital for an hour or two, who was to know. I dressed in my uniform and wrapped up with a scarf to take some of the night chill away from my damaged nose and throat. I grabbed Fred's cycle and set off on the mile or so to the base.

Light was creeping in from the east and the birds were beginning to stir in the hedgerows. I hoped they were cheering not just the dawn but the end of a successful raid. I cycled slowly. I did not want to exert myself and begin to cough. My stomach was tight and my senses taut as I approached the main security gate. The guards asked me to remove my scarf, and could not hide their expressions whilst looking at my still badly hurt face. They checked my security pass and waved me through.

As I rode through the main gates I sensed the activity on the base after a returned raid, but was it my mind or did it all seem rather subdued? Vehicles were moving, bringing aircraftsmen and riggers back and forth from their aircraft.

I approached the Flight Operations Office. There were still two Flight Lieutenants and a WAAF radio operator in there. As I went inside, they all turned to look at me. I saluted the two officers who were both in Intelligence and whom I recognised from previous raids. I removed my scarf again and saw concern in their faces at my own yellow and purple visage.

'Can we help you, Sergeant?'

'Sir, I understand there has been a raid tonight. I am from Flying Officer MacRae's crew. Can you tell me if they were on the raid and if they have returned safely?'

There was a pause of awful moment and the elder of the two officers began to speak. His tone was low and slow and grave.

'We've taken an awful beating tonight, Sergeant, I am afraid. Five of our crews are missing from 13 that departed just six hours ago. MacRae's is amongst them. We know for sure that three were shot down by fighters on the way out, and it is possible that your skipper was one of those. The other two losses we still do not have any information on. In addition to our losses the entire group may have a casualty rate in excess of 20%.'

He paused again.

'I'm terribly sorry to have to give you this news, Sergeant. MacRae and his crew were one of the best. This is a bloody awful war.' The pause was there again. 'Look after yourself, Sergeant. Get well and I am sure you will carry their deeds with you.'

Even in my now numbed condition I found the last comment unusual and disconcerting. I saluted and turned away in a fog of confusion and loss.

I cycled out of the base to our Nissen hut near the little church. The early dawn was still and chilled, as was my heart. Five aircraft with 35 men on board had failed to return. A casualty rate of almost 40%, which was almost unprecedented even in a service that was used to losses on a nightly basis. The Squadron was effectively eliminated as a fighting force for the moment.

I did not want to return to my hospital bed. What was the point? What could I possibly do there apart from send myself mad? Although breathing the chill morning air was difficult and the exertion of riding a bike for a mile up a slight incline to the hut created pain in my throat and lungs, I was quite oblivious.

I wanted to get away from people and the one place I knew for certain I would be alone was in the in the billet of my newly dead comrades!

I had dismissed the idea that they might be alive. I had seen enough of war to know that with losses of this magnitude the night fighters had been amongst them and their toll at 20,000 feet was merciless.

I opened the door of our hut and found in that little room the ghosts of my friends. They had walked out of this place only 10 or 12 hours before in hope, if not the expectation, of return. They were still here in part!

Don and Dan were our perfectionists and Dan's perfectly made up bed and surrounds seemed to reflect his own elegance. It seemed to sparkle with not a crease out of place. A copy of de Tocqueville's *Ancien Regime* lay next to his pillow. On the other end of neatness, Cyril and Geoff had simply pulled their bedclothes roughly straight, and a shirt lay on Cyril's bed in a crumpled heap.

Coats and other parts of uniforms hung from pegs beside the beds and metal lockers stood next to them. My own bed was now an interlopers' as I rather callously regarded the replacement in my crew.

I sat on Cyril's bed and looked down the length of the short narrow and sparse room, which had been our home for several months. I could still see them and hear them, even in the dark and silent room. How could they be gone? How could I bear never to be in their presence again?

I sat in the gloom of the day and of my aching spirit. Time stood still. I was lost in unpleasant reverie and bereavement. Perhaps I should have cried, but the suddenness of their loss in a way removed all softer emotions from me. My feelings were flinty and barren. Young men don't cry. Tears would come but only much later. The tears would be of an old man, when attempting to cross the gulf of time and memory. Now I was simply stripped bare and life had little meaning.

I sat for several hours perhaps, for time meant nothing. Only my head moved occasionally, taking my eyes from the floor across the line of beds and then upward to the cold iron ceiling and back again. As a particular memory or phrase from a man came into my mind my eyes might linger on the place that he once occupied.

I was aware that it was fully daylight and that the sun was well up. The hut began to heat up slightly as the full sun struck its corrugated roof. Shortly afterward I became aware of the crashing gears and noise of a truck pulling up outside. I heard two doors open and slam shut and then the sound of heavy footsteps moving toward the door. It swung open and I recognized an officer and a sergeant from the Adjutant's office. More accurately they were only "attached" to that office, in reality they were from a unit known as the "Committee of Adjustments" which existed in every arm of military service.

The officer looked slightly startled and bemused to see me as I stood, but he then recognised me behind my distorted face.

'I'm terribly sorry to disturb you, Sergeant.' He realised who he was dealing with and understood fully the darkness of the situation. 'You know why Sergeant Donovan and I are here I presume?' His voice was quiet and reverential.

'Yes sir, I fully understand. You are simply doing your job.'

This two person team represented the RAF's efficiency of death! A crew had died and would never return and the bureaucracy of the Service life now swung into action. Telegrams were being prepared to unknowing family. Wills were being read and in this case an officer and his assistant were here in this Nissen hut to collect the possessions and effects of this crew. What little there was would be sorted and reused in the case of uniforms and the rest returned to newly grieving mothers and fathers in accordance where possible with the last will and testament of men no older than 30. It was a gruesome task.

I knew that it had to happen but it was the last and final signal for me of a new world without hope. My friends were dead and could never return and their last possessions were being collected in preparation for their effective elimination from this world.

I nodded to the officer. 'May I assist you,

sir? Some of my own effects are here and I would like to do this one last thing for my crewmates.'

'Of course, Sergeant, we would appreciate your help and you may help us identify any property whose ownership is not clear.' His voice was kind and gentle and as resigned as mine own.

Sergeant Donovan took out a small bunch of keys which were duplicates of the locker keys of those of my comrades so he could gain access to their personal items which had been private only for as long as they lived. He then went outside and brought back a number of kit bags and blank labels to attach to each bag, on which would be written the names of those killed in action.

'Do you happen to know where each man slept, Sergeant?' asked the Officer.

'Yes, of course,' I replied. 'Where do you want to start?'

'Alright! Which is Patterson's bunk?'

'That one next to you, sir,' I pointed to Geoff's bed.

He turned to his work but before doing so he asked me, 'Would you like to assist with

Sergeant Knowles's effects?' He said this whilst holding out a locker key. I nodded and moved to take the key and then opened his locker.

There was little there. Socks, underwear, shirts, old civilian shoes, but then on the top shelf, I was shocked and taken aback to see Cyril's lucky mascot! We all carried some memory of home or some object, which we were convinced would save and protect us from harm. We carried them on each mission and the more we all flew the more precious these objects became.

Cyril's lucky charm was a tiny child's sock stuffed with horse hair or straw, I knew not which, that was sewn at the base and then sewn again with two old buttons to form a pair of eyes. Red thread then denoted a mouth and tiny, floppy pieces of cloth were sewn on as ears. 'Dingbat', he called it and it had been made by his two younger siblings, he proudly told us as he showed us the pathetic but beautiful object shortly after we met.

I saw the crumpled and worn 'Dingbat' sitting in Cyril's locker. It rested on a browning and slightly curled postcard. I picked the tiny sock puppet from the shelf and read for the first time the intimate card.

'Darling C! We all love you and pray for you. Come back to us dearest boy!' It was signed simply "Mum" and next to that in the unsteady hand of young children, "Alice and Charlie."

I was stunned and angry, but I found I could not place my anger. Was I angry with Cyril? How could he forget his precious charm? His failure to take it with him on this mission had doomed him and his crew. It was an absurd thought of course but during the war and amongst bomber crews it carried an insane logic.

Was I angry with the rest of the boys for ensuring that he did not forget to take it? It was an equally outlandish and ridiculous thought, but only in hindsight and long after the war! Its logic was compelling to me in the depression of that moment.

I decided where my anger lay! It was undoubtedly with the RAF and this Order, which sent my dearest friends back out to fly a second mission on the same bloody day as their first. The boys had not had a chance to sleep after they had returned from the early morning raid over Caen.

They had been rushed out of their billets to fly this second hurriedly organised operation. In the hustle and rush and confusion Cyril had forgotten to pick up his ragged and beautiful lucky charm, which I now held in my hand and as a result, the boys were now dead! At that moment I was certain of my righteous anger and perceptive logic.

I might have cried then. Perhaps I should have, but my fury at the way my crewmates had been treated began to fray my nerves further. It is what war can do to a man. It reduces objectivity to superstition and calculation to barren helplessness.

I quickly grabbed Dingbat and the postcard and stuffed them into my pocket before the two man clean-up team could notice. Dingbat would find a different way home, I decided.

I spent the next 40 minutes assisting my new colleagues to extinguish all trace of my friends and our four months of existence in this place. I took my own gear, little that there was.

At the end nothing was left of our life together. The laughter, the banter and intensity of our friendship, and the recklessness of our youth had vanished. We were gone and forgotten. Soon another crew would move into this room and they would know nothing of us, nor would they care. They would have to find another way to survive together.

The efficiency in removing the last miserable effects of five young men did nothing for my mood. It simply reinforced my anger and shock at their loss. Later I was dropped off the hospital block by the Adjustments team who wished me well although by then I could only stare blankly in reply.

It is difficult to describe the utter emptiness and misery I felt in returning to that hospital ward. My lungs and physical structure were pain enough but now I had to endure an aching vacuum in my heart and in my soul. I had no idea what the future held for me. I sat in a trance-like state for the next three days in my tiny room, eating occasionally, drinking water, receiving various medical treatments orally and intravenously, but nothing could assist my dismal mental condition.

On the third day a plain brown envelope was delivered to my room. It simply said "Bobby" on the front in handwriting that looked suspiciously like David's. The Aircraftsman who delivered it apologised, saying Sergeant Lumb had given it to him just before flying on that fateful mission, and it had somehow been mixed up in other papers, which is why he was only now delivering it to me.

He left me and I held the letter unopened in my hand for some time. I looked at it with some trepidation. A letter written in haste by a man now dead! I opened it slowly and turned the page over. It was only a few lines written in David's neat handwriting.

Dear Bobby,

I'm just scribbling this quick note to you as we wait for the bus. We're being sent out again! I just wanted to apologise for my poor show when I visited you earlier today. It's all been a bit hectic here. I've not been sleeping or feeling too well recently I'm afraid, although I guess I am feeling better than you. I hope you get well soon. Only 7 missions to go before the end of our tour! We'll have a party then! Take care of yourself meanwhile.

By the way I never did tell you why I picked

you out of the crowd when we were crewing up. I'll tell you now! It's because you looked like a survivor to me. You looked like someone who could tell our story if we did not make it back. Someone who I know will live a long and fruitful life. Anyway, I've got to rush now. Keep your chin up, my boy.

Yours, David

I held the letter for a long time. These were the last words on earth addressed to me by my friend David. What premonitions and agonies had he seen to provoke him to write this just an hour or so before he flew for the last time. I shook with the fear of his own self-knowledge.

A survivor, he described me! I did not feel like a survivor, nor at this time did I particularly want to be. My own mood was dark, I was physically weak and felt mentally wretched and now my closest friends were gone. I felt close to despair with no hope for the future.

Again, in the years to come I recognised these feelings and symptoms as post-traumatic stress but at the time I had nothing to comfort me or to strengthen my mind or my resolve to go on. Had I actually been physically fit enough to fly I suspect in this mental condition I would have been lethal to my comrades. I was lacking in focus and desire nor had I much will to live. I remained in this state for another week. A time I have no desire to remember other than as probably the lowest point of my life.

A week later my physical health started to improve. I coughed less, my lungs began to feel as though they could actually expand to their fullest extent and as a result oxygen perhaps began to flood into my limbs, my organs, and even my mind.

My spirits started to lift gradually. I turned David's letter over in my mind and my hands, repeatedly trying to analyse its true meaning and what it was he expected of me. I began to think that there was a point to it and that he was working for me and protecting me still. I began to see a purpose to life again.

A few days later I was told that I was being discharged from hospital and that I should return home for two weeks of sick leave to rest and recuperate, after which I was to be medically assessed before any return to active service.

I suppose I welcomed the news and the

chance to get away from the base and from the RAF whilst the dark halo of loss and bereavement still surrounded me. The war had to go on but I, for the moment at least, was still in no physical or mental state to support it.

Chapter 8

Lost Souls

The next day I hitched a lift to the station on my way home to my mother, not sure when I would be back at Sawston Manor. I could have taken the train across to Macclesfield from Nottingham and been home in the day but I had other plans that I needed to fulfil before returning to the love and attentive nursing of my mother.

I needed to return 'Dingbat' to Cyril's grieving family and try to give them some comfort. I do not fully understand to this very day why I felt this urgent need, but finding Cyril's mascot in his locker combined with David's last letter to me set my mind thinking that this was in some way part of my own and their destiny.

I took trains north to Sheffield and Huddersfield and then onto Dewsbury. It was just after 5 pm when I arrived in the soot blackened, sulphurous town. It sat in a wide valley with a steep escapement to the east carved out by the wide sweeping bend of the River Calder. Textile mills belched smoke most of the day and night as the factory workers used the great machines to weave woollen cloth into the uniforms and great coats and blankets that fed the war effort. The area was known as the "Heavy Woollen District," which was exactly appropriate.

I had the address of Cyril's parents and asked a porter if he could direct me to the Saville Town area. He duly instructed me out of the station and right around a grand Victorian era warehouse, and down the hill to the central bus station and across the bridge next to the Parish Church and into the Saville Town area of narrow terrace houses occupied by mill workers and miners which was the working heart of the town.

As I crossed the River Calder I looked into its broiling waters. The name was appropriate I felt: it was a black caldron of industrial filth and poison from the washing and dyeing of cloth and the cooling of steam engines which had rendered its waters dead and un-oxygenated. It gave off the odour of decay and decomposition. Nothing lived in it. It was a running sewer.

I walked into the soot-stained village of Saville Town. To my right there was a patch of green in the grim grey darkness. An area of grass with an anti-aircraft gun at its edge overlooked by another Victorian building of grandeur. I knew this to be the pavilion of Dewsbury Cricket Club where just a few years earlier Len Hutton, Hedley Verity, and other Yorkshire cricketing heroes had played in another world long gone. I had read the obituary of Captain Verity of the Green Howards last year after he had been killed in Italy.

Off to my left ran a series of squat terrace houses, most of them giving off coal smoke even in this high summer. I found Trinity Street as the fifth street along and turned down it. Children of various ages and of scruffy dress played in the street and paused to check the stranger in the blue uniform walking through their playground. The cobbled stones were bare and hard and the pavement ran directly along each side of the street with the houses opening directly onto it. No gardens or fences or demarcations of property here. This was a communal world with only the door of your house giving you any kind of privacy.

A hundred yards down Trinity Street on the left was number 38 with a bare wooden door and grey peeling paint. A window next to the door was clean but black-out curtains were drawn and there seemed little sign of life at first. I took a deep breath, still unsure whom I would meet or what I would say, and then knocked three times.

There was the sound of movement within and I saw the blackout curtain move slightly to one side and a small boy looked cautiously out, his tiny face only just coming above the level of the window. He stared for a moment and I stepped back so that he could fully see me and convey to whoever was inside that I was in RAF uniform and of no threat.

I heard a bolt behind the door slowly drawn back and the door opened half way. A small lady with grey hair and a tired but curious expression on her face looked out at me. Her eyes were reddened and she was trying to straighten a coarse rough apron around her to give her an appearance of smartness.

'Mrs Knowles?' I enquired quietly.

'Yes, that's right,' she said in an accent that I recognised immediately. Cyril had the same intonations.

'I'm terribly sorry to bother you and your family,' I said as I saw two small children standing behind her with wide and curious eyes. 'My name is Bob Astell.' I paused. 'I flew with your son Cyril until recently.'

Her hands flew to cover her mouth and nose in quiet astonishment.

'Oh my goodness,' she said from behind her hands. 'Oh love, we know all about you. Cyril would write about you and all the rest of the crew. He said you had been wounded over Germany in his last letter to us and that you were not flying with them while you recovered.'

Her voice was quiet and low. She lowered her hands. 'Oh love, it's so wonderful that you have come to see us. Thank you so much. Why don't you come in! We haven't got much I am afraid but come in and have a cup of tea. You cannot stand out there. All my neighbours will be watching you now and we won't have a word in private it we're not careful.' Her eyes were moistening a little and her quiet voice was starting to crack. It was an emotional moment for both of us.

'My husband is here. Come inside, love. It's

so grand that you've come. This is Alice and Charlie, by the way.' The two children gave me a small smile of welcome.

I stepped inside into the parlour of the tiny house. The fire was lit and it was very warm. Miners received a free allowance of coal throughout the year and they always used it. Despite the fire it was quite dark and the walls of the room were drab and colourless. There was a small, worn sofa along one wall, with a table next to it on which stood a photograph of Cyril in his full uniform, taken on graduation day from gunnery school I assumed. The frame of the picture was covered in black ribbon. The picture said all that needed saying. Death had come to this tiny house and they were in mourning.

In the opposite corner from the table was a larger, older and equally worn armchair covered in an old blanket. Next to the empty chair was a small wooden stool. That was the full extent of the furniture. A door led off to the rear into a kitchen area and through that you could just make out stairs immediately to the left leading to the second floor.

'Charlie, dear. Go and get your father, will

you, and tell him that one of C's friends has come to see us.' Young Charlie swiftly disappeared up the stairs.

'Tea, dear?' said Mrs Knowles.

'Of course, thank you,' I stammered. 'I don't want to keep you long.'

'Nonsense, love. We need to see you and talk to someone who really knew C and what it was like for all of you. His letters were lovely but I sensed he was trying not to worry us. His loss has been so hard for all of us. Alice love, could you get some tea for Mr Astell.'

'Please call me Bob if you don't mind, Mrs Knowles. Cyril always called me Bob and sometimes things much worse.'

She smiled weakly at my little joke. Alice returned with a large cracked mug of steaming tea. Black and well brewed. Probably the leaves had been used several times. We all got used to that in the war.

I heard heavy steps on the stairs and young Charlie appeared followed by a thickset man with greying hair. I could see Cyril in him immediately.

'Bob, can I introduce you to C's father, Arthur. This is Bob Astell love, who served with our Cyril. We know all about him don't we, from his letters?'

'Pleased to meet you, lad,' and he put out a giant leathery hand for me to shake. Cyril's father could not quite bring himself to look me in the eye and I could not fathom if it was because of his own shyness and unfamiliarity with people outside his normal circle or if he did not trust his own emotions.

'Sit down yonder, lad, will you,' he indicated the old sofa whilst he sat heavily into the big chair which was clearly the seat of the master of the house. 'It's right good of you to come all this way. We appreciate it.'

Alice and Charlie took up a position either side of me whilst Mrs Knowles perched on the stool next to her husband. I carefully cradled my tea.

Mrs Knowles took up the questioning whist Mr Knowles stared off into the middle distance, still not sure of himself.

‘Have you come far, love?’

‘From Sawston Manor on the train. I was discharged from hospital this morning and I am heading back home to Cheshire for two weeks to fully recover from this.’ I indicated my swollen nose and healing forehead. ‘I thought I would come and see you all. I need to return something to you.’

Mrs Knowles seemed not to hear the last comment and continued.

‘When did you last see the rest of the crew, love?’ Her voice was cautious. She wanted to know more about her son’s last hours but was worried about what she might find, I think.

‘Two nights before,’ I hesitated, ‘their last mission. They all seemed in good spirits, but then they always were. We were very experienced and we all got on so well together. We thought we were going to make it through.’

There was silence. Charlie sat closer to me. I cleared my throat.

‘When did you hear?’ I spoke to Mr Knowles but it was his wife who replied.

‘A telegram from the Air Ministry three days after,’ she said. ‘We’ve never had a telegram in our lives before. When the knock came on the door and I opened it ... well!’ Her voice slowed as she tried to hold herself together. ‘Well, I just knew it were bad news. I called Arthur and we opened it together....’ Her voice trailed off as the memory of that awful moment of tragedy caught in her throat.

The air in the tiny room was still and thick with raw emotion emanating from all of us. Cyril had gone from us and his death sat heavily in that hot room, in that terraced house of his home town, in which he had been born just 20 years before.

There was silence again, which I broke very quietly.

‘I have to return something to you from Cyril.’

Everyone turned to look at me and I produced the tiny pathetic puppet figure from my pocket and held it out in the palm of my hand.

‘Oh my, oh my,’ said Cyril’s mother, her voice breaking.

'Look, young'uns. It's our Dingbat. Would you believe it? He must have seen some sights, that dear little thing.'

Alice sidled over to me and slowly took it from my hand as if handling the most delicate treasure. She took it in both hands and kissed it before walking slowly to her brother.

'Look Charlie. Dingbat has come back to us.'

Charlie looked at the tiny woollen object in absolute stillness, almost trepidation, scarce able to believe it was here. He stood in front of his sister and simply stared at it in wonderment. It was as if this tiny rag doll was a small part of Cyril himself. The only real part of him they still had.

'Oh, thank you so much, love,' said Mrs Knowles, her eyes tearing up. 'That little thing means so much to us. The kids made it for him the last night he was home before going off to gunnery school. They took such care over it. He was so pleased when they gave it to him. He called it "Dingbat" straightaway to remind him always of his two little "dingbats" who made it for him. He always called them that, you know.'

She broke off suddenly, not trusting herself to go on.

This tiny little object made of old socks and thread was at that moment the essence of the entire family.

I looked toward Mr Knowles, who seemed in a trance watching his family receive back this beloved object. He sensed my movement and turned his head to look me directly in the eye for the first time. He stared at me for a moment and held my eye and then he spoke, the accent strong and meaningful.

'He were my lad, you know.'

It was a statement of fact but drawn from a deep and profound emotional well within him. There was a pause and he repeated.

'He were my lad.'

His words were slow and evenly paced.

'He were my lovely lad.'

His voice rose as he said this and then it began to crack and descend as emotion began to overwhelm him.

'He were my lovely lad... my lad, my boy ... my lovely, lovely boy.'

He broke and could do nothing as pitiless grief seared through his soul and reduced him to agony.

His wail of pain echoed through the whole house. He leant forward in his chair and began to shake his hands and his head twisted from side to side in his torment and frustration.

His two youngest children rushed to him. They had never seen their father and protector in this state and never would again. They formed a small triangle of emotion. Alice and Charlie had one arm around each other and the other around each side of their father. He in turn now had his arms around his children for comfort. I saw his shoulders begin to shake and heard his wracking sobs but lost in the embrace of his children I never saw his tears therefore!

I never saw the tears of this hard man.

I never saw the tears of this working man. I never saw the tears of this quiet man. I never saw the tears of this loving family man!

Like so many workingmen before him and to come after, he had sacrificed his son to war and was never to see him again. His frustration and pain were amplified because he felt he did not have the words to articulate his grief and love for his son nor to honour him in his death. There was to be no eulogy for Cyril Knowles, and his father's pain was laid bare.

For myself, however I could not think of any greater tribute a father could give his beloved son. He was my flesh, he was my blood, he had said, and he was indeed "my lad".

Mrs Knowles sat beside her family, tears silently streaming down her face. They were united as one in their grief for their lost son.

His sobs slowly subsided and his children withdrew their shield around him. He turned his face to the wall next to his chair and his huge hands balled into fists as he wiped his eyes. It was incongruous to see such childlike movements from the brawny figure of this miner! He turned to face me when his composure had returned.

'I'm sorry, lad,' His eyes were red but I had still not seen the tears that were behind them. 'I didn't mean to go off like that. It's not good for anyone to see, let alone me missus and the young'uns.' He was pulling himself together now and I could see that the catharsis was real and he was healing rapidly.

'I'd like to take you down the pub if you don't mind and meet some of my mates. They all knew Cyril of course from young and would want to meet someone who flew with him. Would you come with me for a quick pint? It's not far, Bob!' He used my name for the first time.

'Of course, Mr Knowles, it would be a privilege.'

He turned to his wife. 'I won't be long love, just a pint and a quick hello to the boys. Will you be alright here?' Mrs Knowles simply nodded. I don't think she trusted her voice. 'Right then, let's be off.' He pulled a rough jacket from its peg behind the door, opened it and stepped outside.

We walked down the cobbled street side by side. 'It's only five minutes' walk, lad. Not far now!' he said. We stepped together in silence for a few yards. I summoned up my own voice.

‘Mr Knowles, I hope you don’t mind me saying this and I hope it brings you some comfort, but that was the finest tribute to Cyril you could have given. He always spoke so warmly of his family and I know he meant so much to you all, and your sincerity and bravery in facing his death is simply magnificent.’

There was more silence for a few more steps.

‘Thank you, Bob. I’ve seen a few deaths down the pit of course and I thought I could get through it, but seeing you in your uniform reminded me of the last time I saw him and then that silly toy! Well, I’m sorry again.’

We said no more and arrived outside the White Hart pub at the corner of a short street. It seemed to me to be simply two terraced houses knocked into one and was nondescript as part of the surrounding industrial architecture. We stepped inside. The walls were dark with generations of coal and cigarette smoke ingrained in them, and the wartime lighting made the room dull and gloomy. Perhaps 25 men were in there. They mostly stood in groups as the furniture was sparse and minimal. A coal fire gave off some light and heat and down the far end of the simple room was the bar that straddled the full width of the establishment.

All the men turned as we entered. There was immediate recognition and as we walked to the bar it was something like a military parade, although in this working mans' environment the salutes took the form of each man looking up from his pint, catching Arthur Knowles' eye for a moment, and giving a simple nod. Occasionally the nod would be accompanied by the words "Arthur" or "Arthur lad" before their eyes would return to their pint. As we walked, we picked up as small gathering of six or seven men who followed us to the bar.

Mr Knowles turned to acknowledge them and with his back to the bar said. 'Lads, this here is Bob. He flew with our Cyril. As you can see, he's been wounded but he's come to see us nonetheless to give us his condolences.'

I shook hands with rough, hard men who greeted me warmly. 'Welcome, lad!' 'Nah then, lad!' 'Good to see thee, lad!' were the greetings.

Arthur put a pint in my hand and then turned to his companions and there was quiet throughout the pub. He raised his glass 'To our Cyril. God bless him.' Everyone drank deeply and repeated the blessing.

Questions then began to come at me, the topics being enquiries about my health and then about what it was like "up there" and then more earnestly about how Cyril might have died. The first two subjects I gave them as honest opinion as I could, garnished with a few anecdotes. The last one I had no answer to other than to assure them it might have been quick. I was as lost as they were. Why Cyril? Why my friends? Why not me?

We talked on. Politics came around, notably in the form as to how long this war might last now that Germany appeared to be in retreat and what then lay beyond it. There was a hint that, in this company at least, there was no love for Churchill. He might become a national and global hero after the war, but to these men he was the man who took Britain back onto the gold standard as Chancellor in 1928 and destroyed their already precarious livelihoods. 'Once this war is over that bastard can go to hell,' was a typical comment, passionately stated in a number of different forms. It turned out that in the not to distant future, politically, this was precisely what happened to our wartime leader.

Talk meandered on. I bought a round and having drunk it I saw that it was after 9pm. I was tired but I also knew that I had missed the last passenger train to Manchester. Nevertheless, I made my apologies and gave my best wishes to Arthur and his friends and I left the pub whilst the last light of dusk was still in the dusty streets.

As I walked back into the station a friendly manager accosted me to inform me of what I already knew, that there were no trains out that night. The RAF uniform helped and perhaps the sign of wounding also.

'I tell you what my boy, why don't you kip down in my office for the night. There is an old carpet on the floor and the cushion from my chair can be your pillow and you've got that great coat of yours to keep you warm and I'll make you a cup of tea before I leave also.'

I took up his kind offer and made myself as comfortable as I could after I had checked with him that the best route home was to get the 06.57 to Leeds in the morning. 'Change there for Manchester and then again for Macclesfield.

Home by 12.30,' he said.

The next morning, I boarded the stopper to Leeds with a few other souls heading to work up the line. I was tired and distracted and after two stops I was ready to sleep but I knew Leeds was only two more stations away. We stopped again after exiting a long tunnel and I suddenly realised that I knew this place. I was back in the deep cut at Morley Bottom station.

On a sudden impulse, I decided to jump off. I had no previous intention to call on another family of my dead friends. I presume it was some unconscious desire to retrace time. The train rumbled out of the station and I stood alone on the platform opposite the long staircase leading to the road at the top of the cut.

I put my kit bag over my shoulder and step by step, ascended. I made the road and turned to my right as I had done a few months before with David. At the end of the small row of houses I looked to my left and up towards Daisy Hill and saw the large squat house on the flat summit across the fields. The morning was still early and life was just beginning on this day. I heard birdsong, but my mind was in such turmoil and my heart so heavy that I couldn't discern the different calls. I stood and looked across fields towards the house and I thought of nothing and everything. There was no pattern or logic in my emotions but David's last letter to me was there as part of the swirl of passions. Was that why I was here?

I climbed the stile and looked up across the fields again. I suddenly sat down on the bottom step. Had I seen movement around the house? Was it a boy and dog emerging in the early morning? I could not be sure and I dared not look up again. Did I go onwards? Was it Stevie? Should I see him and comfort him? What could be said? My mind was racing but my mind was unclear. I remembered the last time I was here and had watched the two brothers say farewell for the final time, David promising his youngest brother on the life of their parents that he would return to them. Now his promise was broken and could never be remade and the ripples of his death had, through my presence, returned to his hometown and his family. How could I make good that promise?

I sat on the bottom step of the stile, hidden from the road and from anyone on it. I was completely alone. Again, I might have cried then. Huge, sobbing tears for my friends and for my crew. For John, David, Cyril, Geoff, Dan, and Don and for Frank MacRae, but the tears would not come. They remained dry and hoarse, cutting and tearing at the back of my throat but never emerging. Tears require acceptance of loss and are part of that process, but my anger was still visceral and real and tears did not fit that emotion. I held my hands to my face as I shook with the energy and adrenalin of rage and I thought of young Stevie and his family facing the world without their sons and brothers.

I don't know how long I sat there but when I looked up again at the house on Daisy Hill the moment had gone. There was nothing I could bring to the family other than more misery and bereavement. I climbed the stile again without looking back and walked back down the steps to the station again.

Several hours later I arrived back home and fell into my mother's arms. I had little to say and felt sorry for her that my taciturn and cautious manner prevented us from making true emotional contact, but she had seen this in my father after the First War and left me the space and time to begin to repair my shattered mind. I was grateful for that.

For the next three weeks my mother fed me and nurtured me. I slept for long hours and as my strength returned, I began to take long walks in the Peak District near my home. I would take buses to Buxton and Ashbourne and stop on the way to walk the hills and valleys of Derbyshire. My joy and love of the English countryside was strengthened further. The weather was kind and my soul began to ease. The fresh air cleansed my tortured lungs and my general mood began to lift as my physical and mental rehabilitation progressed.

Nevertheless, I would awake at night from time to time in the cold sweat of a nightmare with visions of being trapped in a burning Lancaster unable to free myself, or my friends. Occasionally I would awake believing that David and the boys had survived, only to sink into depression in my waking thoughts as reality returned.

After three weeks I was required to attend a military hospital in Manchester to assess my progress. I was warded in for two nights and spent my days carrying out multiple tests to assess my recovery, my coordination, and above all the state of my lungs. I was required to run, climb stairs, do press-ups and star jumps, and various other exercises which were then usually followed by much tapping of my chest, x-rays, and work with a variety of instruments.

I felt exhausted by the entire procedure but during meal breaks and in the evenings, I was buoyed by conversations with my fellow patients who were also being assessed for a variety of wounds. We would compare our suffering and there was general recognition and understanding amongst only those of us who had served in the air above Germany as to our fears for both the past and the future.

After three days of tortuous examination, I was called in front of a formal panel of four doctors and two RAF officers. I was told that due to the damage to my lungs I was no longer fit for active service and would be sent to the reserves. I was free, however, to volunteer for training duties and due to my extensive frontline experience of 20 missions it was felt that I would be able to make a significant contribution to the development of the next generation of bomb aimers. I was given one hour to consider the offer.

It did not take me that much time to think about the situation. I still wanted to serve if for no other reason that I owed it to the boys and did not want to let them down. If I could assist some new personnel to avoid death and destruction over Germany and bring the war to an early conclusion then I would still be playing my part.

So it was that I found myself two months later training several eager cohorts of up to 30 men as potential bomb aimers for RAF Bomber Command. They were good lads in the main – intelligent, keen, and desperate to do well. Many of them were older than myself, but it seemed that my experience of war had aged me and given me a status and confidence that I had previously thought impossible. I knew the answers to all their questions and could back up the theory with actual experience and what could and did happen under fire.

My classes always deferred to me and remained silent whenever I spoke. It was strange. I felt that they regarded me in the same way as I thought of David when first we met. Perhaps they thought I could protect them if they listened hard enough and did as I told them. I did not feel it within me to abuse them of that notion. How could I tell them that fate alone was their destiny and skill counted for nothing: The gods of war would do what they wanted.

There was one question in my classes, which usually went unsaid but which, nevertheless, constantly hung in the air. Occasionally one nervous and worried or simply curious airmen would articulate it.

'What's it like over there, Sarge? What's it really like?'

I tried to be honest but words are generally not enough and no matter how many times I have been asked the same question over the years, I have always found my words inadequate.

Only those who fight might understand what the question means. Unfortunately, the raw hot emotions of combat are beyond description in any language and because of that fact throughout the generations, most fighting men tend to keep quiet and say little. It is a mental defence mechanism as much as anything but also an acknowledgement that war is an evil of human existence that is beyond mortals to explain.

This inability of fighting men to give an exact explanation of what "it is like" is both an historical and personal strength but also a curse, because it means that each generation suffers a curiosity about war and combat that cannot be extinguished. Some novelists, poets, and historians may have come close to explaining the nausea of war, but the fact that it assails every sense simultaneously and destroys nerves and humanity is beyond all of us to explain. In response to the question, therefore, all I could do was to be honest to myself.

'It's hard, it's dangerous, and it makes you so scared that sometimes you cannot think and it turns your bowels to water, but you must always resolve to go on, you must always go forward; otherwise, there is never a way back!'

Every time I said that I saw the acknowledgment of reality in my interrogator's eyes followed by the flicker of disappointment that there must be more. It was ever thus, I suspect, throughout the ages.

In the spring of 1945, it was clear that war in Europe was drawing to a close. I was still training men for that war and indeed I even found myself having been promoted to an officer as a reward for that service. The looks on the faces of my trainees and the words they spoke were now changing. They could sense that time was running out for them to do "their bit" and take part in the war. It was going to be over before they passed out. Some were delighted. Others were disappointed.

I was naturally pleased that things were coming to a close. I did not wish to see any more good men die and the entire country was tired, war weary, starving, and desperate for the end.

During late April 1945 I received new orders. I was directed back to Lincolnshire and to Bomber Command Headquarters near Grantham. Orders were strict. I was to talk to no one and leave immediately. The train journey was ten hours with many stops and changes.

When I arrived at St Vincent's Hall in Grantham, I passed through various security details and was welcomed by an efficient warrant officer who showed me to a tiny attic room with a single bed, a small table, and single hook on the rear of the door.

'This will be yours for the next few days, Flight Lieutenant. There will be a briefing downstairs in the main briefing room on the ground floor in 30 minutes. We shall see you then!'

That was it. I unpacked my small kitbag and hung what I could on the small hook, put the rest under the bed, and found the bathroom on the floor below.

Thirty minutes later I went downstairs to the briefing room. As was usual, a large chart stood at one end of the room covered by a beige curtain and about 25 men were assembling and generally loitering on the rows of chairs. What was unusual was that they were all officers; clearly an experienced bunch. I recognized no one and sat down next another Flight Lieutenant with navigator insignia.

'Any idea what we are here for?' he asked.

I shook my head. 'No idea whatsoever, they seem to have kept this very tight.' As I spoke a senior party entered headed by an air commodore and moved to the raised dais at the front. The room stood as they moved forward and the party of six men took their places.

After introducing himself and his team, the commodore said, 'I will come to the point immediately, if I may. You are all here as some of the most experienced personnel we can spare at present to assist in the planning and implementation of a special operation which we are calling Operation Manna.'

There was a pause and men looked at each other with ongoing puzzlement.

'Gentlemen, we have a major and unusual situation developing in Holland. As you know, a great deal of that country has been liberated, but a number of the western areas including the major cities of Amsterdam, Utrecht, The Hague, and Rotterdam remain in German hands. Following a national rail strike in support of the liberation efforts and the flooding of 500,000 acres of farmland by the Germans, however, no food, medicines, or materials are getting through to these areas and over three million Dutch citizens are starving and in desperate need of assistance.

'Quite simply, gentlemen, it is now our job to plan and organise a program of food drops into designated drop zones in these areas with the agreement of the German Command in Holland. It will be the first time that air power has been used in a sustained humanitarian operation. Rather than drop bombs we will drop food parcels and medicines. There will be difficulties, however. We will have to fly at very low levels, probably at no more than 500 feet, and very slowly as we cannot possibly put enough parachutes together for all the food parcels required and we do not wish to damage the goods. We must also hope that our negotiations with the Germans go well. They will give us specific flight corridors to fly down and we must hope that all their flak gunners are fully informed and do not open fire.'

So it was that just two weeks later, after some furious planning and testing with my new comrades, I climbed back into a Lancaster bomber that was loaded with canvas bags of tinned food and medicines rather than explosive devices.

We were an experienced crew on paper, with our skipper having flown 39 missions, our gunners having more than 60 trips between them, the navigator 45 trips and the wireless operator 42; nevertheless, we had never flown together! This would have to work immediately!

At least we flew in daylight so navigation was relatively easy but we had to be accurate. The Germans gave us just two corridors, one in, one out, which were no more than two miles wide each. Flak gunners had been instructed not to fire on us, although we only had their word on that and at 500 feet and flying at not much over 100 knots we were the biggest and easiest of targets.

We took off in late April leading just over 50 aircraft. As we were low, I did not need oxygen and my lungs felt fine. Sitting in the nose bubble of my Lancaster was a strange sensation. Everything that was physical was familiar but the voices of the men I flew with were not. The routines of flight were automatic but the responses of my crew were new and grated a little at first. It made me realise what a team I had truly been part of and the agony of parting was renewed in me again. And yet, we had a job to do and this time it was life affirming and charitable rather than clinical and deadly.

We crossed the Channel and chose our approach course carefully to ensure we hit the correct flight corridor on time and in the precise location. I was keeping a close look out for all our ground markers – bridges, roads, dykes, windmills – that ensured we stayed on track.

We came up on our target markers, which were white crosses produced with sheets or tarpaulins laid out on open fields and suddenly I could see hundreds and hundreds of people rushing towards the marker locations. Some stopped to wave but most continued on with purpose, desperate to receive the parcels. Starving people who knew that help was coming and their hunger drove them on to their share of respite and relief.

We crossed the target area with our bomb doors open. I released the toggle that held our precious cargo of tins and canisters sitting inside canvas bags and away they went. I watched them fall the short distance to the earth where they crashed awkwardly into the earth and rolled a few feet before coming to rest and they all appeared to stay intact. People swarmed towards them as we wheeled away and took our headings back home. Not a shot was fired at us the whole time. The Germans had kept their word.

I flew two missions a day like this for the next week. At the end of what was to be my last mission I noted that a farmer had cut his tulip field so it spelt out the words “Thank You” to all of us who flew. It was a remarkable sight that I have never forgotten.

I landed for the last time on May 1st 1945 and never set foot in a Lancaster bomber again. The war ended a week later. We were all joyful of course but for many such as myself it was tinged with anti-climax and sadness. So much had been lost by so many. Friends had been lost. Cities lay in ruins and we that were left were half-starved and living with food rationing that was to continue for another nine years, until the economy, which had been geared for total war, unwound and rebalanced itself so that the various niches, cycles, and supply chains of a post-war economy were established.

In the meantime, we had a General Election only weeks after the end of the war. It was the first step to reality and the result reflected it. Everyone and I mean virtually everyone, wanted to forget the war and its sacrifices, as quickly as possible. It was a collective post-trauma decision. Whilst most of us appreciated and understood Churchill's leadership, he now only reminded us of the pain, hurt, and suffering of the previous six years, so we put him away and voted in our millions for the Labour Party of Clement Attlee who promised us all a new Jerusalem.

I was promoted again to the esteemed ranks of a Wing Commander shortly after the election and spent the next month demobilising now unnecessary airfields. In the middle of 1946, I was demobilised myself and began a new life as far removed from the war as possible. As a young man still, I did not want to think about it or go back there. In an understated English way, I wished to be reborn!

Chapter 9

Putting the Pieces Together

I had plenty of time to consider my future in the year or so between the end of the war and my demobilisation in 1946. I could have stayed in a safe and steady desk job with the RAF for the next 30 years if I had wished, but I always knew that such an arrangement was not for me.

I had volunteered to defend my country and my family, to fly, and to rid the world of tyranny. I felt I had done my little bit to ensure freedom and liberty. I had paid the price, physically and mentally, and like the rest of the country I simply wanted to move on and forget.

I chose to become a teacher. I had enjoyed my time in training up new bomber crews and I realised that I had a small penchant for communication and empathy and I felt that I could pass on the ideas and disciplines of knowledge to a post-war generation of children. They were the future and their natural optimism and desire might prevent me from falling into melancholy and depression.

I was, unfortunately, beginning to be increasingly aware of my reflection on "survivor's guilt." The casualty rate in Bomber Command was over 40%; 55,000 of the 125,000 men who had volunteered to serve had died. It was the highest death rate in any service of the Allied armed forces. Why then had I been spared? What fate had decreed my survival whilst David, Johnny, Cyril, and the other boys had died? It was unfathomable. I knew that dwelling too much on this reality could lead to darkness and waste. I needed to escape and I decided that teaching a new generation might be my route to redemption.

As a demobilised serviceman I was entitled to an education grant to pay for my training and I enrolled in the autumn of 1946 at York St Johns College.

I love the city of York, a beautiful historic city of cobblestones and narrow medieval alleys known locally as 'snickleways'. It had escaped the worst of the war as it had no particular strategic industry that required the Luftwaffe to obliterate it.

Most of my fellow students were also ex-service personnel of course, from all areas of the armed forces and support staff. We would talk about our respective war service but only in the most general of terms; as we had been through the same game there was little to declaim upon. We all wanted to forget our pasts to a degree and after checking name, rank, and service corps, generally we would move the discussion on.

Politics was usually high on the list for debate with our new Labour Government making progress in developing what we came to know as the welfare state. The use of the State as a vehicle to assist us all as a means to education, good housing, health, and for our old age we felt to be a fair compromise and a necessary requirement to get the country back up and running. It was also a way to reward and comfort those of us who had fought and suffered. It was only later in my life when the excesses of State intervention began to inflate away my life savings that I changed my attitude.

In the meantime, I enjoyed my training and my new circumstances where possibilities seemed to stretch well into the future and over years, in stark contrast to the constant nagging doubt as to whether I would see the dawn of a new day.

One Saturday evening in late October I and my new friends went out into the city for dinner and a few pints at a selection of the local pubs which existed in abundance in York. As we exited one such establishment, we bumped into a group of four girls walking the other way. The most self-confident of us, which was not me I confess, smiled at them and introduced himself, which in turn was followed quickly by further introductions made by the remainder of our respective groups. The eight of us decided to return to the pub from whence we had come and buy the girls a drink. Four girls, four boys, it was a perfect match!

I found myself instinctively drawn to Mary, a brunette with beautiful blue eyes and a curvaceous figure, which I found irresistible. Just 22 like myself, Mary was working as a secretary in a law firm in the town. Originally from Manchester, she had been in the land army locally during the war and had decided to stay in this more easy-paced cathedral city, with access to the rural locations she had grown to enjoy and love, rather than return to the heavy industrial frenzy of her hometown. Given my own upbringing just south of that dynamic city we had something in common which were the first foundations of our conversations.

Throughout that night as we moved around York, we were increasingly easy with each other and unconsciously found ourselves distancing ourselves from our companions to focus on each other. They did not mind and sensed the burgeoning of a relationship so left us to it. It occurred to me that this was possibly how Johnny felt when he first met Janie, and I felt the pang of loss for them both even in the midst of this sweet moment for myself.

At the end of night, we shook hands in a rather a stiff English manner, each rather wishing we might say or do more, but agreed to meet again the next evening on our own.

Over the next four weeks we found ourselves spending more and more time together and relaxed into each other's company, recognising the similarities and the important differences between us that made us each who we were. After another six weeks of almost constant focus on each other I think we both realised that we should get married although it was never officially raised as a topic by either of us. The realisation occurred once it became almost impossible for either of us to talk about our individual plans, ambitions, aims, and dreams for the future without involving the other. What places we would like to visit in the future, those that 'we really must go and see,' career paths and goals 'that we must achieve,' friends and family 'that you really must meet,' all came into the conversation, usually said with a smile and knowledge of destiny to come.

I decided that I must do the honourable thing. I used up the last of my demobilisation bonus and bought a ring. Not the most expensive or the most glamorous, but quite pretty, I felt. One night in May 1947 after a rather pleasant dinner at what had become our favourite restaurant, we took a stroll by the river in the abbey gardens on a still evening. My suggestion that we take that stroll was a little contrived but I think Mary knew that my slightly nervous demeanour hinted that I had something important to say.

Sitting on a park bench in the gathering

summer dusk, I asked her to marry me. I am pleased to say that she said yes and so after a wedding at a Manchester registry office in August in front of her parents and my mother and with a few friends present as we could afford little else, then followed by a week's honeymoon in the Peak District, we lived happily ever after as Mr and Mrs Robert Astell.

I got my first teaching job in a small but beautiful village in rural Shropshire. A tiny cottage came as part of the salary package, which Mary made to look utterly beautiful with second-hand furniture and hand-sewn curtains and lace. I was the only teacher in the single classroom school, in charge of 22 children at all ages from 7 years old to 15, mainly the children of local farmers and labourers. It was a challenge to teach all subjects to such a wide age range but I thoroughly enjoyed it and the parents reassured me that I seemed to be a doing an excellent job with even the most difficult of teenagers amongst them.

It was a golden time for Mary and I, young and in love, living in a beautiful peaceful part of England with the future laid out before us. It was something of a catharsis for my partially destroyed soul from the war years, although redemption could never be complete and an aching guilt never left me whenever I thought of the men I had loved and lost. Remembrance Day for me became not November 11th, important though that was, but rather July 19th each year, the anniversary of the death of my comrades. Mary knew to give me space on that day. I was distracted and living apart from her in my mind. It did not last and life would resume and we would journey on together.

Together we were in every sense. Such was the peace and tranquillity of our little village, without television and with rather a poor radio signal to hear the Light Service of the BBC, that the nights were long! So it was that we contrived to have four children within the space of five years. Donald, Vera, Hugh, and Joyce came along in rather quicker succession than either of us quite expected, but we were happy and content and very busy.

The years rolled by and every four or five years I would move up the greasy ladder of the teaching profession, gaining promotions and importantly extra money and a larger house to serve my noisy and growing family. Mary went back to work as a secretary to aid the financial effort. During that time, we moved from Shropshire to Birmingham, to Wiltshire, and finally to Hampshire where I became the headmaster of a large primary school with a roll of 180 children and a staff of ten including caretakers and assistants. There I remained for the last 20 years of my working life. My children left home, entered careers of their own, and then got married. Ten grandchildren came along to give us joy and ensure our genetic inheritance. In 1988 I retired with a decent pension, a mortgage free property, and a new life to live, which I admit I had been thinking about for some time.

It is one of the interesting and inevitable stages of the human life cycle that as you age, you reach back to your youth. Why is that? A desire for a time when you are free from the aches and pains of old age perhaps? A time when you had fewer worries and responsibilities such as children and grandchildren? A time when you knew you had more years ahead of you than behind you? As the statistical certainties of age and death reverses against you and time grows shorter you begin to look back perhaps in the hope of justifying your life decisions. In my case

I had a good reason to look back with a certain nostalgia and pride as, seared into my existence and every waking hour, was the memory of my part in the bloodiest conflict known to mankind.

I had begun to go to squadron reunions when I was in my forties. I was nervous at first, not sure what to expect, but I found as the years went by that I could talk about events, feelings, and terrors that no one, other those who took part in a bombing mission over Germany, could relate to. Bomber Command personnel had been badly treated after the war. Our sacrifice had been ignored and deliberately undermined as we were seen as some kind of terrorists who killed women and children indiscriminately. The fact we were required to follow military commands and law at the risk of a charge of high treason seemed to have been forgotten. Whatever the morality, this ill treatment after the war only consolidated the feeling of solidarity between those of us that served and survived.

As the years went by, I began to wonder about my crew and how they might have been had they survived. I remembered them every day but I found myself wanting to know how they were remembered amongst their own families and friends. I wanted them to have an everlasting memory even after I, their only surviving crewmate, had gone. I wanted them to be known not as names on a roll of honour, but as men of blood and reality.

This was brought home to me in somewhat shocking fashion at one squadron reunion in London in the mid-1970s, when, as was always the case, we would discuss mutual friends and comrades who had served around the same time we had. 'Do you remember old so and so? He got divorced, got a new car, moved to Spain.' Whatever the gossip of the day was, even of those who did not usually attend reunions, someone would always know what was going on with someone else. Once a Bomber Boy always a Bomber Boy!

I was chatting to a couple of former aircraftsmen who had looked after our plane at one point. 'By the way Bob, did you hear that Jimmy Naylor died last year all of a sudden! Heart attack apparently. Only 49, would you believe. You knew him, didn't you?'

I was puzzled. I knew the name Jimmy Naylor but couldn't place him.

‘Which Jimmy Naylor, is this Fred?’

‘You know, the guy who took over from you when you were wounded.’

‘Yes, but he died with the rest of the boys on that night. He was posted as FTR with them.’

‘No, mate, he parachuted out and evaded capture. He returned to the base in October of 1944 after three months of being on the run and hidden by the French Resistance. Mind, you had gone by then so I guess you would not have known he made it back.’

I was frozen with my own stupidity and amazement at my thoughtlessness. How could I not have checked this? Men bailed out and survived all the time. Why did I assume all my crew were dead? The one man who could at least tell me what really happened that night was now dead and I had not even known he had made it back. I was in an agony of frustration. Because I had never known him, but instead knew for certain that my crew had gone, I simply assumed he had lost his life with them. What a thoughtless idiot I was. Why had I not checked official records after the war? I just wanted to forget everything at the time I suppose and it was the last thing on my mind. Now life looked so very different and I wanted to know what had really happened to my friends.

I resolved then that when I had more time on my hands, I would seek out all those who had been part of my crew's life and find out what I could of the night of their death and why they did not return. It took me 20 years to get around to the matter, but as retirement approached, I began a serious letter writing campaign to The Ministry of Defence, The National Archives, The Bomber Command Association, and then onto the French Ministry of Internal Affairs and the Luftwaffe Records Office. By the time that I finally retired I was pretty much an expert on all air activity over France in the spring and summer of 1944. I knew all the tactics and organisation behind the raid on the Revigny railway yards in July and the losses; so many losses, on the night of July 18th/19th 1944.

By early 1994 I had established clearly that they had been shot down at 01.21 by a Messerschmitt 110 flown by Lieutenant Eric Zimmermann who claimed two kills that night using his "Schrage Musik" angled, radar controlled weapons system and who had died himself over Germany in March 1945 whist defending his homeland. He was just 23.

I was even sent a copy of a certificate from the "Oberkommando der Luftwaffe" in Berlin, dated 8th November 1944, to Lieutenant Zimmermann confirming that he was indeed the pilot that had shot down "eines britischen viermoterigen kampflugzeuges," a British four engined military aircraft, at 01.21 on the night of July 19th. It may have been a small thing but I could not help but be aware that the phrase was entirely written in the lower case, including the word "britischen". I wondered if that was a deliberate slight and my annoyance was compounded by the fact that the document was the ultimate cold bureaucratic detail confirming the death of my closest friends and comrades. A certificate of death, perhaps even of execution! Their blood sacrifice was simply not a consideration and the pain of their death meant nothing in Berlin.

I was also sent a picture of Lieutenant Zimmerman in full uniform. I spent a great deal of time looking at that picture, trying to analyse the man who killed my friends. It was hopeless! He was a young, good-looking man, following orders, as they had been. It was simply fate and destiny that brought them together for that brief moment one night over the fields and houses of northern France. I held nothing against him.

I began a second letter writing campaign, this time to all the editors of local newspapers in the towns and villages I knew my comrades had come from. 'The Dewsbury Reporter', 'The Border Telegraph', 'The Morley Observer', 'The Northampton Chronicle', and of course the 'Putaruru News' in New Zealand and 'Le Muricien' in Port Louis. I described who I was and my relationship to those deceased airmen and I hoped their remaining relatives and friends might get in touch. I did not know what I might expect. I wrote and then I waited.

Four weeks after my first letter went out, my life changed!

I heard the phone ring in the hallway of our now empty nest. Mary answered and I was vaguely aware of her neutral tone of voice that she used with strangers. She put her head around the door of the lounge and said that there was a man on the phone responding to an enquiry I put in his local newspaper in Morley.

My heart beat slightly faster. I was curious and strangely nervous. I could not put my finger on it but I sensed this conversation might be profound. I felt destiny on my shoulders for some reason as I took the phone from my wife.

'Hello,' I said.

'Hello, Mr Astell, I hope you do not mind me calling you, but I was given a letter from our local newspaper the other day by my Uncle Jack which refers to a Flight Sergeant David Lumb with whom you served in 876 Squadron during the war.'

There was a pause as my caller looked for confirmation. I nervously responded in as neutral a tone as I could manage in my rising excitement.

'Yes, that is correct.'

'I can confirm Mr Astell that we are sure that the man you are looking for was my late father's eldest brother, David, aged 31 who died on July 19th 1944 whilst the navigator of a Lancaster Bomber targeting Revigny in France. Is that correct?'

'Yes, that sounds exactly like the man I am

looking for,' I responded rather stiffly.

I sensed a gathering of breath at the end of the line.

'Mr Astell, I cannot tell you what an honour it is speaking to someone who actually served with my uncle during the war. I was born 16 years after he died. I never knew him of course, but my father would talk of him together with his other brother Tom, who also died in the war, with love and regret. I feel that I know him in some way but not as a man and not as an uncle. He is a distant war hero to me. The saviour of my freedom, as indeed are you and your generation, but in some way, he sits on a pedestal and I wonder if you might help me get to know the man and tell me something of your story also. I am sure it is fascinating.'

There was silence. I was overwhelmed by the introduction and also by the strange familiarity of the voice, which reached back into my soul and my memory of times long ago. I attempted to pull myself together and remember my best headmaster's voice.

'Well! Thank you, young man, for those wonderful words of introduction. I have such fond memories of your uncle. In many ways I owe my life to him, you know. He was an inspirational character. Something of an elder brother and such a good friend.'

We both paused; nervous at our rather effusive introductions.

'Mr Astell, I live near Oxford but I travel quite a lot and I am in Andover on business next week. I see that is only about 40 minutes from you. Could I drop in? I have some family photographs and letters you might like to see and I can assure you that Uncle David's surviving brothers and sisters are very keen that I see you. I have been sent on a kind of reconnaissance mission for the family, if you don't mind me saying so. They all live in Yorkshire so I am closer to you and it is easier for me to travel. Would next Tuesday at say five be OK?'

'Of course, of course,' I said, my enthusiasm rising. 'That would be marvellous. You can meet my wife and let's have some tea. I am so pleased to hear that some of David's siblings are still with us, by the way. Next Tuesday will be perfect.'

'Wonderful,' said the voice. 'I look forward

to it. Well! Goodbye until then.'

'Wait a moment,' I said. 'Before you go, you must tell me your name.'

The breath was inhaled again at the other end.

'My name? Of course, I do apologise. My name is the same as one you are familiar with. My name is David Lumb. I am named after my father's eldest brother! Until next week, then.'

I put the phone down, feeling both elated and slightly dizzy.

'Who was that, dear?' asked my wife.

'Darling, next week we are going to meet David Lumb, the nephew of my greatest friend from the war. You know what that man means to me. I cannot believe it and my God, Mary! He sounds just like him!'

Mary put her hands on my cheeks and looked into my eyes.

'Darling, I know you always feel guilty about surviving the war when David did not, but it was your destiny to have four beautiful children with me. I have always known that and that is why you were spared. It was your destiny also to tell his story and this is part of that same process. This David Lumb is coming into your life now and you and he are going to do something wonderful. I just know it.'

I kissed her and went and poured myself a glass of the whiskey I saved for special occasions.

The following Tuesday came around rather too slowly for me and I watched the clock rather too often as the day drew on. Just before 5pm I heard a car draw up at the bottom of the road beyond our front garden. I stood at the lounge window and watched a figure emerge at the front gate. I went immediately to the front door and opened it to see David Lumb walk towards me. Well over six feet and therefore much taller and broader than "my David" but, my God; the eyes and line of the chin and above all the wry smile as he greeted me. He was almost the same.

'Mr Astell, I presume?' He gripped my hand in a strong, confident handshake as I looked into his eyes.

'David, you must call me Bob. It's is wonderful to see you, my boy. Please come in and meet my wife, Mary.' I indicated that he should turn left into lounge as Mary appeared. 'Darling, this is David. You know all about him.'

Mary reached up quite a long way and kissed him and then stood back to take him in more closely. She had heard me talk about David Lumb throughout our married life and had seen him in old photographs. She wanted to check this new reality.

'David, it's so wonderful to have you with us,' she said. 'I have heard so much about your uncle. My husband may not say it but he loved him very much, you know. I wish I could have known him but now we have you and I know we are going to share some wonderful times together with you and your family. Now let me go and get you some tea.'

She went off to the kitchen and David and I were left with a moment of awkward English emotion to overcome. My wife's introduction had slightly unsettled both of us, although her words were undoubtedly true.

'Sit down, my boy,' and I indicated the sofa

next to my matching lounge chair. I noted he had a large blue folder under his arm, which he carefully perched on the arm of the sofa between us as he sat down. We passed a few minutes of pleasantries discussing his trip down, the state of the traffic, and whether he found our address easily enough. All crucial information!

Mary returned with a tray of tea and biscuits and sat on the sofa to David's right. There was a moment's pause as we all took a sip of tea and then David began.

'I'm so pleased to meet you both,' he said. 'Bob, I cannot believe I am sitting with someone who flew in bombers in the war and who flew with my uncle. As I said on the phone, he remains an enigmatic character for me. I share the name but I don't know him. My father did not speak about him a great deal because it was always quite painful for him to speak of his loss and the effect it had on his family, but I know he loved him and missed him all his life. I have some family photographs here taken before the war if you want to see them. David was the eldest son of a family of ten children you know, and my father was the youngest.'

He reached for his folder and took out a small selection of aging black and white photos of various sizes. Some worn, some torn but all showing a family growing up between the wars in various stages of life and seeming contentment. I was particularly attracted to a semi formal line up of all ten Lumb children drawn up in order of birth from the right.

'When was this taken, David?'

'Around 1935 or 36,' he said. 'That is my father on the left-hand edge, the youngest and the smallest aged 8 or 9 I guess.'

I looked along the line at the similar faces. My David in a formal work suit was second in the line. Young and smiling, the charm and confidence I had known was clearly present even in this aging photograph. I smiled to myself in recognition of my old friend now forever young.

'They look wonderful together, David, don't they' I said. He simply nodded. 'Only three of them left, though,' he said wistfully. 'David and Tom died in the war as you know and the others have succumbed to various illnesses over the years. My father died very suddenly of a heart attack ten years ago, aged just 56.' He shook his head slightly in memory.

'I am so sorry to hear that.' I paused. 'I met him once, you know.'

David looked at me intently. 'Really! When?'

'I came to the family home on Daisy Hill for one night with your Uncle David on leave after our first pilot was killed. He must have been 15 or 16.'

'My God, Bob,' he said. 'I came to hear about you and my uncle, but you have to tell me what my father was like. What did you think of him?'

'He was a good kid. Handsome just like you. I can see where you get your looks. Thick black hair and full of life. He really loved life, David. More than anything he loved life and he loved his family very much I could tell that easily and he seemed very close to his eldest brother despite the difference in their ages. I am sure he became a man to be proud of.'

Again, David shook his head ever so slightly as he looked into the middle distance, his mind trying to capture the image of the teenage father I had met so long ago.

He blew out his cheeks to relieve the tension of memory and loss and then moved the conversation on with a smile.

'So, Bob, come on, let's talk about you and my uncle. I want to know all about you, your crew, how you met, what you did. I am very hungry for all the details you can give me.'

I stood up and went to the sideboard by the door and opened the top drawer. I took out a large and disorderly box file full of photographs and letters and my log book from the war years. I sat down next to David.

'Well, my boy! Are you ready?'

So, we talked for four hours or more, Mary would leave to make more tea now and again and we even ordered in a Chinese takeaway meal, which we ate around the kitchen table whilst we talked further.

I did most of the talking with David interjecting now and again to ask questions – some factual, some technical, some emotional. I explained how we met and how his uncle picked me out of the crowd of hundreds of blue uniformed airmen and changed my life and my fate in doing so. I talked about the characters of all my crewmates. The fierce loyalty we had to each other and the humour and the stories we created together. He was particularly intrigued by the relationship between Danuska and Cyril and the dynamics of class, education, and background that brought them and all of us so much joy and mutual admiration.

He pored over the pictures I had of us as a crew, trying to imprint into his mind the reality of each individual.

'I've only seen these men as names on memorials until now,' he said. 'You talk about Geoff and John and Don as individuals, Bob. You bring them back to life. Thank you for that.'

I talked about the night of their death and what I had discovered about their mission and its ultimate failure. I showed him the picture of Lieutenant Zimmerman and he did the same thing I had done, examining the face for malice and darkness but like me he could find none in that young face.

As we talked and I watched his face and heard his voice and every few minutes I would feel a stab of bereavement that was almost physical. The genetic inheritance that runs through families can be passed down in various ways. The shape of the skull, the arrangement of muscles, the development of the vocal chords, all add to the generational development; many things stay the same, many things alter. Natural selection is a marvel. In this case David would smile, or move his head in a certain way or shape a vocal phrase in exactly the same way that his uncle used to and as they were approximately the same age, the likeness was uncanny. Whenever this happened through that first meeting a frisson of excitement and a pinprick of raw emotion would sear through me and I was left disorientated. It was both a joy and unnerving at the same time.

At around 9.30 David thought he had better head off home, which was over an hour's drive away. We shook hands at the door and promised to keep in touch. This was the beginning and not the end. We promised to carry out more research. David was going to write to the Mayor of Lancy sur Marne, the village where the boys were buried in a First World War British military cemetery, to see if there were any local witnesses to the crash on that night in July 1944, and we promised ourselves that we would shortly make a pilgrimage together to the graves. It was time for me to do that. I had left my crew alone in France too long. I must go to them at least once during my remaining time on earth. I owed them that.

For the next few months we corresponded and called regularly with updates on letters written and received and information gleaned. More than often we just chatted about life in general. We became firm friends and I came to look forward to our regular calls.

One evening David called slightly breathless with excitement to say that he had received a letter from a Monsieur Bernard Elgart, who had been passed the letter David had written to the Mayor of Lancy sur Marne.

'Bob, Monsieur Elgart speaks no English so he has written to me in a beautiful copperplate handwriting in quite old fashioned French, so it is hard enough just to make out the words let alone translate them into English. He is some kind of local historian, I think. He appears very excited to hear from me and it looks like he has some very important information for us. He was only 6 years old when the plane came down, but he remembers it and I think he has a witness to the crash itself. Can I come down and see you tomorrow and let's go through this letter. Get your French/English dictionary out!'

The dashing David appeared at my door the next evening as promised. He brought a letter with a two page attachment, all written in splendid handwriting. The flourishes made it almost a work of Renaissance art. Wonderful though it was it did make certain of the French words and phrases difficult to pick out.

We both spoke limited French although David's written capability in the language was better than my own, having studied a little de Tocqueville whilst at university. After an hour of rising excitement for both of us we had a letter in English and unbelievably, a written eyewitness account of the crash of Lancaster Bomber LM 696. Our Lancaster!

Bernard Elgart was effusive in his greetings to us. He had researched the crash for over a decade. He knew more about the operation than we did, including its effects on Revigny and the surrounding area. The plane had come down just 200 meters from his family home and the noise of its disintegration and explosive end had woken him. It was the talk of the village for months and years afterward. He had joined the end of the cortege with his parents as they followed the burial party that took the bodies up the hill from the crash site to the British Military Cemetery established after the First World War. He had never forgotten that night nor burial of the crew and went to the graves once a week to lay flowers.

David and I looked at each other as we read those words. How profound was this one man's love and respect for these dead men whom he had never met, that he would lay fresh flowers on their graves every week? It was remarkable to think about. We both were silenced by his compassion.

He was insistent that we must come to Lancy sur Marne as soon as possible to meet himself and his family and all the people of the village who held these men and the sacrifice they had made for them in the highest honour. We simply had not thought of it that way, focused as we were on our personal connection to the individuals on that plane. An entire village saw the deaths of these men 50 years ago as a personal sacrifice for them alone and as such held them in their hearts and their memory to this day. We were overwhelmed with emotion as we saw how many lives the crew had touched.

This feeling was nothing, however, to the translation we made of an eyewitness account of the crash itself which Bernard had carefully written and recorded as an historical document. They were the words of a young farmer at the time called Rene Pascal, who we learnt with rising excitement was still alive and who on that terrible night in July 1944, had seen every detail of the crash of LM 696. He had seen the bodies the next morning and had assisted in collecting and identifying the bodies, such as he could. He had led the burial party and remarkably had met the Luftwaffe pilot who had shot them down and who attended the funeral.

Those two pages of beautifully written and crafted French at that instant became holy relics and sacred parchment for both us. Now we knew exactly what had happened to our family and friends. It was a remarkable emotion of release and sadness for both of us. We passed the document between us again and again, as if its very presence was the source of redemption and salvation. We smiled a great deal and shook our heads in our sadness and our newly found awareness and I cried!

The account was breathless, tense, terrible -- but also in some respects exciting and even uplifting.

"It was around 1.15 in the morning. I was awakened by a terrible noise and a bright burning light outside. I rushed to the window of my room and threw back the shutters. It was an awful sight! An enormous bomber was moving from my left up the valley, almost completely enveloped in flames from the cockpit back to the tail. As it moved slowly in front of me the wing tip came within no more than 30 or 40 meters of my house. I could feel the heat radiating from it. The noise of the engines trying to power it forward as they struggled with the weight of the flames was deafening. I could also hear the airframe creaking and groaning as it lost its battle with the inferno.

"The aircraft moved past me a kilometre or

so before the rear end suddenly fell away and it came down near the mill of Sillon in a terrible explosion of flames and noise. Throughout that long night I could hear the sounds of the flames and shells exploding in the heat.

"I went to site as early as I could when the light came. I came across the rear of the aircraft down by the stream. All the trees had been scorched and burnt by the fire but the rear end of the aircraft was still quite intact.

"In the rear of the aircraft was the body of an English Airman. He was dead and his head was covered in blood."

At that point David stopped and looked at me. My eyes were moistening, I knew. I tried to stay calm, but the emotions of this old man could not be held in check. My mouth was dry and the back of my throat was raw with pain and loss. My breath was short.

'Cyril,' I croaked out. 'That would be Cyril. Oh my God.'

I turned away to face the window so David could not see me. Mary in the kitchen sensed something had changed and came into the room.

'Are you alright, love?'

I could not face her or David.

'I'm sorry, Mrs Astell,' said David, who always used her formal title. 'We have been given an eyewitness account of the crash and the details are quite personal and terrible.'

She put her hands on my shoulders to comfort me.

'I should have been with them. I should have been there!' was all I could say as my tears ran.

'I know, love,' she said, 'But you are here with us today! You have their story now and both of you must read it and live it and tell it. You know that is your duty and your destiny now. Their memory is the hands of the two of you.'

She looked at David as she said this and then down at me. I reached up to hold her hand as she continued to stroke my shoulder. I pulled myself together, took a deep breath, and faced the room again.

'You are right of course, darling. Right my boy, let's continue.'

We completed the full version of Rene Pascal's account within the next hour. We learnt of his discovery of other bodies, the arrival of the German search teams, and the collection of various body parts and the arrangements of the burials that afternoon. Finally, we read of the arrival of Lieutenant Zimmerman at the gravesides and his dialogue with Rene. I looked on Zimmerman with admiration and thankfulness when I read this element of the account. He too had died within a year a year of burying his adversaries and I mourned the loss of all of them and the pointlessness savagery of their deaths. The phrase "comrades in arms" was particularly apt for them all.

David and I sat silently for a while on completion of our translation. It had been a labour of love and memory and we allowed the tremendous mixture of emotions that the account had unleashed to wash through us.

It was rare in a war which had consumed millions of lives without pity or memorial to find such an instance where the death of six young men had been recorded in such detail or indeed where those young men had been buried with honour and dignity. We felt grateful for knowing that and grateful to Rene Pascal and Bernard Elgart that they had recorded the death of my crew in such touching and intimate detail and maintained their memory through all these 50 years.

We determined that we must take up Bernard's invitation to visit him and the village of Lancy Sur Marne. I had always been reluctant to go and visit the graves in the past. I was never exactly sure why, perhaps I had been afraid of what I would find. Would any visit alter my memories of the boys and their death? Would I disturb the past?

With David by my side and with the new knowledge of how the boys had died and the esteem in which their memory was held, all the uncertainties fell away. The time was right. Perhaps this was fate, perhaps this was my destiny? The path to the future was now clear and the ripples and tides of history were carrying me forward now.

Over the next few weeks, more letters were written to and from France. Arrangements were made and ferries and hotels booked in advance. David was to drive Mary and I over to France via the Folkestone ferry in his rather swish Mercedes car. We didn't have to worry about anything. We would be visiting The Aisne region of France, where the Champagne was produced, at the height of summer in July. Fifty-two years after the death of my crew!

Two weeks before we were to depart David called and asked if he we minded if he brought one of his cousins along the trip also.

'He's called Stephen Holmes and is the son of my father's favourite sister. He is a keen historian and has helped me a great deal with the research on this project. He would love to meet you and of course David Lumb is his uncle too. He's got a great sense of humour. You will like him a lot.' Of course, I did not mind in the slightest. My love and respect for anyone from the Lumb family was boundless.

Chapter 10

The Message

So it was that early one morning in mid-July of that year David arrived at the front door of our house to collect us for the two-hour drive to Folkestone. Behind him at our door stood a likely looking lad two or three years younger than David, slightly shorter and with dark curly hair and the biggest of grins. He shook our hands as we made our introductions and his smile only grew wider. I liked him immediately.

'This is my little cousin Stephen,' said David. 'But we all call him Stevie. He's here to carry your bags and bring you gin and tonic when you need it.'

'My pleasure always,' said Stevie as he smiled again. We were to get used to that smile over the next few days. Stephen and David loaded our luggage into the car and off we went. It was a noisy but happy party that made its way down to Folkestone. Both David and Stephen were wonderful companions; bright, articulate and clever. It was as if we had known each other for years, which in a strange quirk of history we had. Our family histories were intertwined.

Once off the ferry, we drove the four hours down to Chateau Thierry where we were staying in a rather pleasant hotel overlooking the valley of the Marne. The French countryside was beautiful, the villages and houses were gorgeous, and the weather was splendid. Although a little tired on arrival we were all in good spirits and enjoyed a wonderful meal that evening in a restaurant overlooking the river. We all went to bed early in somewhat nervous but excited anticipation of the tomorrow. We knew it would be an emotional day for us all, but none of us realised at the moment quite how our lives were to be changed and our destinies set on a new course.

The next morning after French croissants and coffee we set off the eight kilometres to Lancy sur Marne through more glorious French countryside. We were to meet Bernard and Rene at the British military cemetery on the edge of the village at 10.30.

As with all of northern France, which had been fought over and, in some cases, obliterated by the events of two world wars, the signposts are everywhere for cemeteries, memorials, and locations of battles. Our road into Lancy from

Chateau Thierry took us past several American memorials from the first war and then as we approached Lancy the red signs to the British Cemetery began to appear.

We drove over the brow of a hill and as we began our descent towards the village, we saw the small, walled cemetery with the large white cross of remembrance in the centre. My mouth was dry with nervous anticipation. There was a small car park adjacent to the road as the cemetery was set back 15 metres or so. I was amazed to see 6 cars lined up neatly and a small crowd of perhaps 15 people gathered around the small entrance gate, who turned to watch us as we pulled in. I was somewhat staggered to see so many people. Surely, they could not be here just to see us?

David and Stephen in the front seats jumped out of the car immediately. I sat in the back with Mary unmoving, as I felt my heart race and my breath shorten. My nervous anticipation rose and my mouth dried up a little more. As I sat several more cars drew up, coming up the road from the village. A crowd was gathering.

I opened my door but did not exit. I don't

think I trusted my legs. A burly man with white-grey hair and a neat grey moustache detached himself from the crowd and moved toward David and Stephen. Just behind him was a young and very elegant lady with long, straw coloured hair, perhaps in her early twenties. She looked delightful. What is it with French women and the word elegance? They fit together perfectly!

I heard David say, 'Monsieur Elgart?' He nodded and held out his hand. 'Je suis David Lumb. Permettez-moi introduire mon cousin, Stephen Holmes.'

Bernard Elgart shook hands warmly with David and Stephen, his affection clear. He then turned to his elegant assistant, who stepped forward.

'Hello,' she said. 'My name is Laura Pascal I am the granddaughter of Rene Pascal.' Her English was perfect. 'I hope I can help with some translation today. I have spent the last year in London. I love England and am so pleased to meet you all. My grandfather is looking forward to meeting you so much. This is a great day for him and for all my family. The crash of this aircraft and the death of the crew are part of our family legend. I grew up hearing so much about that terrible day. We are so honoured that you have come to see us. The whole village is coming out to meet you today. This is a wonderful occasion for all of us.'

David smiled and took a deep breath.

'Laura, Bernard, merci bien, thank you so much. This is all so unexpected. We did not know so many people would be present. It is overwhelming. I have someone very special that I want you to meet, first of all.' He turned towards me in the rear of the car and beckoned me forward. My time had come!

Mary and I got out of the car. Mary whispered to me as we exited.

'Enjoy this day, my darling. This is your day.'

As I stepped forward David said, 'Can I introduce you to my dear friend Mr Robert Astell, formerly of 876 Squadron. He flew 20 missions with the men we have come to see today and knew them all. They were his friends and comrades. He has come to see them for the first time in over 50 years with his wife Mary.'

Laura translated his words and Bernard's face began to light up as she spoke. As she finished, he took several paces towards me with his arms outstretched. He grasped me around both shoulders and kissed me three times on the cheeks – left, right, left. It was the French way but the action took this quiet and taciturn Englishman by surprise. Bernard stepped back and looked me directly in the eye.

'Monsieur Astell, bienvenue a Lancy Sur Marne. C'est un grand honneur de vous rencontrer. Merci pour votre sacrifice et pour votre service pendant la guerre. Ma famille et moi vous serons toujours reconnaissants. Tu es un heros pour nous tous.'

Laura translated his words back to me and when she said that I was a hero to them all, I nodded towards him and in my rather overwhelmed and nervous condition all I could do was squeak out a hopeless "merci" and a weak smile.

Laura spoke again. She recognised the embarrassment I was feeling I think, so she wanted to move matters forward.

'Monsieur Astell, can I introduce you to the

Mayor of Lancy sur Marne, Monsieur Charvin, who is standing over there with my grandfather. Would you like to come over and say hello?' Mary, David, Stephen, and I followed Laura to the gate of the cemetery where the crowd was gathering and growing. They stood back in respect as we made our way towards to a tall, middle-aged man with dark hair and wearing a beautiful tailored suit with his uniform of office in the form of a sash across his shoulders in the colours of the French Republic.

He stopped his conversation as we approached and stood to attention. Laura made the formal introductions in her perfectly modulated English. Monsieur Le Maire, she introduced him as, and he warmly shook my hand and subjected me to the formal three cheeked kiss again and to Mary also.

In excellent English, the mayor welcomed us to his village with warmth and sincerity. The crowd continued to grow as he spoke; by which time we felt we had lost control of events and were simply swept along in a tide of emotion and remembrance.

Laura wanted to move us down the line to

meet other important guests. Standing next to the mayor was a stout, well-built and still athletic looking older man of around my age, I guessed. He had a full of head of hair and his brown eyes sparkled with charm and interest. His eyes scanned his surroundings constantly and it was as if he missed nothing in his visual surroundings.

Laura stood in front of him and spoke directly into his face, although she was introducing us, she did not move her eyes from him. This was initially disconcerting although we quickly discovered the reason. 'Monsieur et Madam Astell, David, and Stephen,' she said whilst still looking directly at the man. 'This is my wonderful grandfather, Monsieur Rene Pascal. He became deaf five years ago in a farming accident but he is perfectly healthy as you can see and he can read my lips, which is why I am talking directly to him. I hope you understand.'

Stephen was the first to reply. 'Of course, we understand, Laura. So, you will be speaking in English and French today as well as assisting your grandfather in understanding our strange linguistic tendencies?'

Stephen's admiration was clear and he sounded smitten already as Laura turned to him and smiled. 'Of course. I hope you will be patient with us all.' Her smile seemed to melt Stephen and he gave her a rather weak, lovestruck grin in return.

David moved ahead of us to shake Rene's hand and as he did so I saw the old man's face change. What was I was witnessing here? Rene's eyes locked onto David. It as if he was exploring every line and pore on David's face. David, realising that something of import was happening, returned his stare, allowing the examination to continue. Rene was searching and remembering.

'Tu es David Lumb!' You are David Lumb! It was a clear statement of recognition and not a question and simply required a confirmation.

'Oui, Monsieur Pascal.'

'Enfin!'

This was the single word that Rene said. David looked at Laura for confirmation, who nodded and simply said, 'At last.' Rene said nothing further, and we all exchanged quizzical looks but moved on.

David introduced myself and Mary. Rene's face softened and he smiled with real pleasure as he took both my hands in his and then hugged me around the shoulders. He did the same with Mary, whispering in her ear as he did so. Laura translated his words for her.

'Your husband is my hero and my liberator. I will never forget his service.'

Now it was Mary's turn to be flattered and overwhelmed by the love and affection that was felt by this small community towards us and my crewmates who had died here. It was not something we had expected or anticipated and the pure joy of it remains in our hearts to this day.

We now found ourselves at the small arched gateway into the cemetery itself. Bernard opened the small wooden gate and beckoned us forward. As with all the Commonwealth War Graves cemeteries around the world it was a thing of simplicity and beauty. The graves of white Portland stone were laid out in ordered rows around a cross of remembrance in the centre of the cemetery. The grass was perfectly cut and the roses and lilies that grew around the grave stones were as if placed by God.

The dates on the stones were all from September 1914, the exception being a row of six graves close to the cross, which were aligned side by side with no spacing. A single crew and a singular team in the solidarity of death! We approached the stones in reverence. My breath shortened in my throat.

It was then that I saw the names.

F MacRae, D Kissonsingh, G Patterson, D Edwards, C Knowles, D Lumb.

Just names carved in stone, with their rank, squadron number, and date of death, but more than names to myself, Mary, David, and Stephen. Our life, our history, our family, our friends, and our memories were carved into those names.

I stopped in front of the line of graves, Mary and David beside me. The crowd of perhaps 40 or so people stood back. They became silent without any request. Everyone knew instinctively that this was a moment of utmost solemnity. I had no choice but to lead this occasion of remembrance.

It was difficult in the utmost. I stepped forward and stood in front of Danuska's grave, which was in the centre of the six. I drew myself to attention and then saluted, holding the salute for perhaps 30 seconds. I then knelt on one knee and simply reached forward with my right hand to trace the letters of his name in the soft, warm stone. It was the nearest I could get to him and lent me a connection to a man who had been long dead but who was still my friend. David joined me on one knee in front of the grave of his uncle and did the same thing, running his fingers over the name. His own name!

I heard the click of a few cameras, but I did not care who witnessed this act of memory and reconnection. My eyes were moist and my breathing was long and deep but I held my composure. What would the boys think if I broke down? I owed them some dignity.

I stepped back and Mary hugged me. 'That was a beautiful thing to witness, my darling. Well done. How do you feel?'

'Strangely better. Strangely serene. It's good to see them again after all these years.' I smiled at her and then at David. I noted too that some of the crowd held silent tears in their eyes. Rene and Bernard simply nodded their respect to us when we caught their eyes.

After that there was a more formal ceremony. Wreaths were laid on each of the graves. A minute's silence was held, which was terribly moving, and then a small cassette player was produced and the national anthems were sung. Fortunately for us Brits, Stephen had a wonderful baritone voice and supported by David gave us a measure of respect on "God Save the Queen," and then the entire crowd joined in a rousing rendition of "La Marseillaise," which I admit has to be the best national anthem of any country in the world. So martial, so uplifting.

The mayor and then Bernard gave speeches of welcome and thanks, with Bernard giving an overview of the night of the crash and subsequent events that brought the crew to the graves we saw before us. The entire event was simple and yet magnificent. I was so grateful and honoured to be part of it and so very happy to find that my friends had not died in vain. Their sacrifice was remembered and honoured in this small corner of France and would be forever.

I asked Bernard after the little ceremony why this crew and these men meant so much to him personally and to this village? I will never forget his reply and committed it to memory later. It sounded so much better and so powerful in the original French.

'Parce que ces hommes sont morts pour moi, pour ma famille et pour La France. Il est mon devoir de les honorer.'

'Because these men died for myself, for my family, and for France. It is my duty to honour them.'

Bernard now informed us that there was to be a reception and a light lunch at the Hotel de Ville in one hour during which we would be the guests of honour, but in the meantime he and Rene wanted to take us to the actual crash site and allow Rene to point out the locations and events of that night over 50 years ago to which he had been such an eloquent witness. Again, this was not something we had not prepared for, but we felt an almost sacred duty to ensure we understood all the events of that night. David and Stephen were particularly keen to do this as historians.

We followed behind Laura's car through the village and down into a wide, lush valley. After 20 minutes we emerged next to an old farmhouse set above the valley floor on a rocky promontory. This was Rene's house and he pointed out the window from which he first saw the flaming Lancaster. I could clearly see how shocking it must have been for a young man to witness my aircraft pass so low in front of his eyes.

I knew MacRae was a good pilot and I realised with greater clarity now, the skill and strength that he had used to keep his flaming aircraft in the air for so long. The valley represented more space and therefore more time in the air and more time to live. He had been tenacious in his desire to stay alive.

What I could not initially understand was why more of the boys had not got out. MacRae had clearly fought hard to stay in the air and give them time, why had only Naylor jumped? I realised I knew the answer. They were either already dead at the hands of Zimmerman's guns or they had decided to stay with the Skipper as he fought his last battle. It made sense to me but I wished with all my heart they had done otherwise.

We drove back up the valley for a mile or so and then Rene walked us down a short farm track to a small stream, which in the July sunlight looked utterly beautiful and at peace. He pointed to a clump of trees next to the stream with a hay field stretching beside it. 'This is where I found the rear section of the Lancaster. It was intact, as were the bodies of your two gunners, Monsieur Astell. I think they had died in the air, however. Their bodies had been torn by bullets or shrapnel before the injuries sustained during the crash, I think.'

I paused to look at this beautiful site, vibrant with green vegetation and fragrant flowers. No evidence whatsoever remained of the blood and pain that this field had seen so long ago. Only our imaginations and Rene's words would suffice to hold this memory of Cyril and Geoff's end.

We followed Rene up the field for another 50 yards of so. He stopped and looked at David.

'Here, Monsieur Lumb! I found your uncle here in this place. He was lying on his own. I closed his eyes here!' He drew his index and middle fingers down indicating the final act he had performed for David.

David knelt down on the grass and brushed it with the palm of his hand, back and forth, as if trying to reconnect with that moment and with the death of his uncle. He stayed in that position for some time and then stood. He blew out his breath in a long, slow exhalation and release of tension. He reached out to Rene and took him in his arms. Gently and softly, he held him and he simply said, 'Merci, Rene,' who returned his embrace. The rest of us stood in silence; the only sound was the distant song of a skylark.

We returned to the cars in silence and drove up the road for another half kilometre or so to where Rene showed us the site where the front section of the aircraft had buried itself in the bank of the road and where the torn and broken remains of MacRae, Dan, and Don had been found. Again, absolutely nothing remained as evidence of that night and only our imaginations lingered.

The full story was clear now. I knew what had happened to my friends during their last moments. It was emotional but it was a form of release and I felt a better man for knowing their fate and knowing that they now lay cradled in the embrace of this beautiful place and its people.

At least, I thought I knew everything at that moment. Emotions had run high all day and I was feeling rather exhausted as my senses were stretched and contorted by events and feelings that occasionally threatened to overwhelm me. Nothing was to prepare me, or any of us, however, for the events that occurred when we returned to the Hotel de Ville!

We arrived in the small reception room at the Town Hall to be warmly greeted again by Monsieur Charvin in his sash of office and a crowd now of 50 or more including a photographer and reporter from the regional newspaper! Numerous pictures were required and statements were taken from all of us on our thoughts of the day, to be welded eventually into a substantial article.

Wonderful canapes and local patisseries had been provided along with local champagne. David had brought photographs of the crew and letters from our files in the car and many people asked questions and made comment, some remembering their role in the day of the crash. Laura dutifully translated the many statements and words as best she could. Stephen's admiration for her only seemed to grow all the stronger! It was wonderful, overwhelming, and exhausting.

After an hour or more we found ourselves sitting at a small table towards the back of the room. The buzz and murmur of conversations were going on all around us and the length of the day and probably the two glasses of highest quality champagne had begun to slow me down further.

Mary and I sat to the left of Rene and Laura to his right so he could easily turn and watch her lips as she translated our conversation back and forth. David, Stephen, and Bernard sat opposite him with some maps and photographs on the table between them. The two boys grilled Rene and Bernard on endless details about the crash. Timings, noises, feelings, the location and condition of the bodies, thoughts on Zimmerman, and a myriad of other matters. Their appetite for information was endless. I was happy. They would take the memory of my comrades into the future and hold their lives in their hearts as I did.

I noted that Rene hardly ever took his eyes from David's face except to look at Laura as she spoke to him. Even then, although his eyes would move toward her, his head remained in David's direction. He seemed to want to explore its depths as if he was reaching back to something and would occasionally seem to become distracted whilst still maintaining his gaze, as if he was considering a matter elsewhere. His enigmatic remark when he first met David a few hours early came back to me as I watched the conversation move back and forth: 'Enfin!' What had it meant, what was he searching for?

After a further 40 minutes or so the noise and questioning began to subside a little. Rene continued to look at David as the two cousins began to consider plans for later that evening. Bars and restaurants in Chateau Thierry seemed to be the point of discussion and the relevant merits of their menus. I was quite clear that Mary and I would not be joining them after such a long and emotional day. A brief meal, perhaps a small glass of wine, and bed would be the order of the day for us old folks.

Laura was enjoined to give her recommendations and thoughts on the local food and the best bars that might stay open until late. She joined in energetically enough. What it was to be young again, I thought. The conversation was now all in English and Stephen suggested to David that Laura might be persuaded to join them in person rather than simply give them advice.

'Why don't you ask Laura out with us. She will be the best guide possible and can even read the menus for us. Saves us making a fool of ourselves.' He said this with a knowing smile directed deeply into Laura's eyes.

David rolled his own eyes a little and shrugged his shoulders at seemingly being requested to undertake the heavy lifting in his cousin's romantic inclinations. He then looked smilingly at Laura whilst directing his comments back at Stephen.

'I'm sorry, I cannot get back to you on that one, Stevie boy.' He paused for a moment, 'Not just yet, at least! Give me time!'

Suddenly, Rene moved with such speed that it attracted the attention of people within a few metres of our table. Faces turned to stare and the atmosphere changed in an instant. With that action we were now in a different place and time! Rene had suddenly grabbed his granddaughter's hand with such speed and vehemence that she cried out in shock.

'Papy, Papy! Mais non! Mais non! Est-ce que c'est?'

More faces turned toward us. The smiles and ease within the room had gone.

Rene's eyes were wide and almost demonic with excitement and insistence. He continued to grip Laura's hand and with his other he pointed at David.

'Laura, Laura, Monsieur Lumb, il doit me redire ces mots. Il doit me les dire maintenant.' His voice was urgent and insistent. The words were a command.

Laura slowly released her hand from his grip and looked at her grandfather sideways, slightly embarrassed for his behaviour. She looked at David.

'David I am very sorry for my grandfather's actions, but he insists that you say the last sentence and words that you used once more, but you must look directly at him when you do this.'

David looked genuinely puzzled as he

searched his memory for the words that had been no more than gentle banter and devilry between cousins and friends when trying to impress a beautiful girl. What words had he used that could have caused this reaction?

'I'm sorry Laura, I don't understand. What words does your grandfather want to hear and why?'

Laura turned back to Rene and put his question to him. Rene looked deeply into Laura's eyes and then down toward the floor as he gathered his thoughts. He then spoke rapidly and urgently to Laura at some length as retelling a story that she had to understand and repeat clearly. As he spoke, he would look and point at David now and again and in doing so Laura's own face began to change to recognition, realisation, curiosity, and excitement.

The room was deadly quiet as she turned back to David and Rene resumed his examination of David's every movement.

'David, this is terribly important for my grandfather and I believe it will be for you also, although I do not yet understand why.' She paused to gather herself.

‘My grandfather wants to apologise because he wants to tell you something about the night of the crash of this Lancaster that he has not told you or anyone else before. He has never given this account before, not even to Bernard, because he thought it was something he could never find out and he thought that if he told this story no one would believe him, or at least they would think he was exaggerating and he did not wish to dishonour the memory of the men who died.

David nodded. His face impassive.

‘My grandfather told me to tell you that as the flaming Lancaster passed in front of him on that night, he saw a man still alive in the cockpit. That man was you, he said! Of course, in reality it must have been your uncle, as you obviously look very similar. The man in the cockpit turned his head as he passed my grandfather and he saw him and he spoke to him! My grandfather saw his lips move very clearly, but of course he could not hear or understand what was being said. It was very brief but my grandfather believes and has always believed that the man, undoubtedly your uncle, was trying to pass him a message. A message for the living, delivered as he went to his death.

'As you know, David, my grandfather can read lips and he recognises you as the man he saw in the cockpit that night and as the man he buried the next day. You have just said the same form of words to Stephen as your uncle used on that terrible night. My grandfather insists that you repeat them directly to him now.'

She paused again.

'Do you understand what I have said, David? Please tell me.'

All eyes now passed back to David. I had in turn watched David's face change as Laura spoke and the realisation had dawned equally on him as it had on Laura and now on myself that the curtain of time had just, for a moment at least, been lifted. We, now all stood on the banks of the River Styx in July 1944 as Charon had come to take my friend David Lumb and my crew to their deaths. David had seen Rene as he saw his death approach and had spoken to him.

David realised now what he had to say. He had held the palms of his hands to the sides of his forehead as Laura's words had passed through him and slowly he had drawn them down the side of his face as if washing before prayer. Destiny was now his and the ripples of events in this village over 50 years ago were now rushing to return and wash over us all.

'Laura,' he said. 'Your grandfather is one of the most remarkable men I have ever met. Before I speak to him, he needs to know that my late father was the youngest brother of Flight Sergeant David Lumb and despite the age difference between them they were very close. My father's given name was Walter but no one ever called him that. He was always called "Stevie" or "Stevie Boy" by the family. I cannot tell you why. Would you please explain that to your grandfather, I will then tell him what I said which I think will explain the message it is apparent that he was given.'

Rene turned to Laura as she translated the words and he nodded slowly. He then turned back to David, as time remained frozen. David leaned forward and took Rene's hands in his and looked carefully into his face. He spoke carefully and slowly and gently and our little world held its breath as he said…

'I'm sorry I cannot get back to you, Stevie Boy.'

Rene looked down at the table again for a long time, reliving that moment and as he lifted his head he nodded slowly with certainty and said simply, 'Oui.'

There was silence and then he said, 'Pourquoi?' Why?

David replied, 'I wish I knew exactly, Rene. I think he must have been apologising to my father for not being able to return to him and the rest of the family. They had just lost one son in the war a year earlier. He must have known that his little brother would be distraught to lose his eldest brother also, but now my uncle must have known there was nothing he could do about it other than to send a message through you. It is incredible that this could have happened after so many years. Words are not enough to thank you, Rene.'

For the second time that day they embraced after Laura had translated.

There was silence for a moment and I spoke.

'David, I know exactly what your uncle was doing and why.' I said this as calmly as possible, to fit with the emotional mood of the moment, I hoped. David and Stephen looked across at me.

'You know I said I visited Daisy Hill once when we were on leave after the death of our first skipper?' They nodded. 'When we left the next morning Stevie, your father, came with us to the station to see us off. It was a very emotional moment between the brothers. Your father was very young and was very upset at seeing his brother leave for the war again. Your uncle, my David, promised him on the lives of their parents that he would return to him.

'Of course, he never did, which is why we are here today. It was a wonderful and tremendously emotional moment between brothers, David. I am so proud and honoured to have witnessed it and be able to tell you about it in the presence of Rene and his family but I'm so sorry they never met again. I'm so very sorry.'

Now I cried the tears I perhaps should have cried years before. It was the bitterest and the sweetest of moments for all of us. We had learned all there was to know about the events of that day in 1944. Rene had delivered the message he had been given and was at peace, but the man who it had been destined for was already dead and could never know. His son now carried it for him. My only consolation was that the brothers I had met long ago were now together and at peace. I firmly believe that.

The words spoken between us now rippled around the room, translated into French for the villagers who were there with us, and there were gasps of astonishment and understanding. Tears, there were too many to count! A tiny moment of history had just been made and recounted and we were all witnesses to it.

Peace and joy had come to us all to mingle with the sadness and the memory of events so long ago.

Three weeks later Mary, David, and I stood in front of another grave headed with a white Portland headstone. This one was in the municipal cemetery in the northern town of Morley.

I read the words of remembrance to a beloved Husband and Father, William Lumb who died in 1944 and his wife Eleanor whose death was recorded as 1963 and then below that:

"Also in memory of two beloved sons who died on air operations. Thomas Leslie Lumb, 1943, buried in Takoradi, Gold Coast and to David William Lumb, 1944, buried in Lancy sur Marne, France."

Below the main headstone was another, smaller one set at an angle to it. All it said was Walter (Stevie) Lumb (1928-1985) Beloved husband and father.

Mary laid a bouquet of flowers as did David, and I left two simple wooden crosses with a poppy insignia made by the Royal British Legion. As we walked from the cemetery, I asked David if he would do one last favour for me. He nodded.

We drove ten minutes back towards the centre of Morley and then up the road to the station. We got out of the car opposite Morley station which still operated. I looked down the long steps towards the platform set in the big cut. Little had changed of the station itself. The old row of Victorian terrace houses was still there also, now boasting modern double glazing in the windows. The old wall and the stile stood as I remembered them and I then I looked up across the fields towards the large, dark house at the top of the hill. A few more modern houses built in the 1960's stood around it now but the view was clear and unimpeded.

I stood looking up at the house and then I reached out and took my wife's hand in my left and held David's in my right. I closed my eyes and in the darkness of my mind made vivid by the memories of so long ago I felt at peace. It was in that moment that I heard them again.

The skylarks were singing over Daisy Hill!

THE END.

For more information on the characters, locations and the reality of the bomber campaign in the second world war, please go to

skylarksoverdaisyhill.com

Printed in Great Britain
by Amazon

21119244R00257